Praise for the Dreamslippers Series

"The launch of an intriguing female detective series... A mystery with an unusual twist and quirky settings; an enjoyable surprise for fans of the genre." — *Kirkus Reviews*

"Clearly author Lisa Brunette has a genuine flair for deftly crafting a superbly entertaining mystery/suspense thriller. *Cat in the Flock* is a terrific read..." — Helen Dumont, *Midwest Book Review*

"Brunette's portrayals of Cat and Granny Grace are nothing short of genius." — *On My Kindle*

"A fascinating plot populated with interesting and engaging characters." — *The Wishing Shelf Awards*

"Filled with twists and turns, humor, a little romance, and suspense, this refreshing take on the world of private investigating will appeal to readers of many different genres." — Janna Shay, *inD'tale*

"A fascinating tale of mystery, romance, and what one woman's dreams are made of. Brunette will keep you awake far into the night." — Mary Daheim, bestselling author of the Bed-and-Breakfast and Emma Lord/Alpine mysteries

"Gripping, sexy and profound, *Cat in the Flock* is an excellent first novel. Lisa Brunette is an author to enjoy now and watch for the future." — Jon Talton, author of the David Mapstone Mysteries, the Cincinnati Casebooks and the thriller *Deadline Man*

"Lisa Brunette's *Framed and Burning* is a brilliant, suspenseful whodunit in its own merit, full of twists and turns, pursued by a unique pair of private investigators —Cat and her grandmother Grace, in a character-as-well-as-plot-driven ride pulsating with the crisis not only in the murder investigation, but also in their own lives. What's more, the introduction of the original practice of dreamslipping—their capability of 'slipping' into other people's dreams—adds to another dimension of the novel. Far from making it semi-sci-fi or something like that, it fantastically blends the Freudian dream interpretation with the crime analysis in a new depth. The book, truly one of the kind, calls for attention of the readers devoted to the genre and in general." — Qiu Xiaolong, Anthony Award-winning author of *Shanghai Redemption*, named one of *The Wall Street Journal*'s Best Books of 2015

"*Framed and Burning* isn't afraid to play with you and then terrify you. It's a mystery with teeth and wounds and loss. Unforgettable, charming in the creation of the characters and world, serpentine and dark, *Framed and Burning* is a mystery not to be missed." — Frances Carden, *Readers Lane*

"This cozy mystery about a family of psychically gifted amateur sleuths possesses enough magic to keep you hooked from the first page until the last." — *BestThrillers.com*

"I've become a Lisa Brunette fan with this read." — Sherrey Meyer, *Puddletown Reviews*

"This is a fun book, much more fast-paced than a cozy, but without the gruesome and gory details of real crime mystery novels." — *Mystery Sequels*

"A savory mystery with a side of supernatural." — Frankie Brazelton, *Mudville Dames*

"Deeply intriguing right from the start! I definitely have to get my hands on the first novel of the series!" — *Book-o-Craze*

"I love a good, eccentric granny character, and Grace is in the top five granny characters I've encountered this year." — *Back Porchervations*

"All credit to the author for holding my interest over the busy festive season!" — *Ali, the Dragon Slayer*

"It was interesting to see how the dreamslippers worked, as each one had a different method of invading and analyzing dreams. *Framed and Burning* is a book I recommend reading." — Michelle Stanley, *Writer Way*

"This book had me hooked right from the beginning! I love the characters!" — *Pari's Books*

Bound to the Truth
by Lisa Brunette

Copyright © 2016 by Lisa Brunette

Cover Design: Monika Younger,
www.youngerbookdesign.com
Author Photography: Regan House Photo

ISBN 13: 978-0-9862377-9-9

Published in the United States of America

Published by Sky Harbor Press, an imprint of Sky Harbor LLC

SKY HARBOR
PRESS

P.O. Box 642
Chehalis, WA 98532
skyharborllc@gmail.com

Direct inquiries to the above address

Author Web Site: www.lisa-brunette.com

Included in this edition of *Bound to the Truth*:

- Book club discussion questions.

>>>Also by Lisa Brunette<<<

Other Books in the Dreamslippers Series

Cat in the Flock

Framed and Burning

Poetry

Broom of Anger

Short Stories

Spy Boy

Birdy

Her Mother's Shoes

Bound to the Truth

The Dreamslippers Series #3

by Lisa Brunette

Sky Harbor Press

For all those who feel trapped

Prologue

Robin Howell sat on the floor of her living room, watching Jin Mae play. The girl stacked yellow block upon blue block, alternating the two colors until she had a tower. Jin Mae seemed to sense when the height would become unstable and stopped. She turned to Robin and said, "Look, I made a building. Just like Mommy Nina does."

The girl's words bloomed like flowers in Robin's chest. She got down on all fours to admire her daughter's architectural feat. The two played together for a long time, until Robin noticed the slanted sunlight stretching out across the floor, suggesting that it was late. She felt for her cell phone in her pocket to check the time. It showed an indisputable 7:36 p.m. and a text message from Nina that she hadn't noticed while absorbed in play: *Taking a client to dinner. Go ahead without me.*

Robin hoisted herself up off the floor, pulling her rough-hewn Guatemalan wrap around her for comfort as much as against the chill. "Come, Jin Mae," she said, beckoning for her daughter's hand. "We need to make dinner."

>>>

Robin woke, her book still in her hand and her reading glasses perched on her nose. She heard running water and saw a slit of light beneath the bathroom door. Nina was home. Robin's heart lilted at the thought of her wife climbing into bed with her, fresh from a shower. But Robin craved more than that. She did not want to wait.

She got up and walked to the door.

The bathroom knob wouldn't turn. It was locked.

"Nina," she said. "Can I come in?"

Silence. A pause. And then, "Oh, Robin. I'm so exhausted. I just want to sleep."

"Okay."

Robin returned to bed, picked up her book and glasses, and set them on the nightstand. Nina finally came out after a few more minutes, and she was wearing a full set of pajamas.

"You used to sleep in the nude," Robin said.

Nina did not respond. Her face was scrubbed of makeup, the ends of her chin-length hair wet. Robin made room for her under the covers, putting her arm around her once she settled.

"How was your client?"

"Intense. But somehow still boring, in the sense that he was utterly predictable."

Robin smirked. "What does he want you to build?"

Nina sighed. "What else? A mixed-use building with apartments above and retail below. It should have all the semblance of sustainability and green living without his having to invest in anything that would really make a difference."

"So no go on the solar."

"Nope."

"Sorry."

Nina turned toward Robin, touching her face. "How's Jin Mae? I looked in on her when I came in. She's fast asleep, with Lambykins in her arms."

Robin felt Nina's touch smoothing the jagged edges of her worry. "She's fine. Building apartment towers with her blocks. Wants to be like you."

Nina smiled. "It would be better if she wanted to be like you."

"A stay-at-home mom? Or who I was before?"

"Both," said Nina, her voice a bit arch. She sat up in bed. "Don't devalue your domestic work. You know it was the right decision for our family."

"It's just hard," Robin said, knowing her voice sounded whiny, but she was unable to stop. "Don't get me wrong; I love raising Jin Mae, and I know economically it made sense…"

Nina cut her off. "Your salary at the shelter wasn't even enough to pay for Jin Mae's child care."

Robin felt wounded. "You don't have to remind me."

Nina's face softened. "I'm sorry. It's been a long day."

Robin took a breath. "It's just … I miss having another purpose in the world. Something to talk to you about at the end of the day, besides what Jin Mae did."

"I enjoy hearing about your time with our daughter," Nina said, but to Robin her voice sounded weak.

Robin thought of a conversation she'd had with a woman she'd run into at the library earlier in the day. The woman was from a feminist group she'd been a part of before she and Nina had adopted Jin Mae. Robin had faded away from them when Jin Mae became her focus, but now she thought it could be the thing she needed.

She told Nina, who shrugged. "If that's what you

want."

"It doesn't pay, of course. It's just volunteer."

"That doesn't matter," said Nina. She flipped off the bedside light and turned to one side, away from Robin.

Robin snuggled into Nina's back, spooning her. "I miss you," she whispered into her wife's ear.

"I'm right here," Nina said, grasping Robin's hand.

But as they drifted off to sleep, Robin wasn't so sure.

>>>

Robin's knitting needles clicked as the women talked, giving their conversation a subtle staccato rhythm. The Wyld Womyn had worked together in the name of social justice for the past twenty-five years. Staunch feminists, they supported an alphabet soup of acronymed organizations that represented the fight against hegemonic patriarchy: NARAL, NOW, EMILY's List, the FMF. More than half their number were lesbians or had dated women at some point in their lives. The ones who were currently partnered with men had chosen SNAGs, or Sensitive New Age Guys, as their mates. These were men who shared in the household chores and child-raising, took their turns in conversation rather than interrupting, and understood that their wives would retain separate bank accounts to preserve their economic independence.

Today's topic: pornography and strip clubs. Marjorie Jackson, an organizer for Feminists Fighting Porn, had been invited to speak about the group's various initiatives.

Marjorie had chosen not to color her gray, which framed her face in dramatic streaks. Robin found the look both stunning and a little intimidating.

"We know that pornography is like a gateway drug for perpetrators of rape and child rape," Marjorie argued. "Notice that I did not use the word 'molestation' in place of 'child rape.' I don't want to minimize the act when it's done to a child. Rape is rape."

Robin felt a surge of emotion that made her drop a stitch. She thought of Nina's father. It had taken Nina fifteen years of therapy to undo the damage that man had done to her. Robin wondered if pornography had had anything to do with his criminal acts against Nina.

"Now it's everywhere, thanks to the Internet," Marjorie continued. "We're long past the days of banning porn from bookstores and convenience marts. Type 'cock' into a search engine, and it's in your face."

Robin fought a snicker at the woman's unintended literalism.

Danielle Everton, a fortysomething financial planner, piped up. "I caught my son watching a YouTube video the other day about how to give a better blow job. The girl in the video demonstrated with a carrot, and she was alone and fully clothed, so I guess the parental filters didn't recognize it as porn."

"I don't know why men like that so much," said a woman named Sharon Koal. She pushed her turquoise frames back up to the bridge of her nose. "I've always found it disgusting."

Robin thought of Sharon's husband, who wore his hair in a ponytail and always smelled of the mushrooms he grew in their backyard.

"Oh, I don't know," said a woman who'd been introduced along with Robin, a twentysomething who was there for her first meeting. "They can be just as good for the woman as for the man."

"Really?" Several women spit out the question at once.

The newbie looked caught off guard, as if she wished she'd kept her mouth shut. "Um, yeah. I mean, why not? It's the variety of sexual expression, right?"

One of the heteros leapt to her defense. "If a woman truly enjoys it and isn't just doing it to please her partner, that would be all right."

Robin remembered her own furtive, awkward attempts at going down on her high-school boyfriend, back when she was trying really hard not to think about her attractions to the girls who were just her friends. She hadn't quite known what to do with that thing. It tasted like the terrible brie hors d'oeuvres her mother served to guests. So she closed her eyes and hoped for the best but ended up cutting him with her teeth. She had to admit, there was something satisfying about causing him pain there. And he never insisted she do it again after that.

"I think we're getting off topic," said Helen Dubus, the host. "And there's been an awful lot of cross talk." She cast looks at Danielle and Sharon, who had effectively derailed their guest's speech.

"Sorry," both women murmured.

There was a pause, and then Marjorie spoke

14

again. "So, anyway, there is not a lot we can do to put a stop to pornography. But what we can do is try to prevent strip clubs from obtaining licenses. They prey on young women who are already victims in society and create centers for drugs and crime."

She distributed a flyer advertising a rally to protest a new strip club opening in a Seattle suburb. "We need as many people to show up to this as possible," she said.

Robin wondered if she could get Nina to go. This protest would be something they'd do together. A question occurred to her.

"Would it be appropriate to bring children to the protest?"

Marjorie considered it. "I think that would be all right. There won't be anything that children can't see at this, not in our signs, and the club itself will be closed at the time. It's during the day."

Sharon spoke to Robin, but she meant her words for the group. "It would be a good experience for Jin Mae. Anyone else willing to bring their daughters?"

"—And sons," Marjorie clarified. "They have just as much to learn as girls do. Maybe even more."

>>>

The day of the protest dawned warm and drizzly. Robin made pancakes, a smiley face on Jin Mae's, with a banana mouth and strawberries for eyes. Nina brewed coffee, Robin's favorite free-trade brand from the shop near their house. She poured in enough coconut milk to turn the

15

coffee tan, just the way Robin liked it.

They told Jin Mae they were taking her to a protest, an important one for women. "Wo-men," the girl said before sticking a strawberry into her mouth.

Robin always let Nina drive. The few times Robin drove, Nina spent the whole trip telling Robin where to go or pressing an imaginary brake on her side of the car.

When they got to the building that would soon open as a strip club, Robin was dismayed to see only a handful of women with Marjorie, and all of them from Feminists Fighting Porn. She, Nina, and Jin Mae were the only ones from the Wyld Womyn, and Jin Mae was the only child.

Still, they held their signs high for the news cameras. A few passersby joined them, including an elderly couple who lived a few blocks away and didn't like the idea of a strip club in their neighborhood.

The building was brick painted black, with a garish pink stripe across the top. A glittery sign spelled out its name: TOP LET'S. The windows had all been blacked out, and there was an enormous satellite dish on the roof. It was on a busy intersection, and the sound of tires swooshing through the rainy streets gave the proceedings a constant white noise, punctuated by an occasional honk, which the protesters took as gestures of support.

Through the constant wash of cars and steadily building commotion as more people joined the protest, Robin sought connection with Nina, who seemed distracted. Robin reached for her wife's gloved hand. Nina clasped hers in return. But Nina's gaze strayed elsewhere, to the gaggle of media people milling about in front of their vans, their crews swarming around them like flies.

One man, holding a tiny microphone, stared right at them.

Or at Nina, rather. He cast a quick, mildly curious glance at Robin, but his stare was directed at Nina.

As if he knew her.

As if there was something between them.

Nina's hand grew limp in Robin's. Robin felt her wanting to break the hold.

But then the man turned away. He fell into conversation with a crew member.

Robin thought she heard the slightest noise come from Nina, just a tiny note, as if she were trying not to react to a sudden pain.

The man turned back around, his eyes scanning the scene but avoiding Nina and Robin. He clipped the microphone to his tie. Robin strained to pick out his voice above the din.

"I'm at the scene of a protest here in North Seattle…"

Robin felt Nina pulling her away from where the man stood, but Robin held her ground.

"Regular listeners of my radio program know I've been covering the Rizzio family saga for the past three years…"

Robin had heard his voice before, when flipping the channels in her Subaru. As soon as his distinct baritone came out of the speakers, in fact, she knew to keep flipping. He was a conservative radio talk-show host, and she never agreed with a word he said.

She nudged Nina, who was already staring at him. "Isn't that…"

"—Sam Waters," Nina supplied. "Yes."

"Right," Robin said in a whisper. "What an ass-hole."

"That's for sure," Nina said, but the look on her face seemed to betray something else.

Sam Waters filled his microphone with his own loud, inflammatory, rapid-fire speech. "…The police have so far failed to provide any solid evidence against the Rizzio family in what amounts to a politically motivated witch hunt. Meanwhile, the radical feminists have de-scended, all eleven of them…"

Robin held one of Jin Mae's hands, and Nina held the other. "You're hurting my hand, Mommy," Jin Mae said to Nina, shaking the hand Nina held.

Nina, appearing startled, glanced down and let go of Jin Mae. "Oh, sorry, honey."

"He just lied about the protest," Robin said. "I count twenty-one of us."

"Like it matters," said Nina, coughing out a laugh.

Someone behind them began to chant. "No more porn! No more porn!"

Robin picked up the chant, and so did Nina. Even little Jin Mae joined in, though coming out of her three-year-old mouth, it sounded like "No morn corn!"

>>>

18

Working late, said Nina's text. Nothing more.

But Robin had received that message at 6:13 p.m. It was now morning, and Nina was not there.

Robin could hear Jin Mae making wake-up noises in her room down the hall. Nina's side of the bed was cold, the sheets still tucked under the mattress.

A panic attack surged through Robin, turning her palms slick with sweat. She felt as if she were being choked.

She leapt from the bed. "Nina?" she called through the house, though she knew her wife wasn't there. She could feel Nina's absence in her bones. She had felt it for some time. Some part of her had known this was coming.

She thought of the man at the protest. Sam Waters. Nina had dated men before, but no one like him. How could she fall for a libertarian?

Robin did not know how to stop it. She couldn't imagine life without Nina, her love, her everything. How would they raise Jin Mae if they weren't together?

It had been a long time since they'd been intimate, truly intimate, Robin thought with alarm. And now it seemed like it was too late to get back there.

She shook the notion from her head. There was still time. She could save this. She had to.

>>>

Robin kept checking her cell phone for messages but found none. She expected to hear from Nina by noon, but lunchtime came and went, with Jin Mae getting parmesan all over the dining room. No matter how many times Robin swept the sponge across the table, she'd find flecks of cheese she'd missed.

Then the front doorbell rang. Robin expected someone selling siding for the house, or cable services. But it was two police officers, a man and a woman. She let them in. They seemed so out of place in her living room in their starched uniforms and shiny shoes. Instinctually, Robin picked up her knitting needles. It seemed important suddenly to finish Nina's sweater. It was taking her forever, and soon it would be too warm for it anyway.

"I'm so sorry to have to tell you this," said the man. To Robin, it sounded as if he were sorrier about his role as messenger than he was about the message itself.

He cleared his throat, hesitating.

"Yes?" Robin prompted him. She didn't look up, though. She didn't want to drop a stitch.

"Your wife was found dead this morning," he said.

Too late, too late. The words Robin had been worrying over all morning rang in her ears. She dropped the unfinished sweater and looked up, but not at him. Her eyes met the woman cop's, seeking comfort.

But there Robin saw only pity.

Chapter One

Cat sat in Siddhartha, her grandmother's Mercedes, conducting surveillance on the neighbor of none other than Seattle's infamous "crow lady."

The crow lady allowed her children to feed the crows, which gathered *en masse* for dinner nightly. The crows left the children gifts in return: a gold hoop earring, a shiny rock. This endearing story had been picked up and reported by BBC News.

But there was one problem. The crow lady's neighbors didn't appreciate the avian food fest, and tensions were running high. This had so far *not* been reported in the news.

The crow lady happened to be a friend of Granny Grace's, who agreed to meet with her and hear her side of the story.

"My neighbors have been yelling at my children, and I think one of those horrible people shot at the crows!" the woman exclaimed, tucking a scarf around her neck as if it could protect her. Henrietta was her name. Cat thought it fitting for a children's book. Henrietta, whose children feed the crows.

Cat had wanted to send the woman packing, but Grace sympathized with her.

"Crows are known for their intelligence," Granny Grace said, sipping her herbal tea.

She agreed to take the crow lady's case. Which is how Cat wound up sitting in a car, spying on some dude's million-dollar home. She'd been there for hours and hadn't seen a thing, except the woman's son coming out to throw peanuts at a murder of crows.

The big black birds kicked up a cacophony of caws. It gave Cat shivers, but the boy seemed to love it.

Cat checked her phone for notifications. She'd recently downloaded a dating app and set up a profile. It was her agreement with Jacob, for now, until they could figure out whether or not to take their relationship in a more serious direction, which would mean a move to San Francisco for her.

She was delighted to find that she already had four "pets," as the app called them. This would be the equivalent to likes or winks on other sites. She scrolled through her petters' profiles. The list of sexual activities they were into were listed candidly, and they were surprising to her. Cat had set her preference to "new at this but open," since she had no idea what she wanted to do in the bedroom, other than the obvious. While setting up her profile, she'd had to search the meaning of half the terms. The experience made her feel as if she'd led a sheltered life. Also, there were so many people of varying demographics engaged in so many different activities that Cat suddenly had the impression that Seattleites as a population must quietly be getting their freak on in the bedroom 24/7.

One of the pets was from a guy she thought really cute, and though he was into a few sexual activities that gave her pause, she bravely accorded him a return "pet."

And then it was back to waiting. The crows had finished off the peanuts, bits of shell littered across the lawn. Cat watched as a fat rat picked its way through the detritus.

Cat had so far failed to slip into any dreams around the crow case, despite valiant effort on her part, not to mention her grandmother's expert guidance. But whatever focused concentration came from having three dreamslippers in one house was lost now. It had worked well in Miami, where Granny Grace engaged in some re-mote-dreamslipping on a suspect. Cat had experienced remote-dreamslipping a few times, but only with people she had some connection to. This case—and a couple of others they'd tried beforehand—gave her nothing. So here she was, engaged in the typical mundane sur-veillance work of a private investigator. For nothing, as it turned out. If they didn't get something soon, she'd have to try to stay the night at Henrietta's in the hopes of pick-ing up her neighbors' dreams. Looking at the messy lawn and the jumble of toys piled on the front porch, Cat shud-dered at the thought of a night in Crowland.

But just as she was about to start up Siddhartha and call it a day, a door opened on the neighbor's bal-cony, and out stepped a middle-aged man. He wore jeans and a fleece sweatshirt, heavy boots that clumped on the decking planks, and gloves. Cat watched, taking pictures with a telephoto lens, as he tied a length of string to the balcony railing and then let the string fall, something dark dangling from one end. A dead crow.

This surprised her. Up until now, she'd felt allied with the neighbors here, for the crowds of crows did seem like a nuisance, not to mention a sanitation issue. But hanging a dead one from your balcony? It seemed like he was trying to send the crow lady a message.

Back home, she told this to Granny Grace, who further astonished her by taking the opposite tack.

"Actually, Cat, what he's doing is perfectly sensible, if you know anything about crows. It's an old farmer's trick I learned when I was growing up. You put a dead crow out to warn its brethren to stay away. Crows are smart. They get the message."

Cat sighed, hating this case all the more. "But you know your crow-lady friend is going to freak out."

"Yes," said Granny Grace. At that moment her cell phone rang, with a ring tone that sounded like sitar music. "I bet that's her."

But it wasn't. "Hello, Robin," answered her grandmother. She paused, her eyes widening. "Oh, my God. Are you all right? Yes, I understand and am happy to help in anyway I can."

Cat listened to Granny Grace's side of the conversation, which seemed to require a lot of reassurance on her grandmother's part. As her grandmother ended the call, Cat said, "I hope this one doesn't involve anything fowl, f-o-w-l."

Grace didn't smile. "I'm afraid it's f-o-u-l. Do you remember my friends Robin and Nina, who came to our last party? Nina works with Simon."

"Right, Nina and Simon are partners. And so were Robin and Nina, until they got legally married. Which they can do now, here in Washington. But Simon and Nina are just business partners, not life partners or sexual partners. Which is what Simon is with Dave. Or are they married, too? It's all a little confusing, but I think

24

I've got it." Cat smiled at her grandmother, who gave her a look.

Nina and Robin were an odd couple, Cat remembered. Robin seemed dowdy in her wraps and sensible shoes, with Nina sharp and metrosexual in her blunt haircut and corporate wear. Maybe it was a case of opposites attract; whereas with Simon and Dave, there were some distinctions, but more similarities than differences.

"Nina's been murdered," Grace said, her eyebrows drawing together. "And Robin keeps going on about how she knows who did it. It's the oddest thing. She's convinced it was Sam Waters, the talk-radio host. She thinks he had some kind of hold over Nina."

"No way," said Cat. "I listen to his podcasts sometimes, when I feel like Seattle's liberalness needs to be balanced out."

"Really?" Her grandmother raised an eyebrow. "I know you've struggled sometimes with your transition to Seattle. Is this your homesickness for St. Louis coming through again?

Cat laughed. "Homesickness? I don't know. Most of my profs back home were pretty liberal, even though I went to a Catholic school."

Granny Grace smiled. "Those Jesuits. God love 'em."

"Yeah, they practically invented the notion of social justice. But Sam's a reasonable guy, Gran. Not like those shock jocks you usually hear."

"Well, he may be politically reasonable, but is he capable of murder?" asked her grandmother. She picked up her purse and slipped it over one shoulder.

Cat grabbed the keys to Siddhartha. "I guess we'll find out."

>>>

Her grandmother gave her directions that put them in front of what looked like a Craftsman home that had recently been given a second story. The two levels meshed in perfect harmony, the design of the newer part calling out the modern aspects that had been embedded in the original Craftsman style.

"Isn't it gorgeous?" she gushed. "Nina designed it. The two of them bought a house that was practically fit to be condemned, and just look at how they salvaged it. Oh, I can't believe Nina's dead! She was so talented."

Her grandmother took a moment at the curb to recover, and they made their way to the door.

Robin opened it right away, ushering them in. "Jin Mae's with the Wyld Womyn," she explained, and Granny Grace nodded.

Aside to Cat, she whispered, "It's a feminist collective. That's how I met Robin, though I haven't been to a meeting in ages."

Cat made a mental note of the collective as she passed through the skylighted entryway and into a beautiful room anchored by a river rock fireplace, a tear-shaped window on either side. Robin Howell sat down in a huge armchair next to an end table piled with balls of yarn and other knitting supplies.

Her grandmother pulled out her old reporter's notebook, but Cat retrieved a tablet computer from her bag and began to take notes her own way.

"Why don't you start at the beginning?" Granny Grace prompted Robin, who looked like she might fade into nothingness within the passing hour.

Robin cleared her throat. "They found Nina in a hotel room just this morning. She'd been—" The woman choked up.

Cat wondered why Robin had called them in so soon. The story of Nina's death had just now hit the local news sites. Cat tapped the *Seattle Times* link on her tablet. The headline read, LOCAL ARCHITECT NINA HOWELL FOUND DEAD IN SEATTLE HOTEL. But it was the subheading that stood out to her: EVIDENCE SUGGESTS HOWELL WAS MURDERED.

"Take your time," Granny Grace told Robin. "We're in no hurry here."

"It's just so hard," Robin said. "I can't believe all this is happening." She broke down in sobs.

Cat scanned the article, which was brief and factual:

> Puget Place Hotel staff found local architect Nina Howell, 43, dead at 9 a.m. today in her room. She had been restrained, with signs of a struggle. The King County medical examiner will formally determine the manner and cause of Howell's death. The police department has referred the case to its homicide unit.
>
> Howell was a partner in the architecture firm Fletcher Green and Howell, which designed the Puget Place Hotel, the same hotel where her body was found

this morning. She is survived by her wife, Robin Howell, and their adopted daughter, Jin Mae Howell.

The rest of the article gave tip-line information. Cat examined the accompanying photo of Nina, which appeared to be a professional shot she used for business profiles. Chin-length blonde hair, cut in a conservative swag. Pale blue eyes. The kind of skin that would easily burn. She had a smart, take-charge air about her, and Cat could easily imagine trusting this woman to design a building.

Robin recovered, but her face was full of rage. "Sam Waters did it. He tied her up. That bastard tied her up and killed her."

Cat swallowed hard, determined to say what she needed to say as delicately as possible. "Why do you think Sam Waters murdered Nina? Were they ... involved?"

"No!" Robin picked up an unfinished piece of knitting, what looked like a scarf or maybe the start of a sweater in turquoise and gold, and began to work on it. "I don't know. If they were, he was controlling her."

Cat didn't know how to respond. She cast a glance at her grandmother for assistance, but she looked as puzzled as Cat.

"Why don't I make us all some tea?" Granny Grace rose, smoothed down the front of her elegant slacks, and walked into the kitchen.

Cat could hear her grandmother banging around and longed to join her so they could talk about how to approach this, but she knew better than to leave Robin alone.

"What are you making?" Cat asked, putting a gentleness into her voice.

"It's a sweater for Jin Mae," Robin said, sighing. "In Nina's favorite colors."

"I'm so sorry for your loss." The words felt wooden to Cat, but they were all she had.

Robin said nothing. She'd stopped knitting and seemed to be examining the sweater now through her thick glasses. "Nina said these colors work together because they're on opposite sides of the wheel. Contrasting colors. See how they vibrate against each other?"

"Yes," Cat said, and she wasn't just humoring Robin. The colors did seem to pulse.

"I only met Nina the one time," said Cat. "But she seemed really strong to me. Not like a woman who'd let someone else walk all over her."

"It happens to the best of us," Robin said. "I once knew a woman who'd chained herself to the gates of the French embassy to protest Chirac's decision to detonate nuclear bombs in the South Pacific. She was as tough as they come. But she got involved in a codependent relationship. It wasn't long before her husband had effectively separated her from all of her friends."

"So you think Nina was codependent with Sam Waters?"

Grace came in with their tea on a bamboo tray and set it on the coffee table in front of them.

"I think so," said Robin, reaching for a cup. "I just don't have any evidence. But I know something wasn't right. Some force seemed to be taking her away from me.

I felt her slipping—but that wasn't my Nina. It was as if she'd come under his spell."

Grace sipped her tea. "You must still be in shock, my dear."

"I guess so," said Robin. "I just—I don't want him to get away with it."

"He won't," said Grace, setting down her cup with a clink. "If he's guilty of her murder, he won't get away with it."

"I don't have any evidence," said Robin. She looked as if she had personally failed her wife. "I just know it was Sam Waters. It has to be."

Cat listened intently as Robin described the strip-club protest, and how Sam and Nina had appeared to know each other that day.

"What happened the night of her murder? Was she supposed to be on a trip or something?" Cat asked.

"No! She was just … late for dinner."

"That was the last thing you heard from her?" asked Granny Grace. Her tone was always less interrogating than Cat's. They made a great team, balancing against each other that way.

"Yes, it happened often. It's a tough job Nina had, working with such demanding clients. She sometimes had to take them to dinner on a moment's notice."

"What time was it when she told you she'd be late?" Cat asked.

"A little after six. I never expected her before six —that's early for us. Nina put in long hours. She liked me staying home with Jin Mae, and I didn't mind her being late. I know it's what she had to do. For us. It was her

30

sacrifice."

>>>

Grace and Cat were silent on the drive home. In the quiet, Grace mulled over the strange conversation with Robin. They were lucky to get a juicy case, though she was sad about the loss of the smart architect, a real leader in her field. The allegation back in December against her brother Mick for child porn, even though it had been proved false, had affected the Amazing Grace Detective Agency as well as his art career. Whereas Cat's case involving a high-profile Midwestern church leader had brought them notoriety and business, the pro bono work they did in Miami to save Mick had cost them a few clients. It wasn't fair, Grace knew, but people tended to react in a knee-jerk fashion to subjects like child porn, no matter a person's innocence.

She took the route through Fremont but got caught when the bridge was up.

As they sat in stagnant bridge traffic, Cat broke the silence. "So is Robin loopy, or what?"

"She's just suffered a tremendous blow," Grace countered.

"Yeah, but seriously? I don't know if I buy any of what she said. Maybe she did it. We always look at the spouse first, right?"

Grace cleared her throat. "Of course we'll cover all angles, Cat. But she's our client, and I don't believe she hired us to cast blame on someone else to avoid her own guilt."

"Fine," said Cat. "So we'll start looking at Sam Waters then. With absolutely nothing to go on but that one time he covered a protest that the victim attended."

"I've started cases with less," Grace said. "You shouldn't let your admiration for the man color your investigation here."

Cat was silent, so Grace continued. "And you should talk to Simon Fletcher. He misses you at church, by the way."

But Cat had pulled out her phone and was busy with some sort of app.

"What are you doing?" Grace asked.

"Petting someone."

"Excuse me?"

"It's this dating app. You 'pet' someone, and they 'pet' you back."

"Sounds like the Humane Society should be involved."

Cat snorted. "Yeah, well, some of these guys look like they need to be vaccinated, too. Check out this one. Would I be dating *him*, or the motorcycle he's posing with? And this one. He says the jacket he's wearing is 3-D. Hard to tell by the picture, huh."

Grace glanced briefly in Cat's direction while navigating the circuitous route to the top of Queen Anne Hill. Cat was right: the 3-D jacket resembled a child's Day-Glo experiment. She looked away, shaking her head.

"Are you just making fun of these men, or have you found someone you want to meet?"

"Oh, I've tried to meet up with them, Gran. You don't understand. This is *Seattle*. You don't actually meet anyone in person here. You waste a lot of time and energy petting each other for days until it escalates into brief but vague text-messaging. We're at that stage. I'm sure the excitement will fizzle out before we reach the coffee-date stage."

"It would be better to meet someone in your own network, in person, in a group where you have shared interests, wouldn't it?"

"Like where, Gran? I'm always working to cover the cost of living in this spendy town. And so is everyone else. That is, when they're not showing up to happy hour with groups of friends in which everyone's busy texting people who aren't there."

Grace didn't know what to say to that.

"Besides," Cat continued. "I just want to experiment right now."

"Oh," Grace said. "What's going on with you and Jacob, anyway?"

"We're keeping it casual," Cat said. "We're both supposed to date other people, unless and until we decide to go further."

"I guess that sounds healthy, considering the circumstances. I mean, one of you would have to move—"

"—Yeah, and it won't be him. He's taking over his uncle's art gallery in San Fran. So if I want this thing with him, I have to move there."

Grace didn't respond. She knew all of this, of course, but hearing Cat put the possibility out there unsettled her.

"You're always telling me to find out what I want, independent of someone else's needs," Cat continued.

"That's what I'm doing."

Grace silently considered what her granddaughter was saying. Maybe it wasn't such a bad thing, she reasoned, for Cat to experiment using whatever tools were available to her. But the specter of Nina's death flashed in her mind's eye.

"Just be careful, Cat."

"Oh, I am. Tell you what. I'll text you my plans, if I ever do meet any of these guys in person, as well as their contact information. Okay?"

"Deal," Grace said.

She'd been thinking about dating again herself. It had been a few months since Ernesto's betrayal in Miami, and she felt ready to meet new people again. There was also the matter of her brother Mick's love life, which clearly needed an intervention.

Grace glanced over at her granddaughter, whose attention had refocused on her app. She'd been keeping the girl under her wing for the past year and a half, ever since her childhood sweetheart Lee had died. Grace knew she'd have to battle her own reluctance to let go of her PI practice if she were ever to properly turn it over to Cat. She'd been at this game for decades, and it was time to move on. What she really wanted was to spend her final years on something full of lightness, something that would nurture her spirit. She didn't know what that was yet, but she knew it wasn't PI work.

It was past time to shift her responsibilities to Cat, she realized.

Chapter Two

He held her hair in a tight nest at the back of her head, the tension making her scalp ache. Like her desire. Pearls swayed in a loose arc beneath her chin. They reminded her of the Newton's cradle on her desk at work, how she'd lift a metal ball to let it drop and hit the next one. The energy would travel through the three still balls in the center, forcing the one on the opposite end to rise upward. For every action, there is an equal and opposite reaction.

How many times a day she did that, she did not know. It was habit. It had been for years.

He released her hair. His fingers massaged her scalp. Her eyes rolled back with pleasure.

"God, you're beautiful like this," he said. "I love it when you let go."

She reset her gaze, and there he was, close in, staring into her eyes.

She touched his strong jaw, freshly shaven, letting herself feel thrilled by his masculinity. "I can only let go like that with you."

The look he returned was one of surrender. She marveled at that. She was supposed to be the submissive one, and yet during their play, they both surrendered, to each other.

"You have no idea how glad I am to hear that," he said.

Funny that he would say that, as she knew exactly how it made him feel. It was part of what drew her to him, his need to know their connection was real, that her responses to him were unique. And they were. He was the only dom she'd ever trusted like this, the only one who could unlock her body.

The only one she loved.

Following her craving, she moved his hands where she wanted them. "Please," she said. "I need you to hurt me."

Cat woke from the dream, feeling a heady mixture of love and arousal, but also thoroughly confused. Where had that come from? It wasn't her own dream, of that she was sure, but it couldn't have been Mick's, or her grandmother's, either. They were the only other people in the house, but in order for the three of them to live together without driving each other crazy, Cat and her great-uncle Mick had learned from Granny Grace how to keep from slipping into each other's dreams. It had worked all right —for the most part. But even if Cat had slipped into one of their dreams, this one didn't seem at all like something they'd dream about.

None of them had ever picked up their neighbors' dreams, either, perhaps because the houses were too far apart, or the walls too thick, or maybe the dreams just didn't warrant it.

Of course, there was the possibility of remote-dreamslipping, which all three of them had done, Mick and Cat involuntarily, when they shared intense connections to someone. Only Granny Grace had trained herself to conduct remote-dreamslipping on a particular subject. But this dream had come to Cat from out of nowhere. She fell back to sleep, still wondering.

He only smacked her where she was fleshiest, and he did it until her skin turned pink, but no more. She enjoyed the feeling of the silk ties against her wrists. When she parted her lips just so, her tongue wet, he would slip his thumb into her mouth.

He seemed to understand everything, without words.

Would he know the sound of her sigh across a crowded room?

But she wouldn't tell him her name. To him, she was only "Dandelion," the nickname at once soft and tough.

"It fits you," he remarked. "You're pretty like the dandelion's flower, but those roots... I couldn't rip them out if I tried."

Cat awakened from this one feeling frustrated and even more confused. This hadn't felt like her own dream either. She got up, grabbed her laptop, and typed up descriptions of both dreams, just like her grandmother had taught her. Otherwise, she'd forget them.

>>>

Granny Grace told Cat she should check out the crime scene by herself.

"What about our whole good-cop, bad-cop thing?" Cat asked.

"That dynamic is overrated," her grandmother said. "Besides, you're pretty good with people when you want to be."

Cat wasn't sure why her grandmother was suddenly turning her loose on such an important first step in the case, but she welcomed the chance to show her stuff.

The Puget Place Hotel was tucked tastefully between two older buildings in the middle of Belltown, and every effort had been made to blend its modern facade with that of its neighbors. Cat could almost hear her grandmother's voice in her head, extolling the wonders of Nina Howell's work. Granny Grace had to be rubbing off on her, because Cat did notice the same tear-shaped windows here that she'd admired in Nina and Robin's house.

The lobby was bright and airy, with bamboo flooring set off by turquoise-and-gold furnishings. Cat introduced herself as a private investigator looking into the Nina Howell murder and was referred to the hotel manager.

"May I ask who hired you?" The manager smoothed the front of his tie down his chest. His tone was polite, if a bit stiff.

"The victim's surviving spouse," Cat said, looking him square in the eyes.

"Isn't she a suspect?"

"I suppose the police have to consider her," said Cat. "But don't you think she's entitled to information? Whatever you have, it can only help."

He nodded. "I get that," he said. "Anything sensitive has been bagged and tagged by the police anyway. And if they ask, I'll let them know you were here."

Cat nodded, and he let her into his office.

"It's like I told the Seattle PD," said the manager, settling back into his office chair and motioning for Cat to sit opposite. "Ms. Howell had never been a guest in this hotel prior to the night of the murder. But of course, she was the lead architect on the design and construction. That was before I was hired, so I never met her, but I believe she worked directly with the owners."

"Did she check in under her own name?"

"Yes. She used a credit card to book the room."

"Was she alone?"

"We believe so. My desk staff says she was the only one who checked in, and she registered as a solo guest."

"Who found her?"

"The cleaning people. They've already given statements to the police. They found Ms. Howell lying on the bed, already dead. Her hands were tied. There appeared to have been a struggle."

"May I talk to your staff directly?"

"I'd rather you didn't. But I have copies of their statements, which I've already provided to our legal counsel. I'll check with our lawyers to see if it's all right to share them with you."

"I'd appreciate that." Cat eyed the manager, who seemed to be cooperating as well as could be expected. She didn't detect anything more than a seasoned manner with regard to legality.

"What was the deceased wearing when your staff found her?"

"Street clothes, as if she'd just come from work."

Cat was surprised by that.

"How was she restrained?"

"With duct tape—both hands behind her back. There was also a strip of the same tape across her mouth."

"Did you review the camera footage from that night?"

"Only from the front desk. It shows Nina Howell checking in at approximately seven-fifteen p.m., as is confirmed by our own records. I haven't seen the rest. All of the footage has been confiscated by the Seattle PD."

"Of course," said Cat. "Do you still have copies? Surely you didn't give them your originals."

"I do," he said, looking a bit tense at this admission, likely in anticipation of Cat's next request.

"I'd like to get a copy of everything pertaining to that night."

The man sighed. "I'll speak to our legal counsel and get back to you." Then he softened. "I promise it won't take long. We're trying to be as transparent as possible here. We want this murder solved and put behind us."

"Has it affected business?"

"Yes."

"May I see the room?"

"I suppose that would be all right. Like I said, the police bagged and tagged everything already. There's not much left in there."

He led Cat toward the elevator, which they took to the eleventh floor. She noted a camera in the hallway. The room was a corner suite, and indeed, the police had taken the bedding, towels, and even drapes, not to mention whatever personal effects Nina had had with her. The room had been picked clean.

Cat walked into the space. Noting the mattress still on the bed, but its pillow-top layer removed, she asked, "Was there any blood?"

The manager shook his head.

She went to the window. The room did not offer the best view from the hotel; that would come on a higher floor. But architecturally speaking, it was an interesting view. Cat studied the outlines of the buildings, which ranged from turn-of-the-last-century to contemporary. The focal point was a low building with what appeared to be a ship's hull forming the roof line.

>>>

Finding the door to the Adorable Amber Attic not only closed but locked, Grace permitted herself a loud knock. "Mick! You in there?"

"Who's asking?"

Grace noted her brother's irritated tone. "It's Grace."

"Grace who?"

"For heaven's sakes, Mick. Just open the door."

A pause—and the sound of a paint can toppling to the floor. "I'm indisposed."

"You're what? Come on, Mick. This is important."

The door flew open. Her brother stood there wiping paint off his hands, a brush clenched sideways in his mouth, the bristles dripping lime-green paint.

"Oh," Grace said. "I didn't realize you were working."

Mick yanked the brush from his mouth. "Well, what else would I be doing in here?"

He stalked back over to an oblong easel, where what appeared to be some sort of alien mothership painted in the same lime green hovered over a field of what looked like tombstones. He stabbed at the mothership with his brush.

"My goodness," said Grace. "What is that? An album cover?"

"I wish. That would at least *pay*."

Grace softened her tone. "It's the mural."

Mick turned to glare at her. "Yes. Your brainchild."

Grace smiled. Her brother had not had an easy time of it in Seattle's art world, what with the stigma of child pornography still surrounding him. Even though Mick himself had caught the real culprit, the initial damage to his reputation wrought by an army of online trolls and opportunists could not be undone. So she'd cooked up a plan to endear Mick to Seattleites, in the form of a large public mural, to be donated to the city as a gift from Mick. He'd been working for a couple of weeks on a prototype to submit to the mural committee.

She surveyed the mothership, which seemed to be emitting bolts of electric-orange rays onto the tombstones. "It's a little more … representational than your usual style."

Mick put down the brush, crossing his arms over his chest. "Did you interrupt me just to give me a critique?"

"I'm just not sure that an alien ship over a graveyard is what the residents of Queen Anne really need."

Mick threw up his hands. "Well, that's what they're going to get, Pris! What else am I supposed to do with this theme? 'Alien visitation.' It's bloody ridiculous if you ask me. But that's what they want. So that's what they're going to get."

"I think they meant it metaphorically."

He gave her a look that would wilt a flower.

"The notion of 'alien' is rather broad," she persisted. "And visitation. Just think of its religious connota-
tions."

Mick picked up the brush again. "You. Are. Not.
Helping."

"I'm sorry, Mick."

"Now what, dear sister of mine, did you wander
all the way up here to talk to me about?"

She hesitated, her hand fluttering up to touch her
throat. Her brother certainly wasn't in the mood to discuss being set up on a blind date.

"Well?"

"Oh, never mind. You're not going to like it anyway."

"Out with it, woman."

Grace swallowed hard, figuring it was now or
never. "I wanted to talk to you about a friend of mine. I
think you'd really like her. She's having an art show—"

"No."

"No, what? I haven't asked you anything."

"I refuse to be set up on a date. Especially with
another artist."

"But Cecily is… You'd really like her, Mick."

"No."

Grace felt frustration welling up inside her. Did
he always have to be such a pain in the keister? She was
only trying to help. "Mickelson Daniel Travers," she said,
raising her voice. "You are impossible."

"Which is exactly why you shouldn't set me up with anyone you're friends with."

"You're going to die old and alone." It was out of her mouth before she could censor it.

Mick put down his brush and sighed. "Really, Pris. Ever since I moved here, you've been up in my business. If it's not you trying to save my fledgling art career, it's you trying to set me up with Seattle's elderly eccentrics. I'm sixty-seven years old, and I've managed perfectly fine without your direction all this time. Please. Leave me alone!"

"But Mick, you could really use the help."

"Get out of my studio!" he bellowed, and for emphasis, he pointed toward the door.

Grace turned on her Etienne Aigners and marched out. Mick slammed the door behind her.

"And stay out!"

She muttered a "hmpf" and stepped back downstairs.

She pulled a flyer for Cecily's art opening out of her bag and left it on the countertop in the Terra-Cotta Cocina, where Mick would be sure to see it. She would not be deterred by her brother's temper. At her computer, she suggested Cecily Johnson as a friend for Mick Travers through a social-networking site.

While logged on, she saw that she'd received a friend request from someone she knew—a former suspect, someone they'd found innocent when investigating the arson in Mick's studio. Grace remembered her fondly: Annie Lin, an artist whose work she greatly admired. She accepted the request and indulged a little, scrolling through Annie's recent posts: A GIF of Frida Kahlo's paintings, a list of Japanese words that had no translation in English. The posts made Grace like the woman's sensibility all the more.

It was time for a new class she was trying out, something called Nia, a dance class that was low-impact and supposedly choreographed with healing movements. She'd watched a few videos online.

The class was at a small studio that had just opened up at the top of Queen Anne, within walking distance of her old Victorian. Though it was a little pricey at twenty-six dollars for a drop-in, Grace pushed herself to pony up the cash anyway, thinking that it was good to support a local business. But lately she had been questioning whether or not Seattle's quickly skyrocketing prices were sustainable for her in the long run. To her delight, she discovered that her first class would be free.

The owner, Yvette Malveaux, wore what Grace could only describe as "yoga clothes with flair." The hems of both her shirt and pants extended past their usual lines into scarves that fluttered as she moved about. A row of cutouts ran down the sides of the legs. She also wore a good deal of makeup, not the usual for yoga teachers in Seattle, more of a theatrical gesture. A magnolia blossom was tucked into Yvette's cornrowed hair.

After the usual questions about her experience level and physical fitness, plus a brief explanation of a "barefoot dance class," Grace walked into the studio and found a place to stand. She surveyed herself in the mirror, being careful to turn off the voice in her head that liked to call attention to the less savory aspects of herself at seventy-nine, like the rings of puffy flesh around her ankles. What was it her granddaughter called them? Cankles.

Soon, a bevy of students bedecked in similar scarf-hemmed attire poured in, and Grace suddenly felt as if she were backstage at a dance show. In her simple leotard and leggings, though, she'd be playing the role of straight man. Yvette waltzed in—literally—and talked about proper form, demonstrating how to pay attention to one's center of gravity and not exaggerate the footwork.

"Small movements sometimes work better," she said. She cued the music, and they were off.

Grace wasn't the least bit intimidated or reluctant as the music swelled. Her muscle memory took her back across time to other moments in her life when she'd danced in a studio: ballet as a small-town girl, modern dance in college, African dance in the seventies, and that undercover work she did serving as a backup dancer for a drag queen. Plus, the movement incorporated a few poses from other practices she knew—yoga, martial arts, tai chi. Yvette's bare, toffee-colored shoulders shimmied and shook, and Grace's followed suit. She mimicked Yvette's quick steps and followed the instructions Yvette belted out through a headset microphone. Grace was mindful not to give herself any trouble for her own missteps. It was her first time, after all. And what a time it was. They alternated between structured dance led by the instructor and moments of improvised "freedance" that allowed the students to whirl throughout the room, letting their bodies move as desired. Grace enjoyed these moments best, using them to work out a kink in her low back that had sprung up during her fight with Mick.

The class ended on the floor, with crawling, slithering movements that to Grace felt luxurious and self-indulgent. She hadn't allowed herself to move like that since the last time she'd gotten down on the floor to play with a friend's kid. By the time the class ended, with everyone taking two steps forward into their day and applause breaking out across the room, Grace wondered where this Nia had been all her life. She vowed to get Cat in that studio as soon as she could.

The lovely Yvette, sweaty and breathless herself, beckoned them to the rear of the studio, where she retrieved towels from what looked like a microwave but turned out to be a newfangled towel warmer. They were hot and scented with eucalyptus. Grace accepted her towel gratefully and, following the others, swabbed her face, neck, and arms.

"How was that?" Yvette asked Grace.

"I feel reborn."

The comment brought a thousand-watt smile to Yvette's face.

>>>

When Grace got home, Mick was in the kitchen eating a bowl of cereal. Grace held her tongue to keep herself from commenting on his aberrant schedule, as it was now three in the afternoon, and he was just getting around to breakfast.

"How's the alien invasion coming along?" she

asked without a hint of sarcasm. She really wanted to be positive in all her dealings with Mick. She had committed to this on her walk home.

"*Visitation*," Mick corrected.

"Oh, right," she laughed. "How could I forget the religious connotation?"

"Where did you go?" Mick asked. "Not that I minded having the house to myself. You just look, well, radiant."

At that, Grace bubbled over with enthusiasm for her new dance practice. She filled Mick's ears with a description of her first Nia class while he munched on his cereal. At least he was eating whole grains, she noted.

Once she wound down, Mick cleared his throat. "You know, you're quite a catch there, sister Grace."

Her senses tingled. Mick hardly ever called her "Grace," even though she'd made it her legal name years ago. He insisted on calling her "Pris," short for Priscilla. This was done, she realized, partly out of habit, as it was her birth name, but mostly just to irritate her.

"Thank you, Mick," she said. It was her policy never to let a compliment go unacknowledged.

Mick waved his spoon at her. "I have a proposition for you."

"Yes?"

"You think you can take charge of my love life. Well, I'll admit I haven't done a very good job of managing that part of my existence on my own. So I'll turn it over to you—"

Grace clapped her hands together. "Oh, Mick! You won't regret—"

"—on one condition," he continued, pointing his spoon at her for emphasis.

She waited.

"You have to let me fix *you* up on a date in return."

Grace protested. "But Mick, you don't even know anyone in Seattle."

He raised his eyebrows. "I know people… Besides, you're just making excuses. Listen, you haven't exactly been a master of your own love life, either. Too busy managing everyone else's, I think."

His words hit a tender place inside her. She opened her mouth to say something but then kept silent.

"I'll take that as agreement," he said.

Grace smiled, placing her hand on his. "I guess we'll see if anyone will have us. A couple of well-worn dreamslippers, we are."

Chapter Three

Cat's findings at the crime scene surprised Grace. "It sounds as if Nina were suffocated—or strangled."

"I agree," said Cat.

"Odd that she was there right after work and hadn't changed. Most women would if they were meeting a lover, don't you think?"

"Yeah." They drove in silence for a minute, Grace running over in her mind the items they needed to pick up from the grocery store.

Cat fiddled with the car radio, tuning to an AM station. "I always listen to his podcasts," she explained. "But I think it's time for his broadcast show."

"Sam Waters?" Grace guessed.

"Oh, here he is."

"...Today's 'Watershed Moment' is literally on the water, floating on it. I can't help but note the irony of Seattle's flotilla of kayaktivists, protesting oil while sitting in kayaks made of plastic, which is derived from oil."

Grace clucked her tongue. "I think they're heroes. Modern-day Davids, taking on Goliath."

Cat shushed her.

"...I'm not the first to point out the irony, and of course the Left is crying foul. They don't think there should be a 'purity' test applied to protests. I agree. But this isn't about

purity. This is about recognizing the hypocrisy of one's posi-
tion. You listeners know I think peak oil is a real problem,
which puts me on the same side as many environmentalists.
But you can't drive your gas-fueled car—yes, even the hybrids,
you Prius lovers—to a protest and then paddle around in your
plastic kayak trying to stop a company from producing some-
thing that you're demonstrating with every breath you can't
live without. These kayaktivists couldn't even wean themselves
from oil for the sake of one protest. Some of them have pointed
out that there are plenty of kayaks made of wood on the market.
To that I say, then why didn't you use one of those? Hey,
kayaktivists, if you want the threat of drilling in the Arctic
Refuge to go away, then stop creating demand for oil."

Grace bristled at his rhetoric. She could see why Cat found his iconoclastic perspective refreshing. But it was not to her taste. She'd felt moved and hopeful, watching those kayaktivists. "I think I've heard enough."

"It's hard for me to imagine him as Nina's killer," said Cat, turning the radio off. She whipped out her phone, tapped a few times, and then showed it to Grace. "He's a hottie, too," she said. "Look."

Grace peered over. Sam had the slightly tousled, charming look of athletes she'd known who could slip from the tennis court to a press conference with nothing more than a towel-off.

"So was Ted Bundy," Grace said.

"Point taken."

"By the way," Cat said, "I can't believe you're let-ting Mick set you up. Do I need to remind you that his ex-girlfriend burned down his beach house?"

"It's our deal, Cat. If I let him set me up, he'll go out with whomever I choose."

"So, who'd he find?"

"An IT director for some company I've never heard of, lowercases their name. I guess that's supposed to be trendy."

"He sounds dull."

Grace wound Siddhartha through a residential roundabout. Most of the inhabitants in the neighborhood had dug up their front lawns and replaced them with vegetable gardens. "I have to admit, he sounds stable, and that's an attractive quality when you're my age."

"Where did Mick find this guy?"

"Through his new job." Mick had taken contract work with a company that supplied art to corporate lobbies, atriums, and the like. His crew switched out the art every few months, taking down the old and setting up the new. Installing art was apparently a specialized skill, with the need to handle it, hang or display it, and then pack it carefully.

"Mick and I have planned a double date. We're going ice skating."

"Ugh, seriously? You people over fifty just don't know how to date."

"I have many more years on you, whippersnapper," Grace said. "I've been at this a long time."

"Yeah, but Gran, you should meet him for coffee first. No obligations. If there aren't any sparks, you're not locked into, like, *a whole day of pain*."

"I think our way is more civilized," Grace said

emphatically, effectively silencing her granddaughter, whose attention went back to her smartphone.

After a pause, Cat looked up and asked, "So who are you setting up with Uncle Mick?"

Grace brightened. She'd gotten Mick to consider a date with her friend Cecily Johnson. She just knew the two of them would hit it off, with so much in common and so much to talk about. Their art styles were even similar.

"You remember Cecily? We went to a show at her gallery."

"Right," said Cat. "Her paintings looked like trail mix. Gave 'mixed media' a whole new meaning."

"You're awfully cynical today, I must say," Grace said. She was beginning to find her granddaughter a bit tedious.

"What? I didn't say the trail-mix art was bad. It's very Seattle, when you think about it. Her paintings could totally hang in the lobby at REI. Hey, maybe with Mick's new job, he can swing it."

"Now you're just being sarcastic."

"What about Mick's ruined reputation? Is she cool since he's actually the hero, not the child-porn perp?"

"I explained the whole thing to her, and she's read the news vindicating Mick."

"Well, that's something. I mean, at least she's willing to give it a go."

"You don't sound very convinced. Don't you think Cecily and Mick would make a great couple?"

"Do you want my honest opinion?"

"Of course."

"Two artists? No way. That's doomed to fail."

Grace felt her hackles rise. "At least Mick and I are meeting real, live human beings. Instead of this virtual thing you seem to be doing. You can criticize when you've earned the right, which you haven't."

"You asked for my honest opinion!"

"Yes, but what I meant was your *civilized* honest opinion."

>>>

Grace chose a pair of microfiber wool stretch pants to wear ice skating. The microfiber would be breathable, but the wool would keep her warm. And the stretch, well, it would allow her to maneuver around the rink without too much trouble.

Not that she wasn't a seasoned, confident skater. Growing up in the Midwest, pre-global warming, when there were still blizzards every winter and the pond on their land froze over, she'd learned to wear skates as if they were her winter shoes. She'd never lost the finesse for it, not even in Seattle, where it only snowed once in a great while, and then just to have an excuse to shut down the city. There were several skating rinks: an indoor one near the base of the Space Needle, an outdoor one over on the Eastside, and an Olympic-sized indoor rink on the north side of town. That's the one they'd chosen for their double date. Grace had once taken a refresher course there.

Her granddaughter had returned to researching the Sam Waters case after they arrived home from shopping. Cat was planning to order in sushi for dinner and keep plugging away at her research, seeming pleased with herself. Grace's plan to hand the reins over to Cat was working.

If all went well at the rink, Grace and Mick's double date could lead to dinner afterward.

To appease Cat, she'd done an online search on her date, the IT director of what turned out to be a company called coplux. The lowercasing was intentional.

"You have to arm yourself with whatever information is available," Cat had said.

But Grace felt as if she were spying. It was one thing to turn to technology to snoop on criminal suspects. But when the matter was purely social, she preferred to let people's personalities unfold more naturally, in the course of her interactions with them.

Still, she had to admit to feeling some relief at learning that George Connors wasn't a known serial killer, not that the thought had crossed her mind. A widower for going on ten years, he was an avid cyclist, an occasional bird watcher, and a lover of classical music. He had been with coplux for a few years, as a consultant. He'd retired from Microsoft six years before.

Mick showed up at her bedroom door, the smell of his aftershave preceding him, just as she slid the posts on her pearl stud earrings into her ears.

"You look too fancy for ice skating," he said.

She glanced over, taking in his jeans and slightly rumpled shirt. "And you don't look fancy enough for a first date."

They spoke in unison. "Will George mind?" "Will

Cecily judge me?"

"Oh, listen to you two," said Cat, who appeared in the doorway behind Mick. "You both look great. Like you're being yourselves. That's probably rare enough in the dating world."

Grace smiled. "Here goes nothing."

>>>

While her grandmother and great-uncle waded into the swirling waters of the Seattle dating pool, Cat buried herself in the case.

Sam was an interesting man. For a conservative talk-show host, he had been decidedly reasonable, mild-mannered, and polite. It probably irked his detractors all the more that they couldn't lump him into the same group as the obviously unhinged set. He forced them to take him seriously, and in so doing, he'd made quite a few enemies.

He was critical of a lot of the sacred cows held dear by progressives. Waters argued the impracticality of solar energy every chance he got, almost to the point of actively fighting it. But he didn't cite biased research done by for-profit entities who stood to gain if solar lost. On the contrary, the scientific evidence supported his charges that solar couldn't pay for itself, that it only worked economically with heavy government rebates and subsidies. Cat found this fascinating, the more she dug into it.

But then her phone buzzed. She was about to hit IGNORE, but then she saw it was Uncle Mick calling.

"So, how are the Ice Capades?" she joked.

"Not good," Mick said, breathing hard. Cat could hear beeping and a loudspeaker in the background. "Your grandmother fell. She might've broken her hip."

Cat tossed her laptop aside and stood up, panic shooting through her. "What?"

"Yeah, it's not good," Mick said. "We're at Swedish Hospital. In Ballard."

"I'm on my way."

As she dashed out to the garage, she remembered that Mick and Granny Grace had Siddhartha, their only car. It would take her too long by bus, so she used her phone to call a service car, in true Seattle style. There were several companies threatening to displace traditional cabs with their app-easy service. The car arrived in less than five minutes. A fuzzy pink mustache adorned the grill, the car company's signature logo.

Twenty minutes later, she found her grandmother lying in a hospital bed in one corner of the ER, a curtain drawn around her. Mick was there, plus Cecily, whom she recognized, and another man who must be George Connors.

"Cat!" her grandmother practically yelled as she approached. "Oh, I'm so glad to see you! Look at me. Can you believe it? I've never been immobile before. I don't quite know how to handle it. Of course I do believe this bed has wheels. They just roll me around whenever I'm in the way here, like I'm some sort of stage prop. That's what this is, isn't it? Quite the show. Broadway in Ballard…"

Cat glanced at Mick, who nodded. "She's a little

high on painkillers right now," he confirmed.

"How did this happen? Granny Grace is an excellent skater."

Her grandmother broke in. "Oh, you can blame George here. A little unsteady on our feet, now, aren't we, hmm? He has the instincts of a four-year-old. You know, when they're learning to skate for the first time. He started to fall, so what does he do? Grabs onto the closest thing—me—and pulls me right down!"

Cat shot a glance at George, who was busy examining the shine on the top of his shoes.

Mick took Cat aside. "It's not her hip," he said. "It's her pelvis, and that's worse."

"Oh, no," Cat said, feeling his words slice through her.

Just then a woman with spiky silver hair appeared, carrying a clipboard. She wore scrubs underneath a starched white coat. Cat noticed a tattoo peeking out from the sleeve of her coat, over her right wrist.

"Are you Grace's family? I'm Dr. Acker." She offered Mick her hand, and he took it.

"I'm her brother," Mick said. "And this is Cat, her granddaughter."

After shaking Cat's hand, Dr. Acker said, "Your grandmother was in a lot of pain when she came in, so we're managing that first. Once the swelling goes down, we're going to manually adjust her dislocation."

"Dislocation?" Cat asked.

"Yes, the bones in her pelvis moved out of place in the fall. She has both a fracture and a dislocation. It's called an *acetabular fracture.*"

Cat took out her cell phone. "Can you spell that for me?"

Dr. Acker complied, and Cat pulled up images on her phone. "Will she need surgery?"

"Not in this case," Dr. Acker said. "She's got strong bones for her age, and she's in good health. The pelvis will heal on its own, I believe, without the need for pins, screws, wires, or plates."

Cat shuddered. "My grandmother will be glad to hear that."

Dr. Acker smiled. "Yes, I know. But in many ways, this isn't as easy as the hip would've been. It's going to take some time."

That made Cat flash on the crucial case they just landed. How would her grandmother handle being grounded while Cat tried to catch Nina's killer on her own? And could Cat do it, without her grandmother's help?

Mick asked Dr. Acker a few more questions, and Cat peered over at Granny Grace, who was holding Cecily's hand.

As Dr. Acker bid them good-bye, Mick turned to his sister, taking her other hand. "I'm so sorry this happened to you."

"Sorry is as sorry does," Granny Grace said, smiling up at him.

Cecily cleared her throat. "Is there anything I can do? Grace, sweetie, tell me what you need."

Cat watched her grandmother's face turn serious as she gazed slowly at each of the people gathered around her. "You can tell everyone to leave, Cecily. It's a bit too crowded in here for my taste."

The four of them glanced awkwardly at each other.

George swallowed hard and then spoke. "Grace, I'm so sorry. I have probably given you the worst experience in the history of dating. Please, when and if you ever want to see me again, let me make it up to you."

Her grandmother did not respond.

Mick turned to George and pulled him away from the bed. "Maybe you should go. But it was just an accident, George. Really. Don't blame yourself."

"I appreciate that, Mick, I really do. But I've been around long enough to know when I've been an idiot. I hope your sister heals well. Please keep me informed." He left.

Cat and Cecily flanked Granny Grace. The two women stroked her hair and hands, trying to make her feel better. But she had a sad look that Cat had never seen before. Her grandmother suddenly looked old, and tired.

Mick came back to her bedside, but Granny Grace shoved him away.

"You, too, Mickey. Go on home."

Mick looked pained, but he nodded in understanding. He turned to Cat. "I'll be in the lobby."

"Thanks, Uncle Mick," said Cat, squeezing his arm as he exited.

As soon as Mick left, Grace sat up, grabbed Cat's and Cecily's arms, and said, "Now, what kind of trouble can we girls get into? You want a little of the juice they're giving me?" She gestured to the bottle feeding into her IV.

Chapter Four

Grace couldn't believe it.

Breaking your hip—or pelvis, she corrected herself—was such a frail, elderly thing to do. What would come next? A shawl and a rocker?

The first thing she'd thought of as she tumbled to the hard ice was Nia. She'd so enjoyed her new barefoot-dance class. Even before she realized how bad things were, that she would not even be able to walk (or skate) on her own two feet back to the lobby of the rink, she knew she wouldn't be able to go back to Nia anytime soon.

All because of a man and his little-boy grab hands.

She knew she should forgive George Connors for his instinctual effort to keep himself right-side up on his wobbly ankles. But that would have to come in time. It wasn't as if the date had been a rousing success even before the accident. George bored her to tears talking about his IT consulting work *ad nauseam*, never once pausing to ask her a question or engage in an actual conversation.

She had tried, too. "I once ice-skated on a frozen lake in Alaska!" she announced. That was his cue to be a human being, to inquire further with something like, "You don't say? Why were you in Alaska?"

But no. He went right on with his incessant IT talk, as if she'd never said a word.

And Mick and Cecily hadn't hit it off either. Before they'd even donned their skates and headed out to the rink, the two were embroiled in a heated argument about art.

"Rauschenberg was a freakin' genius," Mick defended, to which Cecily replied, "Overrated."

"Well, just who do *you* hold up as great?"

"The women of that era got short shrift. Pollock was an ass, and no more a genius than poor Lee Krasner, who put up with him. Ditto Elaine de Kooning. And Janet Sobel deserved far more credit. They all should have better name recognition, and they would, too, if they'd been men. *White* men, that is."

Mick had buttoned his lip at that point, which Grace considered a wise move. Cecily looked so pretty, her cocoa skin set off well by an orange sweater. She had this endearing attachment to body glitter, just a hint of it in her powder so that her skin seemed to glint and catch the light as she moved. Grace could tell that Mick found her attractive, so the fact that they seemed to have differing views on art likely frustrated him.

Grace thought of all this while lying in bed in rehab, where she'd been moved. It was interesting that the first thing she'd thought of when she'd fallen and couldn't get up again was Nia. Why a dance class instead of her case? This time she knew the victim, too. In a moment of pure emotion, her heart had chosen Nia over Nina. Or finding her killer, anyway.

It really was time to move on if she were letting go of the responsibility of solving the world's crimes. That had been her accepted burden for as long as she could remember.

She held the belief that there are no accidents in life. Maybe she'd been grounded because she needed to be. Maybe Cat needed to tackle this case on her own.

But what would Grace do next? She'd never liked the idea of "retirement," which made her think of old people sitting in their air-conditioned Florida homes watching television. Here in rehab, she'd turned the TV off. Several times in fact. A nurse kept coming in, making some silly remark about how it was too quiet in Grace's room, and then turning the TV on again.

It was infuriating how people tended to treat you when you were incapacitated.

And old.

After the third time, Grace hid the remote under her pillow. She rather enjoyed the quiet, as it gave her the space to think. She had begun to meditate throughout the day, which wasn't easy with the nurse bursting in at random moments.

Her meditations distracted her from other thoughts, darker ones, which were otherwise difficult to keep at bay. She found herself reflecting on her lingering feelings of betrayal at her old friend Ernesto in Miami, how he'd been helping a child-porn king launder money all that time, right under their noses. Her nose. That was the thing. It still bothered Grace that it had taken so long to see him for who he really was.

At that moment, Grace's cell phone buzzed. It was Cat, so she took it.

"How are you doing, Gran?"

Grace answered, putting a brightness into her voice that she did not feel. "Fine!"

"Really? You have a broken pelvis."

"Well, tell me something I don't know. What progress have you made on the case?"

"Do you want me to bring you some books?"

"Actually, yes," said Grace. "And my laptop. I want to help you as much as I can."

"Okay, let me grab those things, and I'll be there as soon as I can. We can talk about the case then."

Grace waited for her granddaughter, expecting her trip from Queen Anne Hill to Ballard to last only twenty minutes or so, and that only if the Ballard Bridge was up. But the silence stretched into more than an hour. She wished someone had brought her a laptop. She could at least logon to Facebook to see whether Annie Lin had responded to her last message.

Soon, she found herself in someone else's dream.

"I'll have you know I'm the best ninja clown this side of the Pecos." The words came out of Grace's mouth, but she knew they weren't hers. She looked down at her hands to find them wrinkled and veined, yes, but decidedly manly.

"The best, eh?" An old-time Western sheriff sized up her dreamer, his thumbs tucked into his vest.

"That's right."

Grace realized there was something on her nose, likely a big red clown nose, judging by the feel of it.

"Well, let's see what you've got," the sheriff said, drawing a pistol out of its holster. He shot at the dreamer's feet, and Grace felt her host jump up with some fast ninja moves to avoid the bullets. Then she rode along as he spun and blocked and eventually had the sheriff face down over a barrel, literally.

64

"Now, we won't have you bringing corruption to this town," said the dreamer. He then spun the sheriff around, smacked him across the face, and ceremoniously plucked the badge from his vest.

"Get on with yourself," said the ninja clown, who'd pocketed the sheriff's gun and took it out now to shoot at the sheriff's feet, who hightailed it out of Dodge.

Her dreamer blew the smoke off the gun tip just as Grace was knocked out of the dream by Cat, who was squeezing her shoulder.

"Granny Grace."

"My goodness," said Grace, struggling to ease herself up into more of a seated position, which caused a searing pain to shoot through her right hip. "Ah…"

"Be careful, Gran." She attempted to help Grace, who pushed her hand away.

"Leave me alone. I'm fine."

Cat backed away. "Whoa, you're not doing too well with this, are you?"

"I'm sorry, Cat." Grace crossed her arms in front of her. "I just don't like being in this bed."

Cat sat down next to her and patted her hand. "Well, I don't like seeing you there."

Grace squeezed Cat's hand in hers. "I don't plan to be here for long. Now tell me what you've found on Sam Waters."

Cat's eyes lit up at the mention of the case. She drew Grace's laptop out of her bag and handed it to her. "I haven't seen anything yet that connects Sam and Nina, outside of Robin's *feeling* that they knew each other at that protest. I've put together a list of his known associates. Maybe they met through one of them."

Grace set the sleek computer on her lap and logged in. She kept thinking about beautiful, talented Nina, her life stopped dead in its tracks. It was so unfair.

"I've set up an account where we can share documents and notes, and track our case together while you're in here." She bent over Grace's screen and pointed. "Click on that link to accept my invitation, create an account, and you'll be in."

Grace jumped through these little hoops with no problem and saw that Cat had already added several documents to the site.

"You've been busy," Grace said.

"Oh, you know me. This is all online research. The Seattle PD has not been helpful, by the way. They refuse to tell me anything. And I haven't done any surveillance yet."

"Well, remember Cat, boots-on-the-ground—"

"—work is what solves the case. Yes, I know."

Grace tried to stifle her feeling that she was now a boring old lady known to repeat herself. But she didn't stifle it very well. "I guess I have nothing left to teach you, Grasshopper." It was out of her mouth before she could stop it.

"To tell the truth, Gran," Cat said, "I think I'm kind of in denial about how bad this is." She gestured to Grace's injury. "I keep thinking I have to save the big interviews for when you'll be able to join me. But you know me. I've been researching this pelvis thing, and—"

"—I figured you would," said Grace. "Now don't

give me that sad face. Pay no attention to the stat—

"—You mean the one saying that twenty percent of those who suffer a hip or pelvis fracture die within the year? Don't worry, Gran. I'm sure you're in better shape than most."

"That's right," Grace said, taking Cat's hands in her own. "And I'm well taken care of here with Dr. Acker. But I'm grounded for the duration."

"How long is that?"

"She says it will be two months before I can walk again, three to six before I can practice yoga, and a year before I'm fully recovered," Grace said. "But I'm going to try to beat all that. I'll be stuck here in rehab for a few weeks, though. Then they send me home with a walker."

"Okay," Cat said, sighing. "Well."

"Can you manage the case without me for a while?"

"I'll just have to, won't I?"

Grace remembered an op-ed she wanted to share with Cat. "Grab me that copy of *The Stranger* over there, would you? There's something I want to show you."

Her granddaughter snatched the weekly paper from the windowsill and handed it to Grace, who flipped to the editorial. "Did you read this, Cat? They're defending the kayaktivists from the likes of Sam Waters and his ilk. They make a pretty good argument, if you ask me."

"Oh, yeah?"

"Yes. They point out that demanding the kayaks not be made out of plastic would be like criticizing an abolitionist for protesting slavery while wearing cotton."

Cat considered for a moment, and then shook her

head. "Seriously? *That's* their argument? The analogy doesn't even work. Slavery isn't necessary to produce cotton. But you can't make plastic without oil."

Grace chuckled, feeling simultaneously perturbed and proud of Cat. "You're right."

Cat smiled. "Well, Sam might have some excellent points. But that doesn't mean he's innocent of Nina's murder."

Grace set the paper aside, turned back to the laptop, and opened a doc. She looked around for her reading glasses on the bedside table, but Cat reached over and bumped up the point size on the list in a couple of clicks.

"I don't know that it does either of us much good to go over these names," Grace said. "Maybe you could have Robin take a look, see if she recognizes anyone Nina would have known."

"Sure," Cat said. "Good idea."

"Here's something that's more your style: Ask Robin to put together her own list, and then compare hers with this. You can do that with one of your fancy software tools, right?"

Cat nodded.

"Remember, you need to have a conversation with Simon Fletcher, and have you talked to Cassidy Waters?"

"Sam's wife? Not yet."

"Well, why not, Cat? That's the first thing I would have done." Grace knew she was being too critical, and she could tell by Cat's demeanor that she was making her granddaughter feel bad. But she couldn't stop. The stakes

68

were too high, suddenly. She felt frustrated that she hadn't taught her granddaughter more.

"Really? Because I think checking out the actual crime scene was more important."

Cat's pushback hit Grace squarely on target. "You're right, Cat. I'm sorry. It's just… Oh, this stupid bed!"

Cat put her hand on Grace's, the touch soothing. There were Cat's big brown eyes, sympathizing with her. "It's all right, Gran."

Grace flashed on the silly ninja clown, and it gave her an idea. "Is there a way you can get close enough to the family's home to dreamslip with Sam?"

"I don't know, Gran. I've thought about it. The security is pretty tight out there. Unlike some of the other cases we've had, I'm not sure Mercer Island is the kind of place where you can get away with sleeping in a car out on the street. There's also the possibility that I might pick up his kids' dreams instead, or his wife's."

"Remember what I taught you about popping out of dreams you don't want to be in, and of connecting with your target."

"Yes," said Cat. "But this superhero power of ours sure has its limitations. By the way, I picked up some really strange dreams the other ni—"

Grace heard a knock on her door, and she put her finger to her lips to silence Cat's dreamslipping talk. "Hello?" she called out.

"We heard there was a diva down for the count," said a voice Grace instantly recognized.

"Dave! Come on in here, you rascal."

The door burst open, and in walked Dave Bander and Simon Fletcher, preceded by a mass of glittery, multicolored balloons that would have been perfectly at home on a Pride Parade float. They depicted several beloved drag queens of Seattle. Grace recognized her favorite, Dina Martina, whose deliberate mispronunciation of Seattle as "seedle" never failed to make her laugh.

"We thought you needed company," said Dave. "And I'm not talking about us. I'm talking about the five goddesses here." He bounced the balloons in her direction, and they came to float above her bed as if taking watch.

"What a wonderful idea," said Grace. "Oh, I'm so glad you came by." She reached for both men's hands.

After they were caught up on Grace's prognosis, she fixed her gaze on Simon. "I'm so sorry to hear about Nina."

"It's an awful tragedy," he said, shaking his head. Grace noticed his eyes begin to tear up.

"She was only, what? Forty-three?" added Dave. "Robin's really in a state."

"Yes, we've seen her…" Grace cast a glance at Cat, who had receded as the men crowded around Grace.

"You have?" asked Simon. "Robin hasn't been very social."

"Oh, you're right. I probably wouldn't have seen her until the funeral if it weren't for the fact that we've taken her on as a client."

"A client?" Simon seemed surprised. "Do you believe her theory about this talk-show host? What's his name … Sam Waters?"

Grace found it interesting that Robin had broadcast her suspicions to one of Nina's partners. Not that Robin was particularly circumspect. At times, she seemed to lack the ability to filter.

"We're investigating along those lines," Grace replied.

"Well, they come from opposite ends of the political spectrum," said Simon. "So maybe that set him off. Or maybe they knew each other from somewhere. I don't know, but Robin seems convinced."

"He's our primary suspect," Grace said, and then she glanced at Cat. "But we shouldn't say any more than that."

"Understood," said Simon. And then to Cat, he remarked, "I've missed you at St. Patrick's."

"Yeah, I've just been so busy," she replied.

But Grace knew this was an excuse. Cat hadn't been back to church since Lee died. While she had recovered from the loss, there seemed to be parts of her that had been forever altered by it. Grace was no Catholic herself, but she hated to see anyone parted from their source of divine connection.

Grace's dreaded nurse came into the room then, busting up the gathering. "I'm sorry, but Gracie here needs her rest."

Grace bristled at "Gracie," which made her think of Gracie Allen and George Burns. "My name is Amazing *Grace*," she corrected. "But you can call me 'Amazing' if you like."

The nurse seemed unruffled by this. "Oh, well, we're all amazing here on God's green earth, now aren't we?"

>>>

Cat left her grandmother's hospital room feeling a bit lost.

What Granny Grace said about the case had got under her skin, making her doubt she could truly handle it on her own.

She'd try to figure out a way to dreamslip with her suspect, though. With a murder, it was unlikely the killer would give away his crime in a dream, especially if he or she felt no remorse or lingering guilt over it. But maybe if there *had* been a sexual element, the killer would have a dream about it. So far the Seattle PD refused to release any details on the case, so Cat didn't know if there'd been signs of sexual assault or not. Robin was also still a suspect, so she hadn't been able to get a full police report, either. Cat was flying totally blind on this one.

But there was more than lack of self-confidence bothering Cat after the hospital visit. It hit her seeing Granny Grace in rehab that the woman wouldn't live forever. She was seventy-nine and in better shape than a lot of people half her age, that was true. But Granny Grace's aging couldn't be denied. It was likely that, had she taken that tumble on the ice rink just twenty years ago, or even ten, she would have suffered only bruises.

Cat had done more than research pelvic fractures —she'd also tried to understand the exact effects of aging. Her grandmother's bones were becoming more brittle, her stamina decreasing. Her eyesight was already nowhere near as good as Cat's, and she sometimes didn't seem as sharp as she used to be. Her grandmother was spirited and truly amazing, so it was hard to imagine her frail, or sick, or limited in any way, though.

But Cat had to think about the future. Would her grandmother live another ten years? Twenty? Who knew?

She shuddered, thinking about having to say good-bye to Granny Grace. That would be … impossible.

>>>

Cat went home to regroup, finding Mick in the kitchen. It was getting close to dinnertime and there he was, pouring himself a bowl of cereal.

"You know, you eat like a nine-year-old boy," she said.

"What can I say? I'm just a kid inside."

"Want to go out for a real dinner? It's been a while since we've had some great-uncle, grandniece time."

He stopped mid-pour. "Aw, and waste these frosted loops? Look, they're even healthy." He showed her the box. "Your grandmother made me get organic."

Cat giggled. "C'mon, I bet we can still get in a happy-hour order down at Mo's."

"You're on," he said, delicately pouring the cereal back into the box. A few stray loops fell to the countertop, and both Cat and Mick popped some in their mouths.

"I can taste the organic-ness," Cat said.

"Yeah, that's what makes it suck," Mick said. "I mean, if you're going for *frosted* cereal in the first place, health is not what you have in mind."

At Mo's, she and Mick took a booth in the back, under a red light and a vintage ad for car and axle grease. *A little grease on your pistons, and it's a smooth ride!* an overly exuberant-looking cherub in overalls proclaimed.

Once they were settled with their drinks and a tray of sliders, Cat decided to get into her uncle's business a little. After all, with her grandmother in the hospital, someone had to fill her shoes. "So, that friend of Granny Grace's, the one with you at the skating rink. Are you going to see her again?"

"Cecily? I don't know. Probably not. I think she thinks I'm an ass."

"You kind of are."

"Thanks."

"I mean, in a way that a woman might find … endearing."

"Right."

There was a pause as they both wolfed down their sliders. Then Mick spoke again. "She did call me after your grandmother's, ah, spill. She didn't have to do that. I figured she'd check in with Pris, and that'd be it."

"So, how'd the conversation go?"

"It didn't. It was a voice mail, right after the accident."

Cat nearly dropped her slider. "You didn't call her back?"

Mick looked at her as if realizing he'd done something wrong. "Um, not yet?"

"Uncle Mick," Cat whined. "It's been a week. You better call her. In fact, call her right now."

"Here?"

"Yeah, you've got a phone, right? You know how to use it?"

He frowned. "I thought this was grandniece, great-uncle bonding time."

Cat smiled. "Aren't we bonding here? I feel a definite bond."

Mick shook his head, wiped his hands and mouth, and took up his phone. "All right."

He tapped his phone a bit to find her number, and then hit it. "Uh, hello. Cecily? This is Mick ... Travers."

Cat couldn't hear what Cecily said, but the tone seemed welcoming.

"Listen, I wanted to thank you for your call. I appreciate your concern."

Cat mouthed the words, *Ask her out.*

"So, ah…"

"…I was wondering, you know, with Art Walk coming up next week, if you were planning to go."

Cat shook her head. *Ask her!* she mouthed again.

"I mean, maybe you'd like to go with me."

There was a pause.

Then Mick looked up and smiled. "Good deal. All right. Then I'll meet you at OpCo Gallery at six."

He tapped to end the call, and Cat yelled, "Yay!"

Their waitress showed up to take their next order, looking amused. "Are we celebrating? How about switching it up to something harder?"

They ordered a couple of martinis and another plate of sliders.

Chapter Five

Cat began to wonder if she should have stuck to watching the crow lady. Surveillance on her radio talk-show guy was turning out to be less exciting.

She'd been following Waters for a couple of days, and so far he'd done nothing but make a circuit between the radio station, home, his daughter's ballet studio, and his son's soccer practices. But Cat told herself to stay patient. Nobody could be this boring.

She resisted her grandmother's idea to talk to his wife. If there was anything to Robin's crazy obsession with Sam as the killer, Cat didn't want to risk tipping him off. She'd already done as her grandmother said and de-duped lists of possible acquaintances Sam and Nina had in common. But the two hadn't socialized or worked in the same circles at all. Cat was beginning to think the whole case was a sham brought on by grief. She remembered how she'd totally shut down after Lee Stone died and figured Robin would likewise be twisting in the wind for a long time to come.

Sitting outside the radio station, Cat felt her phone buzz. It was a message, not just a "pet" this time, from a potential date whom Cat found interesting. Exciting, even. *I think we should meet*, it said.

She tapped out a response. *When?*
Tonight.

She glanced at the time in the corner of her phone, then back at the station. It was ten after eight. Waters's car sat in the parking lot. It seemed to give off a station-ary vibe, as if it knew it wasn't going anywhere soon.

Where?

You choose.

I'm on the Eastside. Cat thought that would put him off, since Seattleites typically treat the Eastside as if it were across state lines, or over a mountain pass. True, it was separated by a body of water, but if it wasn't rush hour, a trip across either of the floating bridges would only take fifteen minutes or so. She suspected the true divide was more psychological than physical. The Eastside was affluent and conservative, a place of mostly unchecked growth punctuated by subdivisions and sprawl. Seattle was urban, or neighborhood-centric, and about as liberal as you could get without—Cat imagined, since she'd never been—going to a European city.

But her texter wrote back: *So am I.*

She mulled over the facts on her potential date. He said he was a sommelier for a local restaurant, that he'd been married but was divorced, and that he had a twin brother. He'd sent a picture of himself. Blonde, aquiline nose, strong build, dressed well in a suit that looked tailored for him. Cat glanced back at the radio station. Should she really abandon her post? It wasn't possible to follow this guy twenty-four-seven, she reasoned. It was just too bad Granny Grace was laid up in the hospital and couldn't take over for her.

She searched her phone for a nearby restaurant and told her guy to meet her there. She was famished anyway; otherwise, it would have been better to keep it to coffee. But she felt a reckless hopefulness about this one. They'd been carrying on over text, and things had got pretty steamy.

Cat arrived first and chose a table near the back, where they'd have a bit of privacy. The restaurant was connected to a hotel, and she felt bold about that. If this guy screened okay…

She couldn't believe she was having such thoughts.

Ugh, what her mother would say.

Granny Grace would be more open about it. But still. Thinking of her mother, she nearly bolted up out of her chair and left. But she took a few breaths and texted Granny Grace her whereabouts and this guy's full name: Paul Dorian.

After a few minutes, she saw someone talking to a waiter, who pointed to Cat.

Paul Dorian clocked in at about one hundred pounds heavier than the man in the picture he'd sent. His hair was also not blonde, but rather dishwater brown with bits of gray. He had heavy dark circles under his eyes. He was supposed to be thirty but looked older.

As he moved toward her table, and she realized it was too late to back out now, she tried to stifle a feeling of panicked letdown. While she had a right to be angry about his misrepresentation—after all, the picture *she'd* send *him* was recent—she thought she could give him the benefit of the doubt. Maybe he had an awesome personality. Maybe he'd sweep her off her feet.

"Hey there, gorgeous," he said, pulling out his chair and plopping down.

She noticed there was a stain on his shirt.

He caught her gaze. "Oh, sorry, I'm just off work and didn't think to change."

She tried to let that relax her. He did work in a restaurant. But it was the "think to change" that got her. So he had an opportunity to change into fresh clothes, but he didn't "think" of it.

"Classy place," he said, picking up the menu.

"I'm just off work myself," she said. "I just left a stakeout. I'm a private investigator."

He laughed, as if she were pulling his leg. "You're kidding, right? You look too young."

"Nope. I'm a PI."

"What, like Magnum?"

She had no idea what he was talking about. It was probably some reference that signaled his actual age.

"You know, *Magnum P.I.* On TV?"

"Sorry," she said, staring at him blankly.

"You call yourself a PI and you don't even know who Magnum is? Tom Selleck?"

When she continued to stare at him blankly, he shook his head.

Thankfully, the waiter arrived and asked them what they'd like to drink. Cat decided she needed something to fortify her.

"Hey, you're a wine expert," she said, though she was having trouble imagining wine expertise coming from this guy. "Why don't you choose something for us?"

Paul looked at the menu briefly but then turned to the waiter and said, "Oh, just give us a couple of glasses of the house red."

As the waiter exited, Cat said, "What about all this fancy sommelier business?"

"Well, that was a bit of an exaggeration," he said.

"What do you mean? You do work in a restaurant, right?"

"Oh, yeah. But I'm more of a ... chef."

"Really? Which restaurant?"

He scratched his head, looking away, as if he didn't want to tell her.

"Are you embarrassed?" Cat felt a pang of sympathy for him. "Look, I won't judge. We've had a really good text exchange, and I want to know about you."

"Yeah, our sexting got pretty hot, didn't it?" he said, winking. He grabbed the edges of the table and pulled it toward him. "Too bad this table isn't bolted down. Think it would take us?"

Cat cringed, tried to politely laugh it off, and then a thought occurred to her. "Are the tables in your restaurant ... bolted down, Paul?"

He looked caught. "Yeah," he said. "It's the restaurant in the old Titus Motel, out by the highway."

"Oh," she said. "Well, there's no shame in that. I bet you have a lot of good stories."

"Sure," he said. He laughed. "One time, this gay guy worked back in the kitchen with me, and he had AIDS. Cut himself chopping a tomato. Can you imagine? His blood in your soup."

Cat had been settled on the spicy tomato soup for dinner, but when the waiter returned, she switched to a spinach salad. She'd decided there was no way this homophobe was getting any closer to her than the length of the table between them. At this point, she was sticking around only for the food and for whatever she could get out of the evening in terms of her ongoing study of human behavior. Or animal behavior, as the case may be.

"You look just like your picture," Paul said after they'd ordered. "That's good, by the way, in case you were wondering."

"So where was your picture taken?" she asked. "I'd assumed it was in your restaurant, since you're dressed up and holding a wine glass."

He smiled. "Oh, that was at a wedding."

"How long ago?" She asked the question as brightly as she could.

"Just last year."

"But you look so ... different."

He laughed again. "Well, okay, it's not my picture. That's my twin brother. You know, same difference, since we're twins. I just don't have any good shots, you know?"

The waiter brought their food, and Cat dove into her salad as if she were in a salad-eating contest.

"You've got a good appetite," he said. "I like that in a woman."

"Yeah, that's good," Cat said. She motioned to the waiter. "Could you bring us our check soon?"

"Sorry," she said between forkfuls of salad, "but I've got to run."

"Oh, okay," said Paul. "So, uh, will I see you later?"

"I have an idea," Cat said. "Let's text each other when we get home to see if we want another date. You know, it's more civilized that way."

Granny Grace would be proud of her use of "civilized," but maybe not the fact that she wasn't going to let this guy down in person. She felt like she'd already put way more into this than it deserved. Still, maybe there was a way she could help the guy save face. He was a misrepresenting jerk in addition to the homophobia, so part of her didn't want to spare his feelings, but Granny Grace was rubbing off on her.

Back in her car, Cat decided to swing by the radio station to check on Waters.

But his car was no longer in the parking lot, just an empty space to mock her for wasting time. She drove to his home and didn't see it in the circle drive there, either. Tired, she decided to head home.

Propped on her bed in the Grand Green Griffin, Cat sent Paul this text: *It didn't seem like we had any mutual chemistry.*

His came back, *Yeah, me neither.*

She stared at it for a few minutes.

Then she launched herself off the bed, bent down, and pulled a box out from under it. A whiteboard on an easel, which she'd bought when her apprenticeship with her grandmother began nearly two years ago and had never used.

She took it into the Daring Damask Den, spilled the contents out on the floor, and put the thing together. Then she printed out photos of Nina and Sam. She taped these to the board, took a whiteboard marker out of a bag, and went to work.

Chapter Six

After losing Sam Waters while out on a date that nearly made her lose her lunch, Cat decided it was time to shift from mundane PI work and into dreamslipping.

She wouldn't be able to sleep in her car nearby without alerting Sam or seeming too suspicious. But during her surveillance, she'd mapped out the surrounding neighborhood and got a sense of the general layout of the Waters household. A greenbelt backed the property, so Cat left her car on the street and brought camping gear into the strip of woods with her. After sunset, she planned to scale the fence and set up her sleeping bag in their backyard, just under the second-floor window of Sam and Cassidy's bedroom. The kids were on the first floor, which presented a logistical problem for dreamslipping, but Granny Grace had trained her on how to isolate the various dreams to enter the one she wanted. From her vantage point in the woods, she had a peekaboo view of their house. She sat on her rolled-up sleeping bag, a cushiony prop for her butt, and waited. It was still dusk.

She'd been sitting in the eerie suburban quiet for about twenty minutes when she heard a twig crack behind her, and then the shuffling of footsteps in the underbrush.

"Hey, who are you?"

Cat turned. A chubby boy of about ten, his neck wrapped in too much scarf, stared at her.

"Hi," Cat said, trying to make herself sound

friendly, but not too friendly, when what she actually felt was panicked annoyance. "I'm Cat. I just like coming out here. It's so quiet."

"Me, too," said the boy.

He stood there for a minute that stretched into two. Cat sensed the shifting light as the sun began to slip behind the mountains in the west.

"Can I sit on your sleeping bag?" he asked.

What she really wanted was for the boy to go away, but that didn't seem to be happening. "Sure," she said, scooting over to make room for him.

"My name's Roland," said the boy, offering his hand.

Cat shook it, noting a stickiness, though his fingernails were clean.

"The kids at school call me 'Roly-Poly,' but I don't like it."

"That's not very nice," Cat said.

"It's mean," said Roland. "The teachers make a big deal out of it. There's like this zero-tolerance-for-bullying thing they do. But sometimes that makes it worse."

Cat thought of something. "Does Zach Waters go to your school?"

"Yeah, he's in my robotics club. So is his sister, Chloe."

"What do you know about their parents?"

Roland thought for a minute. "Their mom is, I don't know, busy with mom stuff. Their dad is nicer, especially to our teacher."

Cat made a note of that. "What's your teacher like?"

"She just started working there. So she's still like nice and stuff. And she's pretty."

"Ro-land! Roland!" A voice called from the other side of the woods.

The boy beside her ignored it.

"You're pretty, too," he said. "How come I've never seen you before?"

"Thanks, Roland," Cat said, standing up. She stretched out her back. "I guess I never thought about coming here before."

"Roland! Come home *now*!"

"Sounds like you better head home."

"Yeah," Roland said, unmoved. "We're having tofu stir-fry for dinner. I hate that stuff."

"Roland!"

"I hear ya, dude. But, you know, it's good for you. And you didn't have to make it yourself."

He had nothing to say to that but seemed to be turning it over in his mind.

"What's your teacher's name, by the way?"

"Miss Adams. She says I'm too advanced for my grade, but I don't want to be put in there with the fifth graders. That'll just make everything worse."

"You better go."

"I know," Roland said, standing up. "But I wish I could stay here. Looks like you're camping out."

She hoped he wouldn't blow her cover by telling his parents about her, but she balked at the idea of asking him to keep their little meeting a secret.

Cat offered him a fist bump. "Keep it real, Roland. And tell those morons at school that someday they'll be asking you for a job."

He laughed. "That's what my mom says."

"Roland Jefferson Hayes, you come home *right this minute*!"

The boy ran off through the woods. Cat heard him say, "I'm coming, Mom, I'm *coming*!"

She settled back onto her sleeping-bag roll and waited for the dark.

Luckily, no one came looking for her. Around 9:30 p.m., the lights finally went out in Sam and Cassidy's bedroom. She knew them to be early risers, so it would make sense they'd turn in by ten. The lights in the kids' rooms had been out by eight. She made her way to their backyard. This meant having to jump a wooden fence, but at least they didn't have a dog. Yoga with Granny Grace kept her in pretty good shape, so she managed it with ease. Previously, she'd cased out where the motion-detection lights were, and she kept to the fence perimeter so she wouldn't set them off. She crouched behind a rhododendron next to the house, spreading out her sleeping bag on a foam pad she'd brought as much to cushion her body as to keep the damp earth from reaching her. So close to the house, she decided to turn her phone off to keep it from buzzing every time Granny Grace texted her, which lately had been often.

On her grandmother's suggestion, she'd brought two things that would help her sleep: melatonin and a mug full of hemp milk with freshly grated nutmeg. Cat wasn't sure either would work and had argued with her grandmother about using pills from the drugstore instead, but Granny Grace insisted. And yes, the nutmeg had to be freshly grated. That apparently made a difference.

So Cat swallowed the melatonin, washing it down with her mug of not-really-milk. She had to admit, hemp was a pretty good substitute, creamy and thick.

A whirring sound, then clicking. Cat looked down at her hands, and they weren't hands; they were metal claws. As she moved, the whirring and clicking matched her movements. She saw a stuffed animal on the floor, a frog with googly eyes. She picked it up in her claw hand, shook it to get its eyes to move. Zach stood above her with his hands on his hips.

"Chloe, you're not really a robot," he said.

Cat felt something in her rebel at this, focus its strength, and push. "I am, too!" she yelled, and her robot self shot up to Zach's height.

"Whoa!" he yelled, stumbling backward. "That's so cool! Can you teach me to be a robot, too?"

"Maybe," she said. "If you're nice to me."

Cat realized at this point that she needed to pop out of Chloe's dream and find Sam's headspace. So she thought about herself asleep under the rhododendron outside, so separate from Chloe in the house in her bed, and when Chloe the Robot whirred out of the room, Cat stood still, letting Chloe rip away from her. This ejected her from the girl's dream and bounced her into another one.

She was on stage, and the lights were so bright that she couldn't see the faces of the people in the audience. But she could feel them there, watching her. Judging. Waiting for her to make a mistake.

"Zib zab zot," came a voice from stage left.

"I don't know what that means," Cat hissed. She looked down at her hands and noticed the smooth, slender fingers, the tasteful, pearl beige manicure. This must be Cassidy, Sam's wife.

"Zib zab zot!" insisted the voice.

"Oh, just shut up!" Cassidy hissed. She began to sway, but stiffly, as if she weren't comfortable in her body.

The crowd roared with applause.

"You trained them to like anything I do," hissed Cassidy. "I can't tell anymore whether they love me or not. This isn't fun. I'm canceling the show."

"Zo," said Stage Left.

Cat felt torn about staying in Cassidy's dream. It didn't seem pertinent to the case, but you never knew. She decided to linger.

Cassidy picked up one foot, stomped it down, and then did the same with the other. The crowd gave her a standing ovation.

"I hate them all!" Cassidy said, her hands clenched at her sides.

A large tarantula crawled out from stage left.

Cat was forced out of the dream, which probably meant Cassidy had awakened, or else she'd dropped from REM sleep. Cat became conscious of sleeping outside again, the cool air filling her nostrils. She heard the wind sighing through the pine trees in the greenbelt. Her lower back ached, so she stretched into a more comfortable position and focused her mind's eye on Sam. His radio voice filled her head, a deep one with a reedy quality when he got excited about something. Cat pictured the way his face lit up when he saw his kids. Toward Cassidy, Cat had observed that he was, if not exactly affectionate, then kind, at least.

"There are no buns like cinnamon buns," Cat sang. She patted the apron over her tight abs, sending a swirl of flour into the air in front of her. On the marble counter was a ball of dough. She leaned over and kneaded it with her strong hands. A man's hands. Sam's.

She hadn't figured Sam for a baker. Right away this dream seemed irrelevant to the case, but Cat stifled her frustration.

"There are no buns like cinnamon buns," Sam sang again. Cat could feel the enjoyment he was getting out of all of this, the singing, the kneading. There was something else, too: He was looking forward to feeding his family with what he made. That was the biggest source of pleasure for him, to take care of them.

She stuck with the dream, though it wasn't helping to paint a picture of a killer. Magically, the dough turned into cinnamon buns in a fraction of the time it would take in reality. Cat thought she was living in the game Candy Land for a moment as cinnamon and icing leapt off the countertop and swirled around Zach and Chloe, who laughed and laughed with Sam.

Then Cassidy entered the room, and for a moment, Sam and the kids stood still, as if they were afraid of the consequences of being caught making a mess. But Cassidy smiled at them. She dipped her finger in a glob of icing on Chloe's face and stuck it in her mouth.

"My, my," she said. "I could eat you all up."

Sam offered to feed her a piece of bun from his fingers, but she refused. Cat could feel his stark disappointment.

Cat woke, feeling hungry, and for more than just food.

Chapter Seven

Grace was tempted to throw the flowers that George Connors sent her into the trash. She couldn't help feeling as if she wanted to punish her bad date for landing her in rehab, but she knew punishing people put negative energy into the world.

He'd certainly spared no expense in sending her a tremendous vase full of Lisianthus roses, which Grace knew stayed fresh only for a couple of weeks after cutting, making them so spendy. They were white with royal blue tips, the petals like the ruffles on her favorite blouse.

They were far too pretty to toss. The card that came with them said, DEAR GRACE, PLEASE ACCEPT THIS SMALL TOKEN OF APOLOGY. YOU ARE A LOVELY WOMAN, AND I AM ASHAMED OF MY BEHAVIOR. GEORGE.

So she let the flowers be. And worked on her angry heart.

Stuck in bed, she'd been texting her granddaughter more than Cat seemed to appreciate lately. Not getting an answer, or getting terse responses that told Grace little, further fueled her frustration. So she was working on that, too.

Mick visited her often, and she was pleased to see he'd gone on another date with Cecily despite all the drama of the first. He'd finished the prototype for the mural, and the Queen Anne Neighborhood Association approved it. He would begin work on the mural itself soon.

She'd had a thrilling exchange online with Annie. They discussed yoga, which they'd both practiced all their adult lives, as well as art, and Eastern philosophy and religion. Grace pined for a chance to introduce her new friend to Nia, but besides the fact that she herself was stuck in the hospital, Annie lived in New York, so it wasn't as if she could pop in for a visit. Living so far away from the artist, the best Grace could hope for was an acquaintance, someone to see the next time she traveled to New York. It made her sad.

Cat seemed to be making some progress on the case, and Grace was eager to hear how the dreamslipping had gone.

She was happy for everyone that life seemed to be moving on so well without her, she really was. At least that's what she told herself.

"You look as blue as those roses," said a voice at her door.

She glanced up and recognized a man she'd seen yesterday in the cafeteria. They were finally wheeling her out of her room on occasion, and she'd had a chance to eat with some of the others stuck there in rehab like her. He'd met her eyes more than once across the cafeteria and seemed about ready to come over and introduce himself, but the dreaded nurse had whisked Grace back to her room before he could.

"Oh, I'm fine," Grace said. "Just not used to being grounded."

He chuckled. "You seem like a flier, all right. A spitfire, maybe. One of those daredevil planes."

Grace smiled. It had been a while since anyone

had flirted with her.

"May I?" he asked, leaning onto his cane and gesturing to the empty chair next to her bed.

"I suppose that would be all right," she replied.

"Should we share injury stories?" he asked, once settled in the chair. "Or let's try something different. What would you be doing if you *weren't* in this hospital bed?"

"Well, I'd be tracking down a killer."

He glanced over at her with surprise. "I hadn't figured you for a cop."

She laughed. "Nope. I'm a private investigator."

"You don't say!" He stuck out his hand. "Ed Maxwell. My résumé lacks the excitement of yours, however. I'm just a retired lawyer."

"Maxwell..." Recognizing the name, Grace scanned her memory. "Of Maxwell, Kreiser, and Shin? Why, you're a legend! You got them to release that information about the poison on apples—Alar, I think it was."

He smiled, revealing a nice set of teeth, an old gold crown visible near the back. "The public had a right to know."

"Of course."

"It doesn't sound like you're retired," he said, directing the focus back on Grace in a way she felt was gentlemanly.

"I'm retired to this bed, I'm afraid," she said, feeling the blue come back over her.

"But not for long, I hope?"

"For the duration," she said, tears springing to her eyes.

He shook his head in sympathy. "I saw you in the cafeteria yesterday. You didn't look like you belonged in that wheelchair. Rather on the dance floor, I'd say."

The thought of not being able to dance made the tears in Grace's eyes pool up and spill over. Ed produced a starched white handkerchief from his shirt pocket.

Grace took it. "Oh, look at me. What a mess."

"I didn't mean to—what is it the young people call that now? Trigger you." His eyes were full of teasing mirth. It made Grace laugh. She told him about discovering the Nia dance class only to have it whisked out from under her.

"Oh, I think you'll be dancing again in no time," he said. "And when you do, I'll be at the top of your dance card."

They talked of their lives. He was a widower with two grown children who'd moved elsewhere, chasing jobs. He'd hoped his son would follow in his lawyerly footsteps, staying in Seattle, but he was a writer in his forties still struggling to make it in the TV business in LA. So far all his son had managed was work as a "punch-up" writer on scripts for a failed series. His daughter was more successful in her tech career, having recently been named a director.

"Honestly, she'd be a VP by now if it weren't for the glass ceiling," Ed admitted.

Grace told him about Cat and Mick and the detective agency. They did get around to relating their injury stories, and she regaled him with an account of her awful first date with George. When she got to the part about how she told George she'd ice-skated on a frozen lake, Ed interrupted. "You did? What brought you to Alaska?"

At that moment, Grace knew for sure she'd be spending more time with Ed.

Her dreaded nurse shooed him out before they'd finished talking, but Ed kissed Grace's hand and slipped away without a fight.

>>>

While staking out Sam, Cat barely saw her great-uncle, only long enough to notice he seemed … perkier. In the kitchen one day, she caught him making a salad.

"Don't tell me the foodies finally got to you, Uncle Mick," she said, gesturing at his bowl of greens. "Oh. Em. Gee. Is that *kale*?"

"Yep," he said, popping a leaf into his mouth. "It's a super food, I'll have you know."

"It's super gross," she said, making a face at him. "What happened to the frosted loops?"

"I just thought I should eat better."

Cat poured herself a bowl of cereal and drowned the pale organic O's in a torrent of cow's milk, which she'd purchased instead of Granny Grace's usual hemp, almond, or rice milk since her grandmother wasn't there to fight her on it. "Does this have anything to do with Cecily? Because I just realized your beard is all trimmed up, too."

"Maybe…" Mick looked sheepish.

"Whoa, dude! You're dating her?"

He nodded.

"So you guys, like, resolved your artistic differences."

"Sort of." He hesitated. "Let's just say I have allowed for a different perspective than my own."

"That's impressive, Uncle Mick. I guess you're not too old to become a feminist."

"I've always been a feminist."

"Right," Cat laughed. "Remember, I've met at least one of the women you've dated in the past. Candy Port wasn't exactly Gloria Steinem."

"You're going to judge me on that one relationship alone?"

"Well, come on, now. You yourself once admitted to me you tended to keep to the shallow end of the dating pool." She shoved a spoonful of loops into her mouth and grinned.

"I guess that's true."

"So Cecily does it for you, eh?"

"Yep." He sat down at the table and began to pick at his kale.

"So, have you two done the deed yet?"

"That is none of your business."

"Fine," she said. She marched over to the fridge, took out a bottle of ranch dressing, and set it on the table in front of him. "Here, this'll help you choke down your salad."

>>>

The truth was Mick *hadn't* slept with Cecily yet, and he could tell she was wondering why he was being so old-fashioned with her. It was just that he knew she'd want him to spend the night, and that meant sleeping. And sleeping meant dreamslipping. With someone new like that, who wasn't family and definitely not a dreamslipper herself, he knew he wouldn't be able to keep out of her dreams.

They were on their fifth date, a stay-in date at Cecily's apartment. She'd offered to cook. Mick knew what this meant, and there was no way he could say no. He didn't want to say no.

"You're officially the only person in my social network who isn't avoiding some kind of food," Cecily said. "So I decided to make this a no-holds-barred night." He watched as she drained a pot of pasta in a colander, admiring her well-defined arms.

"You have biceps like Michelle Obama," he said, wondering for the millionth time why a brilliant, hot fiftysomething like her would want to lower her standards by dating him.

She smiled, obviously flattered. "You just keep grating that cheese, Travers."

He resumed his work on the other side of her kitchen island. As they continued in silence for a while, he realized for the first time in perhaps his entire dating career, he was actually curious to know what Cecily's dreams were like.

"Penny for your thoughts?" she asked gently, breaking the bubble on his reverie.

"Oh, nothing," he said. "Should I set the table?"

"Here," she said, giving him a curious look.

He took the napkins and silverware she offered him. Once they were seated, they fell into their usual conversational rhythm, which ranged from art, of course, to music and literature. She knew far more than he did about the latter and had been trying to get him to read more. He was kind of a reader, but his habit was to pick up books and read parts of them in no particular order until they sparked something in him to paint.

She'd called him on it once. "You're just using literature as reference material. Try reading a book start to finish. Let yourself get lost in it."

She'd given him *The Catcher in the Rye*. It was a good read; he liked the narrator's voice immensely, though he had to resist the urge to get up and paint at every page.

After dinner, he helped her clean the kitchen, and then he offered to give her a massage. She needed it; she held a lot of tension in her shoulders, he'd noticed. But he also craved the feel of her body in his hands, like he was sculpting.

He was determined not to treat the massage like a pretense for sex. He insisted she take off her shirt and bra, though, as they would just be in the way.

They went to her bedroom. She lit candles. He considered putting Boléro on but decided that would be too obvious, and cliché. So he went with Bartók.

The strings seemed to pose a tense, maybe even dark question that a lone flute tried to answer, its response light, suggestive. Mick let his hands be the strings, kneading the knots above her shoulder blades. Cecily sighed.

But the music crescendoed, the horns joining in a wave that crested dramatically.

"Mick," Cecily said. "The music…"

"A little too intense?"

"A bit."

He flipped through her selection and chose a mild Chopin for piano.

She smiled. "That's better."

Still, his hands picked up the subtle drama in the piece. He found himself choreographing his movement across the planes and curves of her back, her neck. Mick pressed into the tightness, following its lines with his fingers. He felt her relax, felt the muscles give way. She sighed again. She began to make sounds that keyed him in to her pleasure, and that aroused him.

He stemmed it, though. He wanted her to feel the full benefit of his work. And maybe there was something else going on, too. Maybe he was holding back. It was as if he were the sand on the beach, and Cecily the tide. His fingers nudged the edge of her jeans, which she'd kept on. His hands traced the sides of her body, under her arms. He felt the swell of her breasts, noticing how she did not resist his further explorations but seemed to suck him further in…

She turned, her breathing rapid. In the candlelight, her eyes glittered. Her lovely mouth.

They kissed. And broke away. "You've been holding back with me," she said, panting. "I've sensed you … struggling."

He kissed her, hard this time. "I'm not holding back now."

She broke away. "Tell me I'm not the only black woman you've ever been with."

He smiled. "You're not." He felt a pang of sadness that she'd mistake his fear of getting too close for some vague racism.

Her face relaxed, and they embraced. Mick expressed with his body what he could not with his words, and she responded. Oh, how she did.

It was the most intense, yet sweetest, sex Mick had ever had, lasting till the candles began to gutter, the Chopin long since come to an end. Mick drifted to sleep.

Cecily entered a room lit only by candlelight. A man wearing a fedora sat playing Chopin on a grand piano, his back to her. She approached him. He played as if it were the only thing in the world. She thought it was Mick at the piano.

Cecily touched his shoulder, and he turned.

But it wasn't Mick. It was a man she recognized.

"Daddy," she said.

"CeeCee." He smiled. The two embraced. Mick was lost for a moment, noting the resemblance between Cecily and her father. The same wide foreheads leading into a heart-shaped face, though her father's jawline was harder. The same button noses. Cecily's blue eyes, though, those must have come from her mother, as her father's were a deep brown, like the rich wooden bannister in Pris's old Victorian.

"Mama's gone now, too," Cecily said to him.

Her father nodded. "Gone to the other place, I'm afraid."

"Hell, Daddy?"

"Not as simple as that, CeeCee. There are all these dimensions, planes... It's hard to explain. We're like mists, clouds. Passing into and out of each other. I see her sometimes.

Or maybe it's just pieces of her, like strains of music."

"Bartók," Cecily said.

"More like German death metal." Her father laughed.

"I didn't think I'd miss her, but I do," said Cecily.

"Me, too," said her father. "I try to pick out her music sometimes, in the noise."

"I miss you more," Cecily said.

"I miss you, too," said her father.

"Do you like Mick?" asked Cecily. "Do I have your blessing?"

"It doesn't work that way. I can't see him. It's not like I'm looking down on y'all like I'm in the sky."

Cecily began to cry.

"Sometimes I can see his pictures," her father said. "Hoo-wee, that white boy can paint."

Cecily woke up, and Mick was flung out of the dream. He could hear her sniff. She must have really been crying.

"Are you all right?" His voice was as soft as he could make it.

She grabbed a tissue from her nightstand. "Sorry, I didn't mean to wake you."

"What is it?"

"Just a dream," she said.

Mick wanted to say something to her, let her know he understood. He'd felt everything along with her so powerfully that he was now fighting tears welling up in his own eyes. But he had no words. He was afraid.

"Oh," was all he could muster.

She looked at him for a minute, as if unsure why

he was there. In the dark it was easy for him to close his eyes and pretend he was falling asleep again. Soon she settled back onto her pillow. He touched her arm, but their connection seemed to have broken.

Chapter Eight

Cat realized she'd been watching Sam through an entire wardrobe cycle when she recognized an emerald green-and-jet-black houndstooth tie she'd seen before, notable for the way it set off his green eyes. Sam Waters was way too old for her—like that ever mattered to anyone—and if crazy Robin was right, he was a killer. But Cat began to develop a crush on him anyway. A mild one, from afar.

Maybe it was the endearing way he always remembered to check his mirrors before reversing out of the radio station's parking lot. Or the way his face lit up when his son Zach piled into his arms after soccer practice. But what really got her was his calm control. She never saw him lose it with anyone, no temper tantrums or dicey moments with the kids, not even when Zach wiped his chocolate frosting-encrusted lips all over the aforementioned houndstooth tie.

It made Cat want to lean into his arms and let go.

Which was a pretty strange feeling to have toward a guy she'd never met. Despite having stalked him for weeks, she'd never actually *spoken* to him, after all. But then there was that strange baking dream. Cat had to admit, even as young as she was, a guy who knew his way around the kitchen had a sexy, domestic appeal.

Watching Sam gave Cat an opportunity to observe Cassidy a little, too. Like Sam, she seemed to be in control, but she wasn't relaxed. Her kind of control was pinched, seemingly calculated. She dressed impeccably, was never late, and flashed a plastic smile on the people she needed to please, turning her face in indifference to those she did not.

Cat found herself feeling sympathy toward her suspect. This was not good. She knew better, too. She remembered from her college study of serial killers how well liked many of them were, how charming.

So she worked harder to bust Sam.

Her first lead came when, finally, after a long stretch of perfect behavior, he ducked out of the radio station early, about two in the afternoon. Hoping he wouldn't lead her to a dental appointment or something equally mundane, Cat followed cautiously. She'd chosen a different rental car this time, parking it at the strip mall across the street from the radio station to blend in and avoid raising Sam's suspicions.

As his car continued across the floating bridge and into Seattle, Cat kept tailing him. She followed him across Lake Washington and into Seattle proper. He finally stopped near Capitol Hill, where he slid effortlessly into a parking space. Cat thought she'd lost him when she searched for her own space and took a chance on one that was probably closer to the end of the street than allowed. The sign said, NO PARKING TEN FEET. She ran to catch up with him as he turned the corner and saw a glimpse of his sporty rain jacket as he ducked into a place called Leather Underground.

The shop's name kicked up her adrenaline a notch. She thought of the duct tape found over Nina's mouth and securing her wrists behind her back. Cat debated going inside, but it seemed like a small place, and she didn't want to risk having Sam see her. So she waited. There was a bus stop sign a few feet from the shop entrance, so she stood there and pulled out her phone. Soon a bus paused at the curb, and she waved it by.

He reemerged about twenty minutes later with a large package in hand. She followed him back to his car, where she watched him take a duffel bag out of the back seat and place the package inside.

Cat returned to her own car to find a ticket under the wiper blade, for parking too close to the end of the street. She stifled her rage at the hefty fee: $97.

She tossed the ticket on her front seat, and letting a car ease between her and Sam, she followed him downtown to the Seattle Athletic Club, a fancy gym for the downtown's well-to-do. He entered the SAC's underground lot, leaving Cat to fend for herself on Seattle's busy downtown streets.

It took her more than ten minutes to find a spot that wouldn't fetch her another ticket. Fearing she'd lost him, she marched into the SAC lobby only to realize she didn't possess the required membership card that would convince the desk staff to buzz her in.

"Can I help you?" asked a guy in a maroon shirt that seemed like it would split from the force of his pecs pressing from underneath.

"I'm, uh, sort of looking for someone."

"Got a membership card?"

The question infuriated her by its obviousness. "Nope."

"Sorry, but we can't just let you in to look for

someone. It's kind of against the rules." He flashed over-ly white teeth at her.

Thinking fast, Cat said, "Well, my, uh, friend was going to give me a tour. I'm thinking of joining."

"Great!" he said, producing a clipboard as if out of thin air. "Here, fill this out, and I'll give you a tour my-self. I'm Randy."

Yeah, great, thought Cat. Peering through the questions, she chafed at the choices under household in-come, which started with a range that was double her current salary. Defiantly, she left that blank, as well as some of the others, too. There was no way she was going to give this place the names and email addresses of three of her friends "who might also want to join." It was bad enough that giving her own was a mandatory part of the form. She saw an "unsubscribe" in her near future.

After Randy plugged her info into the desktop with all the urgency of a ground sloth, he led her past the front desk into the poshest gym she'd ever seen. A juice bar flanked one end of an enormous workout room filled with machines. A group of kids rappelled down a climb-ing wall. There were two pools, one resembling a tropical grotto, complete with faux waterfall, and another of the Olympic variety. Stacks of fluffy white towels sat free for the taking.

Distracted by the luxury only for a second, Cat scanned the rooms for Sam, tuning out Randy's script about the member benefits and gym highlights. She didn't see Sam on any of the machines. He wasn't in the weight room or running the track. If he was swimming in the pools, she couldn't pick him out from the others.

Randy finished his pitch and began to lead her back to the lobby.

"Hey, Randy," Cat said, touching his arm. "Do you mind if I, you know, check the place out on my own a bit? To make sure it's where I want to work out."

Randy winked. "You're still looking for your friend, aren't you? Be my guest, but don't stay too long. And if you want to work out, your friend will have to sign you up for a day pass as his guest."

"Okay," she said and then did a double-take. "Hey, how'd you know my friend was a dude?"

Randy smiled. "You seem … a little, you know, interested in him."

Cat let that one pass.

She scoured the gym and finally found Sam in a racquetball court. She'd missed him before because of the goggles he wore, and the fact that he wasn't in his familiar work clothes. His opponent was another guy, taller and blonde. Cat watched them from the gallery for a while, but there didn't seem to be anything special about their relationship, no extra familiarity or intimacy. She wondered if she'd hit a dead end. Maybe Sam had come to the gym only as a cover for his little shopping trip.

Cat watched him play for a good fifteen minutes but didn't want to push her luck with Randy.

Back in the lobby, Cat decided to take Randy into her confidence. "I have to be honest with you," she said, pulling out her business card and handing it to him. "I'm investigating someone."

Randy's eyes widened. "For real? Like, who?"

"I'd rather not say, at least at this point." She did

not want to risk that Randy would tip off Sam to her surveillance. "But thanks for your assistance."

Cat couldn't help it. She liked the way Randy looked at her now.

"Sure," he said, reaching out to shake her hand. "Let me know if you need any help."

"I will."

Cat retrieved her car and circled back around to Leather Underground, which appeared to be at least partially a misnomer. Brightly lit and decidedly at street level, the place did reek of the leather that took up most of its racks. Not that the leather items were made of very much leather. Many of the pieces were comprised of nothing more than crisscrossing strips secured with heavy metal loops. Cat perused the racks of harnesses. They reminded her of the odd pair of dreams she had had, the woman's craving for the man to hurt her.

"Need anything?" asked a woman behind the counter. The ends of her wavy brown hair were dyed hot pink, and she had piercings in both eyebrows and through her lip.

"Just ... browsing," said Cat.

"For you, or your partner?"

Cat didn't know how to respond. "Me?"

The woman laughed, revealing a tongue piercing as well. "Those would be too big for you, seeing as how they're for men," she said, nodding at the rack in front of Cat. "Here, these are more your size."

Cat sauntered over to where she pointed.

"Dom or sub?" the woman asked.

Cat hesitated.

"Oh, switch," the woman concluded. "Here. We've got corsets on this rack, waist cinchers mixed in if you just want that. Collars over there in the back, crops and whips behind the boot rack. If you want to try anything on, let me know."

"Hey, I actually wanted to ask you about a guy who was in here about an hour ago," said Cat, showing her a picture of him.

"What, are you like stalking him or something?" She laughed. "'Cause I can't help you with that." The woman spun on her Doc Martens and went back to emptying boxes of their corset-y content.

Cat followed her while searching her own purse with one hand. She located her stack of business cards and pulled one out. "I'm a PI," she explained, handing it to the clerk. "Investigating the guy who was in here earlier. Is he a regular?"

"I don't have to tell you anything," the woman replied. "We don't fink on our customers."

"I just need to find out if he's been ... in here with anyone."

The woman folded her arms across her chest. "He always comes in here alone."

"What does he buy?"

"I'm really uncomfortable telling you about my customers' purchases."

"Please," Cat said. "He might've killed a woman."

The woman's demeanor changed. "Well, fuck. Why didn't you say so?" She ran her hands over the pink ends of her hair. "Okay, so what he bought today was different. It was like he was ... memorializing someone."

"Show me what he bought."

The woman led her toward a part of the store that looked as if it were dedicated to bridal wear, at least to what might be worn *underneath* a wedding gown. "These are for collaring ceremonies."

When Cat drew a blank, the woman sighed. "When a dom and sub decide they want to cement their relationship, the dom formally collars his sub. Some play it up like a wedding. It just depends."

She pushed past a row of white lace veils, drawing out a black one. "Most go for traditional-wedding white. But some prefer the Goth, or BDSM, look."

Cat took the veil. "What else did he buy?"

"A whole black outfit," she said.

"Show me," Cat said.

She watched as the clerk moved through the boutique, assembling the outfit on the sales counter for Cat to see: black satin heels, about three inches high; black thigh-high stockings, which would fasten into the clips that hung from the bottom of the velvet corset; a black velvet collar; and the dark lace veil, which could be worn fully covering the face.

"It's really just the veil that makes it look like a sexy funeral, right?" asked Cat.

"Yeah, but that guy usually goes for color. He like greens and blues especially, with an occasional red for, like, Valentine's Day or Christmas. This is his first real Goth blowout. And another thing"—the woman pulled on her lip ring—"he seemed really sad. I don't know. It was just … weird."

111

>>>

Cat decided to follow up on the only other lead she had, which came thanks to her new friend Roland. The kids' teacher, Bethany Adams, was a redhead, and the boy was right about her looks. An adorable widow's peak topped a cute round face with almond eyes and lips that would probably never need Botox. Cat had easily secured a lunch meeting with the woman, who showed up in a modest green jumper and flats.

"Thanks for taking the time to meet with me," said Cat. "Lunch is on me."

"Oh, it's no problem," Bethany said. "I'm not sure how much help I can be since I've just started out myself, but I'll try."

Cat had asked Bethany to lunch on the pretense of interviewing her about the ins and outs of teaching certificates and getting a job. The market was tight, especially for the prime positions in Seattle, and teachers literally had to wait for someone to retire before they could even apply for a job, which would get numerous applicants. Cat had learned all this in her research previously, and it came in handy discussing the field with Bethany like a pro, she thought. Her plan was to slowly steer the conversation in a certain direction, once she felt as if she and Bethany were connecting.

It wasn't hard to connect with her, as she really was nice. Between how easy it had been to set up the lunch date and how warm the woman acted toward her, Cat realized Bethany must not have been in Seattle for very long. "Where are you from?" Cat asked.

"St. Louis," said Bethany, and Cat could swear she heard the sound of cathedral bells. This kicked off an excited conversation as the two compared people and places, reminiscing over Ted Drewes Frozen Custard and the Missouri Botanical Garden. Cat nearly forgot her mission but then circled back around to it by discussing dating. She opened the topic by telling Bethany about her disaster date with Paul Dorian. The woman nearly choked on her green tea, she was laughing so hard.

"Do the fathers of your kids ever hit on you?" Cat asked.

"Oh, they flirt," said Bethany. "But I try not to flirt back. That's the last thing I need, you know?"

"You must have some VIPs in your parent group," she said. "I mean, your school district is one of the wealthiest."

"Yep," said Bethany. "All the more reason to be careful."

"But if you could, are there any you'd be … tempted by?"

"Not really," said Bethany. "Well, okay, there is this one guy. Sam. He's easy on the eyes, that's for sure. But I don't share his politics, so I just think about that every time he bats his ridiculously long eyelashes at me."

Cat laughed. "Do you think he's just a flirt? Or would he, you know…?"

Bethany considered it. "There's a vibe, but … I don't know. I think maybe I'm too young for him, I mean, not just age-wise… I realize that kind of doesn't make sense. I just get the feeling that guy needs, like, *more*, you know? He's super intense."

Cat still felt creeped out by the memorial outfit, and Bethany's characterization of Sam clicked him further into place as a suspect. She was beginning to feel as if they had a legitimate case, not to mention a huge leg up on the police, who according to the *Times* had not made any arrests. She left the lunch date with a new friend but with more questions than answers.

So she decided to drop in and see her grandmother.

Who, it turned out, wasn't alone.

As Cat approached Granny Grace's room, she heard the sound of her grandmother *giggling*. She hadn't heard that since the very beginning of their trip to Miami, before things with Ernesto Ruíz had become strained.

Cat peeked into the room to find Granny Grace playing cards with an elderly gentleman who must have also been a patient, as he wore a plastic identifying wristband. Cat wondered how he'd convinced them to let him wear street clothes instead of the requisite hospital gown. Her grandmother, she now noticed, had also shed the gown and was wearing a ruffled blue blouse. She looked better than she had in days, the color back in her face.

"Why, Cat!" she exclaimed. "What a great surprise. This is my friend Ed Maxwell. Eddie, this is Cat."

Ed rose, with only some difficulty and the use of his cane, to shake her hand. He let the cane stand on its own—it was hospital-issue with four tennis balls on each of its legs—and placed his other hand to enfold hers in both of his. "Grace has told me so much about you."

Flustered, Cat glanced around the room for another chair but didn't find one.

Ed remained standing.

"It's, um, nice to meet you, Ed," Cat said, remembering her manners after a pointed look from Granny Grace.

"Well, I should let you two ladies catch up," he said. "Your grandmother was just about to beat me at gin rummy anyway. I better get out while the gettin's good."

Cat watched him bend down to kiss Granny Grace on the cheek and then saunter off.

"Are you two…?"

"Oh, like I can do anything naughty in my state."

"Of course," Cat said. "But that didn't look like … friendship."

"Well, I don't know what it is, Cat, but just let me enjoy it for now, all right?"

"Right," Cat said, feeling shame heat her face. "Sorry."

"Now what brings you here? I was beginning to think you were doing better on this PI thing without my meddling. Or that you were busy dating. Or both."

"Yeah, sorry I haven't come by as often as I promised." Cat noticed that the pretty blue-and-white flowers from George were tinged brown on the edges now, as if stained with tea.

"I've missed you, Cat. Now tell me what's wrong."

"I'm beginning to think Robin's right, Gran." Cat briefed her grandmother on what she'd discovered so far.

"Good work, Cat," Granny Grace beamed. "Sam's emerging as a complex suspect. Your dreamslipping with his family paints an interesting portrait. Sam the nurturer, his children loved and cared for. Of them all, Cassidy comes across as the most emotionally conflicted."

"I've wondered that, too. Of course that was only one random night of dreams," Cat said. "The hard evidence speaks loudest: He bought a memorial outfit intended for a woman he regarded as his submissive."

"Have you told Robin?"

"Not yet." Cat feared confirming Robin's suspicions, especially now that Sam might be continuing to fetishize Nina after her death. That could further upset the grieving widow.

As if reading Cat's mind, Granny Grace said, "Just tell her you've found evidence suggesting she might be onto something."

Cat nodded. "I wish I knew where he was planning to hold this little memorial, or whatever. I mean, without Nina's body, since it's at the morgue? I don't think he'd go back to the Puget Place Hotel, but I can ask the manager to call me if he does."

"By the way," she continued, "I canvassed the hotel, and Nina had never checked in there before, despite having worked on its architecture. That's an odd coincidence, don't you think?"

"Yes." Granny Grace smoothed down the edge of her bed comforter. "What about Sam? Did anyone see him there that night?"

"No," said Cat. "Of course, the police have been all over the hotel, interviewing witnesses and grabbing security footage. Not that they'll share any of that with me. They've denied all my requests. But none of the hotel staff recognize Sam from that night, or any other time."

"Maybe he was disguised."

"Maybe," Cat agreed.

"Well, you could talk to Robin again, see if she's centered herself enough to let you go through Nina's things."

"All right," Cat said.

"And don't forget about those dreams you had at the Waters house," said her grandmother. "Did you write them down? Remember, we tend to forget our dreams immediately after waking."

"Yes, I did," Cat said.

"I'd like to see you use your dreamslipping even more," Grace said. "I think you could surpass me, in time."

Her comment surprised and touched Cat. "Really? I still feel like I'm bumbling around with it."

"Oh, Cat. Quite the contrary. When I was your age, I was just using it as a card trick."

"Gran…"

Her grandmother took her hand. "Tap your connection with him. See what else is in his psyche. He can't just be the fabulous baker man."

Cat thought about the other two dreams she'd had that didn't seem like her own. The image of the Newton's cradle came back to her, the woman's pearls swaying. The two seemed like lovers involved in a power-play dynamic, but unlike with Nina's murder, the woman was a willing participant, maybe even the instigator. She hesitated to bring the dreams up to Granny

Grace until she understood what they meant. She was eager to prove to her grandmother she could handle this case on her own. Maybe they'd been her own after all, a result of the exposure she'd had to Seattle's dating scene. She hadn't had dreams like them since.

"Oh, and one more thing," said her grandmother. "Are you going to call Henrietta, or should I?"

Cat drew a blank. "Henrietta?"

"Your crow lady."

Cat had completely spaced on that other case. "You mean *your* crow lady," she shot back.

"I guess she is mine since you've ignored her calls on the land line. She finally tracked down my cell." Granny Grace waved her phone at her. "Six messages. She's accusing us of moving on to another case."

"Well, that's true."

"Yes, but it's not very professional."

"Gran, I can't hang out in Crowland when Robin expects me to bring Nina's killer to justice."

"Fine, fine. I'll deal with Henrietta. You better sleep on it."

"I see what you did there."

Her grandmother smiled.

>>>

Cat was not at all surprised when Roland Jefferson Hayes tromped through the bushes with a mug of coffee for her.

"My mom doesn't know I took this," he said, as if that made it even better.

Cat accepted the coffee in one hand and fist-

118

bumped Roland with her other.

"How's it going, Ro-Ro?"

He smiled at the nickname. "It's okay, Cat."

She sniffed the mug of coffee and pretended to sip before setting it down by her foot. It was the worst thing for her since she planned to fall asleep again.

"Are you, like, on a stakeout?"

"Why do you ask?"

"Because you're always staring at Chloe and Zach's house."

"Oh, I just like the trees in their yard." Cat pointed to the tall blue spruce occupying one corner of the Waters family's expansive lawn, but Roland seemed unconvinced.

"I had a dream about you," said Roland. "A villain tied you up with a rope, but I saved you."

The rope reference made the hair on the back of Cat's neck stand up. "Thanks for saving me."

That made him smile bashfully. "It was just a dream."

"You have no idea how important dreams are," she said.

"My mom says it's just your mind getting rid of junk you don't need."

Cat didn't want to contradict the kid's mom, so she let that one settle.

"Hey, Ro-Ro, did you tell anyone about meeting me back here?"

The kid looked thoughtful. "Just Chloe."

"Okay," said Cat. She didn't feel right interrogating him further.

"I better go." The kid adjusted the scarf around his neck. "We're having hamburgers tonight."

She gave him a parting fist bump and watched him make his way home. Now she'd wait till the sun went down and the lights in Sam and Cassidy's master bedroom winked out before settling into her spot beneath the rhododendron bushes. Luckily, it was a typical Seattle weather night, the rain just the lightest drizzle. Sky spittle, her grandmother called it. Easily combatted with a wool scarf and cap, not to mention the waterproof jacket she'd found at the Salvation Army. When she'd bought it, the tags from the high-end store it came from were still attached.

Later, as she drifted off to sleep with the taste of nutmeg in her mouth, she focused on Sam, like Granny Grace said. How he gave off a confidence that was only slightly arrogant but also sensitive, highly sensitive, in fact. He seemed very in tune with whoever was around him, especially if he cared about them. But was this the pretense of a sociopath? With a little fear now in her heart, Cat felt for him with her senses instead of trying to understand him logically. She pictured him with Cassidy, with his kids, and at the gym. She tried to envision his manner with Bethany Adams, his kid's teacher. She imagined him carefully choosing the memorial outfit at Leather Underground.

And she slipped into him. Though it wasn't a dream exactly, just brain waves at this point. It felt as if she were floating atop waters that consisted of Sam, his essence. She caught flashes of his life: Street scenes, the inside of the radio station. His daugh-

ter dressing her robot in a pink tutu. Then Cat felt as if she were being submerged, deeper.

"Nina!" Cat's voice, Sam's voice. "Nina Howell!" It echoed.

He trudged through ankle-deep water. A sewer tunnel. His pants legs were wet, his shoes ruined. He didn't know where he was or how he'd get out. But none of that mattered. He needed to find her.

He saw something floating in the water, something familiar. A red bow. He grabbed it. The bow was sewn to the top of a long black stocking. A gift for his sub, to wear for him. It was torn and dripping gutter water.

He stuffed it into his pocket. "Nina!"

Finally he could see the end of the tunnel. He ran, splashing water as he awkwardly made his way through the sewer.

There were cuffs chained to the wall.

They dangled there, empty. He spotted strands of hair caught on the brick wall, medium-length, the same blonde as hers, like hay.

"No!" he said. Pain engulfed him. It was so intense that Cat recoiled from the force of it.

This seemed to break Sam out of his convulsions of agony. "Nina?" he asked.

Nothing.

"If you're not here, why do I sense you? It feels like you're in my dream!"

Panicking, Cat tore herself away from him.

She sat up, knocking her head on a thick rhododendron branch. Stifling her "ow," she rubbed the spot to calm

121

down the pain.

Unfortunately, she hadn't thought to bring any aspirin. She considered bailing on her mission, especially now that her connection with Sam seemed to have gone too far. But she remembered what Granny Grace said about Cassidy and decided to see if she could slip into one of her dreams as well.

She lay back down and fell asleep easily. But instead of falling into a Cassidy dream, she began to have one of her own. In it, Granny Grace danced on one leg. "My other leg is just fine, Kitty Cat." That had been Lee's nickname for Cat.

"Who the hell are you?"

It wasn't Granny Grace. Cat began to awaken, realizing the voice came from elsewhere. A bright light in her face. She couldn't see anything; it blinded her.

"Do I need to call the police?"

It was Sam.

Shining a flashlight at her.

"Wait," she muttered. "Sorry. I-I'm getting up."

"My daughter said something about a girl in the woods. Her friend told her. I thought it was her imagination."

"I can explain..." Cat said, scrambling for something that didn't include dreamslipping or investigating her suspect for murder.

"It's all right," his voice softened. "Are you a runaway? Can I get you some help?"

"Sam?" a voice called from behind him. It must have been Cassidy, his wife.

"It's just ... that's a strange place to sleep." He

turned off the flashlight and helped Cat to her feet.

"I know," she said. And then she lit on an idea for a cover story. "I … used to live in this house, years ago. And … I'd come out here and sleep under this bush. I guess I got a little nostalgic about it."

"A little?" He laughed. "I'd say you're bona fide obsessed."

"What's going on, Sam? Who are you talking to?" Again, the woman's voice.

"Come on inside," he said.

Cat groaned inwardly, unsure she could keep up the ruse.

Sam explained to a robed but somehow still elegant Cassidy that Cat used to live in the house.

"You did?" whispered Cassidy, appraising Cat with her eyes. "Well, that couldn't have been long ago, judging by your age. But we've lived here for a decade."

"I-I was really young," Cat said, matching Cassidy's whisper. She didn't want to make things worse by waking up their kids. "It was only for a short time. But it made a huge impression on me."

Cassidy gave her a look that said she didn't trust Cat or like having her in her house in the middle of the night. To Sam, she said, "Are you sure we shouldn't call the police?"

"My car's around the corner," Cat interrupted, trying to head off the answer. "I started out in the green-belt—one of my favorite places to go—and then I thought it would be all right if I slept under your bush. I'm really sorry to cause you this trouble. I'll just go home now. I live over in Queen Anne."

Sam placed his hand on Cassidy's, resting on the kitchen counter. "Tell you what," Sam said. "Let me take down your driver's license number just to ease my wife's mind. And you're free to go."

Cat was reluctant to let Sam know her identity, but refusing would be a bad idea. So she agreed.

He jotted down her name, commenting on "Cathedral," her full name, as just about everyone felt called to do.

"My mother is a very active Catholic," she explained, and thankfully, he didn't joke about a brother named "Mosque," as she'd heard a few too many times. Cassidy wandered back to bed with one last suspicious look at Cat.

When Sam handed Cat back her ID, as well as her sleeping bag, which he'd rolled up tighter than she'd ever been able to get it, he looked at her quizzically for a moment and asked, "Do I know you? I mean, before tonight. You seem ... familiar."

"I don't think so," she said, too quickly, she realized.

He paused for a moment as if considering whether or not to trust her words.

"We had the kitchen redone," he said. "It must look nothing like you remember."

"You're right," she said.

"Come, I'll show you the downstairs on your way out. But not the bedrooms. I can't wake up the kids. I'm sure you understand."

"I don't want to trouble you anymore than I already have," she said.

Sam took her by the elbow and steered her down a hallway.

"Here's the living room," he said. "We haven't changed a thing. You might remember this wallpaper."

Cat walked over to the wall and put her hand on it, as if to show the old-fashioned hunting-themed paper meant something to her. "My brother and I had names for these horses," she said, drawing on her college acting class to make herself sound wistful about the past. "Mine was Butterfly. His was Lightning."

Cat was an only child, but she figured as long as she was making up a past for herself, she'd throw in a brother as well. She'd always wanted siblings.

"Mmm…" Sam said. "Was he an older brother?"

"No. Younger," Cat said.

"And where is he now?"

Jeez, why the twenty questions? "Joined the Army," she said, giving him Lee Stone's background. "Rangers."

"Your parents must be proud."

"I better get going," Cat said, edging toward the front door.

"Yes, you should," he said, opening the door for her.

As she stepped out, he caught her arm and held it. She twisted back and met his gaze, which bore an intensity that startled her. "My wife had that wallpaper put up just this spring."

He held her arm a moment longer. She said nothing. He let go.

Chapter Nine

Grace smoothed the "Winter Spice" balm across her lips, conscious of Cecily standing there, expectant. Grace pursed her lips together, smearing the balm evenly.

"What do you think?" asked Cecily.

Grace inhaled the scent of cinnamon and cloves that the balm gave off. "It's like wearing Christmas."

Cecily frowned. "A little too much?"

Grace shook her head. "I like it, but it might smell too much like potpourri to some people. The lavender and mint balms will probably sell better."

Cecily nodded. "I'll make it a seasonal item."

Grace smiled, happy to be part of Cecily's latest product scheme, this time a line of her own handcrafted oils and balms. She grew the herbs on the rooftop deck of her Seattle high-rise, with her landlord's blessing, though he didn't know they were being used for commercial, rather than culinary, purposes.

"So, now that I'm done serving as your guinea pig," said Grace, "do you want to tell me what's going on with you and Mick? You haven't mentioned him once, and we've been at this an hour."

Cecily busied herself packing up the small tins and bottles she'd laid out around Grace. "I'm just not sure we're compatible," she said, avoiding Grace's gaze.

"Is that what you really think?" The voice wasn't Grace's, though the question had been on her lips, too. Mick himself stood in the doorway.

"Mick," Cecily said, visibly flustered. "I-I didn't mean for you—" Her voice changed to indignant. "This is a private conversation."

Grace's heart went out to Mick for the crestfallen look on his face. "Oh, come on in, Mick. Why don't the two of you stay a while? I've been so lonely lately." In truth, Mick had just been by the day before, and Ed had kept Grace company earlier, so she wasn't feeling lonely this time, but she'd use whatever it took to get these two to tango.

"How have you been?" Cecily swept the last of the balms into a bag and sat in the chair next to Grace.

"All right," he said, settling on the edge of Grace's bed. He talked a bit with Grace, the conversation flat.

"I feel like my words are lingering in the air, putting a damper on this little gathering," said Cecily. "I'm really sorry, Mick."

"If that's how you feel, that's how you feel," he said, putting his hands in his pockets. "But I'd be lying if I said I felt the same way. I think we're great together."

"It's just—" Cecily looked away from him.

"What?"

It seemed to Grace that Cecily was struggling to put something into words. "Maybe the two of you should talk without me here."

"No, it's not you, Grace." But as soon as Cecily said that, something flickered across her face, as if a thought had occurred to her. "Then again, maybe it is. This is going to sound strange, but it's as if you both keep who you are to yourselves. Grace, you and I have been friends for what? Ten years. And all this time, I've always

127

felt as if you were holding back on something, some kernel of yourself. It's the strangest thing. I thought maybe it was just the dynamic between you and me, until I started falling for your brother here."

Well, Grace certainly hadn't expected this, and she wasn't sure how to respond. She glanced at Mick, who seemed to be at a loss for words himself.

"So what is it?" Cecily continued. "Some horrible family secret? I can understand that if so, but this just feels like it's … in the way." She turned to Mick. "For us. I can handle it with a friend, but if I'm going to love someone, I need to have all of him."

Grace could see tears in Mick's eyes. She watched as he swallowed hard. "Cecily, that's the best thing anyone's ever said to me."

He stood up. So did she. They embraced.

Mick held Cecily's face in his hands. "I promise, I'll open up more." He broke away, looking at Grace.

Grace, whose heart felt as if it had grown two sizes in the last minute, nodded at him. She'd rarely told people about her dreamslipping ability, and neither had he, but surely it was time in this case. It only remained to be seen how Cecily would take it, and if she'd believe him.

"May I buy you dinner?" Mick asked Cecily, and she agreed, after checking in with Grace, who said she was fine.

"What's this?" asked Ed, who appeared just then in the doorway. "A family reunion?"

Mick and Ed hadn't met before, but they seemed to hit it off. Ed was charming to Cecily, complimenting her art, which he'd seen in a gallery downtown.

After they left, Ed sat in the chair by Grace's bedside. His presence next to her brought to mind her own romantic predicament, which was the fact that today was Ed's last day in rehab.

"I like Mick," said Ed. "He's not one of those pretentious artists. You know, stuck on his own genius? He just paints."

"That's a fairly accurate description of my brother," said Grace. "I'm amazed you picked that up so quickly."

"Sweetheart," Ed said, as if trying out the endearment, as he wasn't the type to slather it on like butter. "Now that they're springing me from this joint, I won't have the luxury of dropping in on you like this or commandeering your attention at the cafeteria table. But I'd like to keep seeing you, and when you're up and at 'em, which I suspect will be sooner than anyone in this place realizes, I will insist upon taking you out for a real date."

She reached over and took his hand. "I've enjoyed getting to know you, Ed."

He smiled, placing his hand over hers.

Grace closed her eyes, thinking of the various dreams of Ed's she'd been able to slip into over the course of their mutual hospital stay. After she'd figured out from their conversations that he had been her ninja clown dreamer, she'd been privy to dreams about his ex-wife and children, their presence often mingling with those of the other people in rehab with them. Like a lot of people, he had a recurring anxiety dream associated with his work, and for him it was a day in court with no opening statement prepared, so that he had to wing it. Sometimes while naked. Grace got a kick out of those, even though they made Ed squirm.

"What's going through that gorgeous head of yours?" he asked.

"Oh, nothing," she replied. "I was thinking about the oddity of a rehab romance."

"I think you just invented a new fiction category," he joked.

"Or a fetish," she shot back.

"Naughty girl."

Just then her dreaded Nurse Ratched showed up to truly put a damper on things. "I'm afraid you lovebirds are going to have to take a breather," she said, pulling the blinds shut. "Gracie here needs her rest."

>>>

Cat was convinced now that Sam had to be Nina's killer, and she was going to nail him for it. Why else would he have encouraged her to lie about the wallpaper? He had to know she was onto him. She reasoned he thought she was spying on him that night and maybe simply fell asleep on the job. That part made her self-conscious. She felt like proving her prowess by getting him for the crime.

There was also the dream about losing Nina in a sewer tunnel. She wondered if she should take it literally as indicative of a location for his creepy memorial.

Cat decided to tell Robin about the memorial outfit. This time Robin responded with outrage instead of crumbling in grief. She'd quickly mobilized the Wyld Womyn, and they had all convened at the Howell residence to help. While Cat was upstairs poring through Nina's belongings, the WWs were in the living room, digging up whatever they could on Sam Waters.

Their voices occasionally floated upstairs. "Here's an online commenter, a woman, who's accusing Sam of sexism." Cat recognized the voice as belonging to Sharon Koal, who wore her hair bobbed, a perfect frame for her turquoise glasses.

Cat tuned out their conversation and concentrated on the box in front of her. It was a tidy plastic bin full of Nina's keepsakes, the kind of thing an adult woman wouldn't want to throw out, but wouldn't want to have displayed in her home, either. Her high-school class ring. Valentine's Day cards from Robin, spanning the length of their eleven-year relationship and two-year legal marriage. Correspondence from their adoption of Jin Mae.

There was nothing that helped her with the case.

"I don't know how anyone can listen to this drivel," said a voice downstairs. Cat remembered the financial planner, Danielle-something, who'd agreed to listen to Sam's radio show archive to see if anything stood out that could be used in the case. He took calls from listeners all the time, and Cat was interested in those. "He's a fucking moron!" Danielle continued. "I'm so tired of these libertarians. They believe in the free market like it's religion or something."

"Let me know if you want to switch off," replied Sharon. "Although I don't know that reading these mostly illiterate online comments will be any better."

Cat got up and shut the door.

She appraised the couple's closet. There were a few more storage bins on a top shelf to go through. What she was looking for was something, anything, that tied Nina to Sam. As far as she knew, the police hadn't talked to him. She was the only one looking at him for the crime. But she knew that there had to be some moment when the two of them had crossed paths, and finding that moment was the key.

She didn't see what she wanted in the other bins, but she did discover something interesting. An obituary. For Nina's father. Only it was an obvious fake.

Someone had mocked it up, in the style of an actual newspaper listing, but Photoshopped. It was dated more than six years ago, in September 2008. She wondered if the details were accurate. She knew his name was Norman Jeffers, but not much else about him. The obituary described him as a retired chemical plant manager, survived by his wife Tina Jeffers and a daughter from a former marriage, Nina Howell. It also said he'd "been tragically murdered at age seventy-two, the victim of poisoning." Cat set the obituary aside to discuss with Robin later.

She exhausted Nina's physical holdings without finding anything else of interest. The woman must have been OCD, in Cat's opinion, the way her socks were perfectly folded and sorted, and even the detritus of her past organized in neat bins.

Cat's cell phone buzzed, and she glanced at it, expecting a text from Granny Grace. But it was Bethany Adams, the schoolteacher and her new friend.

Sort of new friend. Cat liked her all right, but Bethany was part of the case, at least tangentially. Cat had pretended to be a fellow teacher looking for a job, so right off the bat, their friendship was built on a lie. Cat shuddered, recalling what happened with Wendy, another woman she'd met while undercover. Wendy was a devout believer who turned out to be a source of key information in a case, and that had had to come before any friendship concerns. Cat still felt guilty about it, even though Wendy forgave her when the truth came out.

Bethany's text read, *Hey, Cat! You free for happy hour this week?*

Cat felt lonely and craved conversation with someone her own age, especially someone who was also single and a recent transplant from the Midwest to Seattle. Could she come clean about being a PI? She weighed that possibility, running through the hypothetical conversation in her mind. Nope, there was no way Bethany wouldn't keep bugging her to find out exactly which of her students' parents was the target of Cat's investigation. So she had two choices: Give Bethany the brushoff, or keep pretending to be a schoolteacher. Both made her wish for a moment she could trade places with her grandmother. Well, without the pain component, anyway.

She decided to ignore the text for now and turn back to the task at hand. Next were Nina's personal laptop, tablet computer, and phone. Robin had given Cat the passwords. Again, she found the files organized into neat folders: Household, Jin Mae-School, Anniversary Trip. She found the Photoshop file of the obituary in a folder marked Archive. But nothing else. Nothing to connect Nina to Sam. While she was on the computer, which was still automatically picking up the couple's Wi-Fi, Cat searched Norman Jeffers and found that the man was still alive and well and living in Texas. Tina Jeffers was indeed his wife's name. He had little online presence except for a bit of activity on a few public forums frequented by UFO buffs. It seemed like a strange hobby for a man whose daughter had been well grounded, maybe even scientific to a fault. Granny Grace's only complaint about Nina had been that the woman regarded New Age practices and religion as silly, make-believe stuff.

Tired and feeling a headache coming on, Cat sauntered downstairs. "How's it going?" she asked the WWs, who were tucking into pizza that looked homemade. The smell made Cat's stomach growl.

Sharon looked up, her turquoise frames falling down to the edge of her nose. "Sam's a mansplaining neocon who cuts off his female callers about twice as often as his male callers."

"I guess that doesn't surprise me," said Cat. "But anything linking him to Nina? Or anything suggesting he fixates on certain callers?"

That drew blank faces. Danielle, who'd pulled the earbuds out of her ears at Cat's approach, said, "He calls us *feminazis*."

"Would you like some?" Robin asked, offering Cat a slice of pizza on a terra-cotta plate. "The crust is gluten-free."

Later, after the other women had gone home, Cat drew the obituary out of the folder where she'd hidden it and showed it to Robin, who clamped her hands over her mouth in response.

"You weren't supposed to see that," said Robin. "I didn't realize she'd kept a copy. We had a ceremony one night, she burned it…. Oh, I wish you hadn't seen that!"

"Why? It's not like he's really dead."

Robin made a sour face. "He was to Nina."

"Oh," Cat said, confused, and wondering why Robin hadn't told her about this before. "They were estranged?"

"Ever since Nina was in undergrad," Robin said, getting up to take a stack of plates back into the kitchen. Cat followed. Robin scraped hardened cheese off a plate before setting it in the dishwasher. "He was abusive."

"So, Nina created the fake obit as, like, an act of catharsis?"

"You're not supposed to know about this," Robin said, shaking her head. "Nina kept it in here." She gestured toward her chest. "She called it 'the vault.' I'm the only one she ever told about her father. She wanted to have a normal life, a career. She didn't want people to know. When we got married, we came up with our own last name, Howell. One we could share."

With that, Robin broke down crying. Cat reached for a paper towel and offered it to her.

"I'm sorry," she said.

"It's two words," Robin said, sobbing now. "*How* and *well*."

"I'm sorry," Cat repeated.

"It's okay," said Robin, wiping her eyes and calming down. "A reporter from *The Seattle Times* was here the other day. I didn't tell her about this either. I don't want to destroy Nina's memory. They're keeping the details of her murder out of the obit, but I think that's more to protect the investigation than Nina's reputation or us. I thought I would write it myself, but Nina was just important enough in Seattle to warrant a pro write-up, I guess."

>>>

She took the belt out of her trousers and, lying down on the bed, tried to smack herself. The sensation was mildly pleasurable, but nowhere near the same. She needed him, the one in the mask. That didn't frighten her, the mask. She could lock eyes with him, see the communication there. He anticipated her needs so well.

The calendar where she'd marked the days away from her masked man flew up off her desk and grew to fill the room. Twenty-seven days, each marked with a red X on paper. It was a long time to feel such need.

But then the waiting was over.

He stood before her. "I want to be your everything," he said. "Your boss, your lover, your owner. Even your daddy."

"No," she said. "Not that one. Everything else, but not daddy."

If he said that again, she would have to stop everything. She would have to use her safe word. The name of a bird: robin.

"It makes me think of flying away," she explained. She gave him coy eyes, but from the look on his face, she knew he'd heard the sadness in her words.

"I don't want you to have to escape," he said. "I want

136

you free, to choose me. I want us both to be free."
But she knew they were each in their own cage.

When Cat woke, she grabbed her journal from the bedside table and wrote up a description of the dream before it dissipated. This dream and the other two like it seemed like splinters to her, as if they were only the remnants of dreams. Could they belong to Nina? Or was it just a coincidence that her dreamer's safe word was "robin"?

Nina was dead.

Do the dead dream?

Chapter Ten

"I don't like this stuff about Nina's father," Cat told her grandmother.

Granny Grace's face was still flushed from her appointment with the physical therapist, who'd left the room as Cat came in.

"Whew," she said. "If I hadn't already gone through the change, I'd think I was having a hot flash. That's the most active I've been in days."

Cat realized she'd dived right into business without asking her grandmother how she was. "I'm sorry, Gran. Here I am, acting as if you're just here to consult with me on the case. How are you doing?"

"Oh, it's not going fast enough for me. But Dr. Acker seems pleased. Really, Cat. I don't mind your focus. I'm flattered that you still need me."

"I'll always need you." Cat's voice caught in her throat.

"Cat..." Her grandmother reached her hand out. Cat took it.

"I'm sorry I've been such a sad sack in here."

"It was totally understandable. I mean, I kind of abandoned you for a bit ... but at least you had Ed to keep you company. Is that going anywhere, by the way?"

"I don't know yet," said Grace. "He's not all I've had. Mick and Cecily visit often. Other friends have called, too. Including a new one, Annie Lin."

"From New York? Mick's old girlfriend?"

"The same."

Cat gave her a mischievous smile. "Why am I not surprised? It seemed as if I'd disappeared the day we interviewed her. Like it was just the two of you in her apartment."

"She's a lovely human being," said Grace, her feelings for the newfound friendship bubbling over. "Do you know she's on a first-name basis with Yoko Ono?"

"Really? Isn't every artist?"

Grace rolled her eyes. "Oh, you don't want to hear about her anyway. Tell me what's happening with the case."

Cat sat down and got her grandmother up to speed on the new developments. Of course, Granny Grace was not happy about the close call with Sam.

"Did you at least tell Mick what you were up to? I realize he's not a licensed and bonded PI and all that, but he is a dreamslipper, and your great-uncle besides. You don't have to be alone in this. Bring us in when you need us."

"You're right, Gran." Cat wondered about her tendency to fly solo. Maybe it was because she'd grown up an only child. She hadn't even considered bringing Mick in on the case, or even clueing him into her whereabouts, for safety reasons, the way she had with her grandmother when she'd gone on that disaster date.

About Nina's father, her grandmother had this to say: "Nina's past does seem to further suggest that Robin has been right all along. Maybe Sam had some psychological hold over Nina. Maybe she could never fully heal from the damage her father did."

"You might be right," Cat said. "It's just… Nina had a stellar career. She was the youngest partner in her firm, she'd won a number of top architectural design awards, and she'd been involved in several high-profile Seattle projects. I'm just having trouble seeing her as a tragic, codependent victim."

"It is a rather depressing thought," Granny Grace said. "But even the strongest women are vulnerable to abuse."

"The obit suggests she had an outlet, at least, assuming what Robin says about Nina's father is true. It seems like a good way to express that, you know? It's something I would do."

"I agree."

"We could talk to Norman Jeffers," Cat suggested. "See what we think. I have a number for him. Maybe he's home. He is retired."

"All right, but I hope people don't assume I'm always home when I retire."

"Oh, Gran," said Cat. "You'll never retire!"

"Never say never," said her grandmother.

Cat decided to ignore that for now. She put her phone on speaker and dialed. When Jeffers answered on the second ring, she gave her grandmother an I-told-you-so look. The man's Texas twang came through right away in his greeting, which sounded like "Yallo!"

"Hi, Mr. Jeffers. This is Cat McCormick, calling from Seattle."

"What can I do for you, Ms. McCormick?"

"First, I want to express my condolences at the loss of your daughter, Nina Howell. It must be a tremendous blow."

"Thanks for your kind words, ma'am. It's never right when a parent outlives a child, is it?"

"Certainly not," Cat replied. "I'm sure you wish for justice to be done. My partner and I have been retained by Robin Howell to investigate Nina's murder."

"I see," said Jeffers. "You'll have to excuse my ignorance. I didn't realize Robin had hired a PI."

"No worries," said Cat. "We're calling to ask you a few questions."

"I've told the police everything I know, but sure. Shoot me some questions."

"Do you know a man by the name of Sam Waters?"

"I know of him, from the radio? We get his programs out here in Waco. A little on the liberal side for my tastes."

Cat and Granny Grace exchanged looks.

Cat pressed further. "But you've never met him, nor come in contact with him?"

"No, I haven't."

"Did Nina ever mention him?"

"Not to me," he said.

"Were you and Nina close?"

"I'd say about average for a father and daughter. She came to visit me not too long ago. I'm grateful I got to see her before—" His voice broke. "Excuse me."

Cat glanced at her grandmother and mouthed *A visit?* Granny Grace shrugged. They waited a minute before he returned.

Cat resumed questioning. "When was this, exactly?"

"Oh, just a few weeks before she died. It's a nice time to visit Waco, in late February. You can smell spring right around the corner." His tone sounded bittersweet.

"Did she stay in your house?"

"She stayed in a fancy hotel in downtown Waco," he said. "The Grant, I think they call it, on account of President Ulysses S. Grant having once tethered his horse outside. I'm sure back in the day it cost nothing, with a bathroom down the hall, but now they charge an arm and a leg—for the character. Character seems to come at a premium these days."

"But my wife and I did offer to put her up," he continued. "You know how it is. She's an architect. In other words, a sucker for character." He laughed good-naturedly.

Cat noted his use of the present tense when referring to Nina.

Granny Grace cleared her throat, motioning at Cat to let her talk.

"Mr. Jeffers, I have my partner, Grace, on the line here, too."

"I *thought* it sounded as if I were on speakerphone," Jeffers observed.

"Hello, Mr. Jeffers," her grandmother said. "Where were you the night of Friday, March 14, 2014?"

"The night Nina was killed," he said soberly.

"Yes," said Granny Grace.

"On a fishing trip," he said. "Lake Whitney."

"Did you go with someone who can verify that?"

"Nope. I like to fish alone. But my wife saw me

142

leave. And return."

"How long were you gone?"

"Oh, I guess about ten days."

"You can check with the state park office to see that my reservation was claimed, and my spot occupied."

Cat decided to redirect. "Mr. Jeffers, I have to ask you a really tough question."

"Tougher than what you've already asked?"

"I'm afraid so."

Cat drew out what she had to say. "There seems to be a suggestion that Nina's childhood was ... not a happy one."

He did not reply. Cat went on. "We're following up on reports that you ... that there was some ... domestic abuse in the family."

"Are you talking about me?" he asked. "As some kind of ... wife beater?"

"Yes," said Cat. "Not just your wife, but Nina, too. Did you? Hurt them?"

Cat waited through what sounded like an emotional response, close to a keen. "You'll have to excuse me," Jeffers said, his voice breaking. "This is so upsetting."

"Take your time," Cat said gently.

When he came back to the phone, his voice was hard. "I don't know where you're getting your information or how this could possibly help you find the bastard who killed my daughter. But I'm sorry. I'm done. This is good-bye, ladies." He hung up.

"Well, I honestly don't know what to think," said her grandmother.

"Me, neither," said Cat.

"It's hard to tell on the phone, but he seemed genuine. It sounds like his alibi will check out, too."

"Maybe Robin's lying."

"If Nina did visit him recently, that certainly doesn't sound like estrangement to me."

>>>

Cat accompanied her grandmother to dinner in the rehab cafeteria. She felt a great deal of sympathy for Granny Grace as she slurped down the bland applesauce and pushed a few wrinkled peas around in their tray compartment, thinking about how the woman hadn't once complained about the food.

After they ate, Cat wheeled her back to her room, pausing to kiss her on the top of the head before helping her back into bed, noticing she could move around more freely now, without pain.

"Don't forget to ask Robin about Nina taking a trip to Waco."

"I won't."

Granny Grace's phone, sitting on the nightstand, buzzed.

"Oh, it's your mother," said Granny Grace. "I should take this."

Cat nodded.

"Mercy, how nice of you to call. Cat's here, too. All three generations."

Cat watched her grandmother's facial expressions as she talked. Mercy had been an only child as well, and

Cat knew her mother had dreamed of a house full of children. Cat felt a pang as she remembered a dream of her mothers that she'd slipped into the last time she visited St. Louis. The dream was full of the sorrow her mother still felt about not being able to have more children. A staunch Catholic, she'd taken it as "God's way" and had not pursued infertility solutions.

"...yes, I'm coming along nicely," said her grandmother. "Would you like to speak to Cat?"

Cat took the phone.

"How is your grandmother *really* doing?" asked Cat's mother. "I know how she runs everything through her positive-thinking filter."

"Oh, she's recovering well," Cat said, winking at her grandmother. "Her doctor seems pleased with her progress."

"Your father and I were thinking of coming out there."

It was as if a needle scratched across a record, or so she imagined. She'd only ever heard it in old movies and TV shows. "*To Seattle?*"

"Yes, Seattle. Where else? We want to be of help to your grandmother. And you."

Cat looked to her grandmother for help. "I-I don't know if it's such a good idea for you to come here..."

Granny Grace's eyes widened. She drew a slash mark across her throat, which would have made Cat laugh if she weren't herself feeling panicked about the idea of her parents showing up in Seattle right now.

"...We're in the middle of a case. Kind of an intense one. And Mick's here. He's very helpful."

"Well, I doubt your Great-Uncle Mick is all that much help," her mother countered. "And we won't intrude on your case."

"Oh, well, you know, Gran's still here in rehab.... I'm not sure it's a good time."

"Cathedral," her mother said, her voice coming across as severe. "It sounds like you don't want us there."

Guilt rained down on Cat. "Oh, no, no, Mom," she sputtered. "It's just—"

"Put your grandmother back on the phone."

She handed the phone back to Granny Grace, who didn't fare any better against Mercy, with her mind made up.

After a few rounds of polite attempts at dissuasion, her grandmother said, "Well, it's all settled then. You'll stay in the Perfectly Pink Parlor, that is, if Joe's comfortable enough in his masculinity to stand it for a week or two."

A week or two! Cat shook her head, waving her hands for Granny Grace to put a stop to this crazy talk.

But her grandmother ended the call.

And sighed.

Cat slunk back into the chair beside her. "How are we going to survive this?"

"Well, it has been a while. We're overdue. It'll be nice, won't it? With Mick here, too? An old-fashioned family reunion."

Cat recognized her grandmother's characteristic way of putting a happy face on everything. Her mother'd been right about that.

"I don't have time to clean the house to the level

of my mother's expectations," said Cat. "I have a killer to catch, remember?"

"Just give it a cursory straightening. You know your mother will clean it herself regardless."

"Yeah, you're right. I'll go do that now and see if I can get Uncle Mick to help. And then I'm going to drink that bottle of whiskey you've got stashed for just such an occasion."

As soon as Cat got home, she texted Bethany. In order to survive this parental visitation, she'd need a friend into whose company she could escape. The risks be damned.

Mick was less opposed to the idea of her parents' visit. "Good deal," he said. "I haven't seen Mercy and Joe since ... well, since you were a girl."

"Then I guess you won't mind helping me clean this place up a bit." Cat gestured around the Daring Damask Den, which was strewn with paper copies of *The Seattle Times*, a subscription her grandmother insisted upon keeping despite the fact that anything she really needed to read could be found online. There were also crumpled sketches that Mick had excised from his notebook and some of Cat's clothes, which she had a habit of leaving in the den. Then there was her evidence board, with its photos, connecting relationship lines, and questions she had yet to answer.

WHERE DID NINA AND SAM MEET?

The question seemed to mock her.

"What should I do with this?" she asked, not expecting Mick to have an answer.

He was busy smoothing out one of his crumpled

sketches. "This isn't half bad..."

"Are you going to help or what?"

The sharpness in her voice seemed to startle him.

"Sorry," Cat muttered.

The two cleared the den and attacked other parts of the house together when the sun showed itself outside —so rare Seattleites call it a "sunbreak."

"Well, I've reached my limit," Cat announced. "Have a drink with me? It might even be warm enough to sit outside."

Mick grabbed an old towel and dried off the deck chairs in back. Sunlight glinted in puddles of water all over Granny Grace's backyard.

"Cheers," Cat said, lifting up her whiskey.

"Salud," said Mick in return.

Cat surveyed the garden, and with a pang of worry realized the late Seattle spring was fully upon them. "Gran's not going to be able to tackle this garden like usual," Cat said.

"Hmm..." Mick stared at the sun turning the whiskey in his glass to a honeyed hue that seemed to glow.

Cat used to feel frustrated at her Uncle Mick when it was hard to get his attention, but increasingly, she found it amusing. She waited for whatever observations he was making about color and light to die down.

"There are a lot of weeds out here that need pulling," Cat tried again.

This time he shaded his eyes from the beams of blasting, sudden sun and looked at the yard. Cat watched him take in the small Japanese garden in the corner, which now looked ragged and unkempt, the strawberry patch succumbing to dandelions, the English ivy growing over the azaleas.

"I'll do it," he said. "I've got the time. You need to work on your case."

"You sure?"

"Yep," he took a swallow of his whiskey. "But tell me all about this killer you're stalking. Your grandmother seems to think you need my protection."

Cat filled him in on the case. As she talked, she walked over to the edge of the deck, near where an ornamental cherry grew, its coils of peeling bark like strips of cellophane. She held one up between her hands, in front of the sun. It caught the light as if she'd lit it on fire.

"Does your grandmother know your suspect has learned your identity—and your address?"

Cat let the bark curl around her fingers. "No, I might've left that part out when I told her."

"Great," said Mick. "I'd say it's only a matter of time before the stalker becomes the stalked."

"I'm aware of that," Cat said.

"Maybe you should get a gun."

"Granny Grace won't have guns in her house."

"Well, keep it in the car."

"She won't have them as part of the agency. She doesn't believe we need them."

"What do *you* think?"

"I know how to shoot. I took lessons."

"That's not what I asked."

"I don't know," Cat admitted. "I like to think Gran's right. A gun wouldn't have saved Lee that day. It all happened too fast. But sometimes I think I'd feel better if I had one."

"Well," Mick said, pouring himself another whiskey. "I guess that's your decision."

"Yeah," said Cat. She didn't feel the need to run out and get a gun right away, but she had to admit her uncle was right. It was time she thought about what kind of PI she wanted to be, independent of her grandmother.

"So things with Cecily are good again?" Cat asked, taking the focus off her.

"I think so," said Mick. "But if we're going to make it, I'll have to fess up about being a dreamslipper."

Cat nearly choked on her whiskey. "What?"

"This one's for real," said Mick. "The realest I've ever had. But she feels like there's this big thing between us. Something I'm not telling her."

"Because there is."

"Yep."

"Well, good luck with that."

"Thanks."

Cat thought for a moment about what it would be like to find out the person you shared a bed with could see all your dreams. Would it feel as if they'd read your diary? Probably worse. Way worse. There's just no way this could go well.

"She won't believe it," Cat said. "Which means you'll have to prove it to her."

"Yeah, I'm not looking forward to this."

"Are you going to tell her we're all dreamslippers? Gran and me, too?"

"I don't know." Mick ran a hand through his thinning red-and-gray hair. "She's sort of accused your grandmother of the same thing. She thinks there's some dark family secret."

Cat laughed. "Well, I guess there is."

Mick smiled. "And your mother will be here, too."

"You know she still doesn't even like to talk about it."

"Maybe she's mad that it skipped her generation. Maybe she feels left out."

Cat had never considered that. She'd always assumed Mercy was glad she'd been spared the family curse, especially since she pretended to not really believe in it. Even when Cat was a child and described her mother's own dreams to her, Mercy shrugged it off as coincidence, or accused Cat of having too much imagination. If it weren't for her grandmother, Cat wouldn't have known anything about her dreamslipping ability.

"What about your dad?"

Cat smiled at the thought of her father. "Oh, he's always made sure I was getting a bona fide education in criminal justice. He didn't want me to use dreamslipping as, like, a crutch or something."

"A crutch," Mick said, laughing. "That's what I'll tell Cecily. It's just my crutch, till I can walk on my own again."

Cat clinked her glass with his, and the two of them watched as the clouds encroached on the sun again, burying it in a gray shroud.

>>>

Early the next morning, Cat called over to Robin's house.

"Have you found anything yet?" Robin asked right away.

"There is something," Cat said, hesitating. "But I'm not sure yet. I need your help."

"Okay," Robin said. Cat could hear Jin Mae playing with a xylophone in the background, methodically going up the scale. It sounded like *Do, Re, Mi...*

"Did Nina take any trips recently?"

"She travels all the time for work."

"This would have been in late February."

"Oh, yeah, of course. The AIA meets then. That's the big conference everyone goes to—the American Institute of Architects."

Cat ran a quick search using the laptop sitting in front of her. This year's conference had taken place in Dallas, only an hour and a half from Waco.

"Did she mention a side trip to Waco? Because her father says she visited him."

Silence.

Jin Mae made her way down the scale. *Do, Ti, La, So...*

"Robin?"

Cat heard a sniff. "Nina didn't say anything to me about a trip to Waco," she finally replied. "Her father's lying."

"Okay, Robin, okay. Sure. He might be lying. But could you do me a favor? Go back over your bank records from that time. See if there are any charges from Waco. If you don't see that, look for large cash withdrawals."

Silence.

"Robin? Will you do that for me?"

"How does this help us catch Sam?"

"You've got to trust me, Robin," Cat said. "We need to form an exact timeline preceding your wife's murder."

"Fine," said Robin.

"Call me back as soon as you can," Cat said. Then, thinking better of it, she added, "Or I can just stay on the line and walk you through it."

"I'm already looking," said Robin. Cat heard her typing.

She sighed heavily. "It's here," she said.

"What do you see?"

"Cash withdrawals, from a bank in Dallas. More than her usual for a conference."

"I'm sorry, Robin. This must be hard."

"No," Robin said. "She must have had a reason. I'm sure she was going to tell me when she was ready. She liked to protect me, you know. She always said I was very sensitive." Robin's voice changed to melancholy, romantic. "She used to call me her hothouse flower."

Chapter Eleven

The building housing Fletcher Green and Howell was shaped like the hull of a ship—because it used to be one. Cat realized it was the same place she saw from the room where Nina was killed.

Cat gazed up at the spine of the old boat bottom, which, a plaque on the far wall informed her, was that of a one-hundred-year-old halibut schooner.

"They made them from old-growth lumber back then," said Simon, who'd come out to greet her. "You literally cannot make a ship like that today. You can't make *anything* like that today."

She nodded, and he said, "Nina's office is this way."

Cat followed him down a long corridor lined with black-and-white photographs depicting street musicians.

"Here you go, Cathedral." It was her full, legal name, but Simon was one of the few people she allowed to use it. She figured that, as an architect, he basically studied cathedrals for a living, so he'd earned the privilege. He used a key to open a spacious office with a peekaboo view of Pike Place Market. Nina's desk was situated to take best advantage of the view, as well as the natural light pouring in through the oversized window. The furnishings were spare, making Cat realize that the home Nina shared with Robin likely reflected Robin's aesthetic more than Nina's, outside of the architectural design. On the walls were original paintings, none by the same artist.

Even so, the artwork had been chosen with an eye for the harmony between them. Cat caught herself wondering what Jacob, who worked in his uncle's art gallery, would think of these pieces.

"May I?" Cat asked, gesturing toward Nina's desk drawer.

"By all means," said Simon. "The police have already been all over this room, though. I'm not even sure what they took, but they left with several bags of evidence."

Cat was not surprised to hear that, and maybe it didn't matter, since she was looking specifically for ties to Sam Waters. It hit her that she and the Seattle PD were in a contest to find the killer.

"What kind of person was Nina?"

Simon straightened the knot in his tie. "The best. Ridiculously skilled at her job—every aspect of it. A brilliant architect, and good with clients as well. That combination isn't always there, unfortunately. She wasn't driven by ego. She really loved the design, and she was passionate about sustainability."

"And personally?"

"She tended to keep her work life and private life separate. It's odd, I suppose, but she never talked about her childhood or parents. I can tell you that she and Robin have been together since the same year Nina and I became partners. That was—gosh. Nine years ago, 2005? A lot changed for Nina that year, for the better, I'd say."

"And before then?"

"She'd taken a hiatus, called it career burnout. But sometimes I think there was something personal going on. It's not my way to pry."

Cat wished he'd been nosier.

"I've got to get back to work, but take as much time as you need," said Simon.

"Thanks. Before you go—here," she said, taking a sticky-note pad from Nina's drawer, along with a pen, and handing it to him. "Write down Nina's password for me."

"Sure," said Simon, taking his phone out of his pocket. "I've got it in here. The police kept asking for it—they made copies of all her files. I'm not sure what you'll find. It didn't seem to help them any, not that I've heard, anyway. Nina was meticulously neat."

He scribbled the password down for her. "There's a break room down the hall if you get hungry or thirsty."

"Thanks, Simon."

Cat checked the drawers, which didn't hold much. Office supplies, and a tidy grouping of what looked like marketing swag: mouse pads, pens, and an architect's compass all inscribed with the logos of various firms, both construction and architectural. On top of the desk sat a Newton's cradle, six silver balls suspended by nylon strings. All six balls were still. Cat lifted one on the end and let it fall. The force traveled through the balls in the middle, which remained stationary, and the one on the opposite end rose. Cat watched as this repeated now of its own volition on each side, back and forth.

"I can only let go like that with you."

Cat jolted in recognition. The swaying pearls, the Newton's cradle. The woman's desire to let go in a way she couldn't with anyone else.

"Please, I need you to hurt me."

The mystery dream, the first one. It seemed to belong to Nina.

Control, said that voice in Cat's head, the one that could be God or her own higher self. She didn't know, but she knew to listen to it when it spoke. *This is about control.*

Nina had seemed very *in* control. Of herself, of her career, even within her marriage.

But her death was messy.

And when she died, she'd been restrained. Under someone else's control.

Cat sat down at Nina's desk, turned the computer on, and went to work. The partners kept a paperless office, so any files Nina saved would be stored there. Cat needed to learn more about their business, starting with the Puget Place Hotel project.

>>>

They were at Cecily's again. Because she lived alone, and Mick decidedly did not, they preferred her place to his.

But this time he was cooking, a dish Pris had taught him to make: quinoa with barbecue tempeh.

As he mixed up the sauce, he braced himself for what he was about to do. And he made sure to keep Cecily's wine glass full. She was perched on a stool at her countertop, drinking Chardonnay with gusto, going on about how nice it was to have a man cooking for her. But then she stopped, as if a thought had just occurred to her.

"Wait a minute. Why am I making such a big deal

out of this?" she laughed. "I already cooked for you once. Why is it such an extra-special treat that you're now cooking for me?"

Plying her with a dish of cheese, Mick said, "I didn't say any of that. You did."

"You're right, Travers. And you're a good guy, too."

Her words, and the cute way she was looking at him tonight, made Mick feel undone. He nearly blurted out "I love you," but he had something else he needed to say first.

After dinner, he told her to head into the living room and relax while he cleaned her kitchen. She obliged. It gave him time to think about what he should say. He realized there was only one way to go.

He joined her in the living room, bringing the bottle with him to fill her glass again.

"Are you trying to get me drunk? You know you don't need alcohol in order to take advantage of me."

He sat down on the couch and turned toward her.

"Damn, Mick. You look so—oh, shit. This is it, isn't it? The big family secret, once and for all."

Mick cleared his throat. "You dreamed about your father, the first time I ... stayed over."

Cecily looked at him, her expression a mixture of surprise—and curiosity.

"He was playing the piano. I think it was influenced by the music we were listening to that night. You wanted his impression of me, maybe even his blessing."

Cecily stood up. Wrapped her arms around her chest. "No," she said. "This can't be happening."

Mick stood, too. "He called you CeeCee. It's a cute nickname. I've wanted to call you that myself."

Tears pooled in Cecily's eyes. "What the hell, Mick? This can't … This can't be happening."

"I was there, in your dream. I—saw everything. I felt what you felt."

Silence, as Cecily's hand went to her mouth. She shook her head. Stared at him, wild-eyed, accusing. It seemed to Mick as if a lifetime went by before she spoke again.

"No, no, no, no, no, Mick Travers. You're trying to tell me you're some kind of fucking psychic or something? No."

Mick didn't know how to respond. "I guess. I don't know. Psychic? If you want to use that word, sure. Pris says we're spiritually attuned."

"You're telling me Grace is psychic, too?"

Mick slowly nodded. In a hoarse voice, and knowing it wouldn't help but unable to stop himself, he added, "She likes to call us 'dreamslippers.' I told her it sounded like something you wear, but she—"

"Uh-uh. No way. I don't buy it. Back in the 'hood, we'd call you the bogeyman. Some Boo Radley shit you're handing me here, Mickey. Well, I don't buy it. You are *not* the bogeyman! You're supposed to be my *boyfriend*!"

Cecily collapsed on the couch. She wasn't crying anymore. Just staring into space, her head going back and forth, over and over again. Then she began to vocalize her thoughts. "No," she said. "No."

Mick didn't know what to do. His script hadn't

159

gotten this far. He had one other thing to say, and leading with it had seemed like a cheat, a setup. But he realized going there now would be equally bad. So he said this: "Do you want me to leave?"

For a long moment, Cecily didn't answer. Then she started to laugh. "He's been in my dreams!" she said. "Of all the crazy, nonsense shit…"

"Cecily?"

She finally turned to look at him. "Yes, please, you trifling artist. First it was the child-porn thing, but Grace explained it to me, and I actually felt sorry for you. But here you are, making me waste my time, falling for you, and for what? This wackadoo shit? I don't have time for this. Get out!"

Mick could hear her sobs down the hallway of her apartment building. It took everything he had not to go back. He knew she wouldn't want him to.

>>>

The Pike Place Market sign glowed neon red against a charcoal sky. Simon had long gone home, but Cat was still in the office. He'd given her permission to stick around when he left.

She'd had a split-second's excitement when she located a document labeled GYM MEMBERSHIP CONTRACT, but it turned out to be for a different gym than the one Sam attended. Rain, it was called, with an orange logo.

The Puget Place Hotel project files were either squeaky clean, or Cat just didn't know what to look for yet. She copied everything over to her thumb drive for

160

future reference.

She was about to give up when she discovered a doc titled ADDRESSES that listed no names, just the addresses for several Texas locations. They appeared to be residential addresses, judging by the names of the streets and the lack of suite numbers or other corporate identifiers. Cat wondered what other family Nina had left behind.

Performing a reverse lookup, she saw that one of the addresses was the last known for Nina's father. The other two had different last names but were presumably family, too. Locating them on a map, Cat could see they were all within a twenty-square-mile radius of Waco. She had to assume Nina had either been in contact with these people recently, or she had intended to be. The file had been created only three months prior to Nina's death and was last opened a couple of weeks before her death. The Seattle PD had either ignored it or copied it over to their thumb drive in a batch without opening it.

Cat needed to get her hands on whatever else they'd removed from Nina's office.

Chapter Twelve

Cat stood in line for the third time at the Public Request Unit of the Seattle PD's headquarters. She had the report from Nina's murder already in hand, but it was just a basic one with a bit of narrative. It didn't tell her anything she didn't already know. What she wanted was to be able to look at the evidence taken from Nina's office.

As she waited, she thought about their decision to confiscate Nina's office files but not anything from her home. They must be exploring the theory that Nina's murder had something to do with its location—in a building she'd designed.

Once Cat advanced to the front desk, she presented her credentials and request to see the evidence from the crime scene.

"Didn't you already make this request once?" asked the same government employee Cat had spoken to previously, a matronly woman who would have looked more at home behind the desk at the library.

"Yes," said Cat.

"And what did they tell you that time?" The woman smiled, revealing yellow-tinged teeth.

"Look, I'm a private investigator—"

"—I'm sorry, but PIs have no more special dispensation than does the general public. This unit is for requests of police and collision reports, clearance letters, fingerprinting, and concealed-pistol permits." The woman said all of this politely, smiling at Cat with each pause.

"Is there someone else I can talk to?"

"Not at this unit. You can try Homicide."

Cat rolled her eyes. She'd already tried appealing to the Homicide Division, but the desk gatekeeper there wouldn't let her talk to the detectives on the case, whom he said were overwhelmed with tips. He took her information, but so far, no one had returned her query.

Maybe they would get around to her eventually, but she didn't like having to wait.

"Cat?" asked a voice behind her.

She turned. It was "Mr. M&O." His real name drifted to mind: Greg Swenson. He'd just entered the same line she'd come through. With nothing else for her to do at the window, she thanked the woman behind the counter and walked toward him.

"Nancy Drew," said Greg, using the silly name he'd called her back when she worked for him as a security guard. "Fancy running into you here."

Cat wasn't sure if she should hug him or give him a handshake. With the stanchions marking off the waiting queue for the Public Request Unit between them, she settled for the latter.

"I know," said Cat. "It's been—what? More than a year."

"A year and a half, almost," said Greg. "Not that I'm counting."

Cat glanced away from his deep brown eyes, which seemed to invite her in for flirtation. At the same time, seeing him again made her feel a stab of loss for

163

Lee. She still missed her childhood crush, her Ranger hero. The pain was no longer debilitating, but she sometimes still ached for him, wondered what could have been.

"Next!" said the woman at the desk.

Greg offered his spot to the person behind him and then unhooked the stanchion, stepping out of line.

"So, what were you requesting?" Cat asked.

Greg smiled. "Requesting? Um … as I recall, the last time I requested something from you, I was turned down."

She laughed, remembering how she'd backpedaled when he asked her out on a date, telling him she was "sort of seeing someone," meaning Lee. He had kidded her about it, saying that "sort of" implied there was some doubt. She'd left the door open on that. But then Lee died.

"Actually, I was talking about there, at the window," Cat smiled, gesturing to the counter for the Public Request Unit.

"Oh, right. Of course. Just renewing my pistol permit." He moved his black leather jacket aside to show a glimpse of his holster. That didn't surprise her, since she'd never once seen him without a firearm.

There was an awkward pause, and then Cat said, "I-I'm sorry I never got in touch."

"Hey," he said, putting a hand on her arm. "You didn't owe me anything."

His kindness brought up feelings that surprised her. "But I do," she said, making herself gaze into his eyes. "If you hadn't been there…" she whispered.

This time it was Greg's turn to look away. "I did what I was trained to do. That psycho had just shot your boyfriend, and I had to take her down. End of story. Besides, you saved my sister's life. Twice. So if anything, I owe you."

Cat gestured to the queue behind him. "Are you going to get back in line? Or let me take you to lunch?"

Greg didn't hesitate. "I'll go to lunch, but I'm buying."

"We'll see about that."

They walked down the street to a place called Verve, the closest eatery that wasn't a crowded walk-up counter.

"I feel as if I've stepped into a video game," said Greg as the waiter took them to their seats. "From the 1980s."

As Cat gingerly sat down in her chair, which was covered in pink fur and swiveled aggressively, she said, "This does kinda look like one of the Pac-Man ghosts."

"Do you play those old games?" Greg asked excitedly.

"Nope," said Cat. "I only know what the ghost looks like because of *Sandi and Silvie*."

He looked disappointed for a moment, and then confused.

"The YouTube stars?" Cat prompted.

He stared at her blankly.

"Seriously? They're like the best thing happening on YouTube right now. They use screenshots from the original Pac-Man game in their intro. And sometimes Sandi dresses up as Ms. Pac-Man, with Silvie wearing a tie and moustache and calling herself 'Mr. Pac-Man,' to make a point about how sexist it was to put a bow and lipstick on basically what was just a pie with one piece missing and call it a girl."

Greg looked amused. "I guess I'm not very with it."

"How old are you, anyway?" asked Cat. "I never really knew. I mean, you were my boss. Sort of."

"Just turned thirty-two," Greg said, pressing the starburst scar on his temple with his fingers. She remembered how he got it, from a tweaker who hurled a bottle at him.

"You've got eight years on me," said Cat.

Greg nodded, looking down at his menu.

"Now that we've established we're both old enough to drink," said Cat, pretending to peruse the drink menu, "how about a cocktail?"

"Not while I'm carrying," said Greg, gesturing to where his weapon was concealed.

"Right," said Cat, her face burning. She hid behind her menu, this time reading it. "I guess we're getting one of these healing smoothies, then," she said, pointing to the list. "Look, you can get turmeric as an addition."

Greg laughed. "Turmeric?"

"Yeah," Cat giggled. "My mom calls that 'the poor man's saffron.' Leave it to Seattleites to take a bottom-shelf spice and imbue it with healing properties."

When the waiter came, they both ordered smoothies with their lunch, adding turmeric, of course.

"Are you still with M&O?" Cat asked, referring to

166

the security firm they'd both worked for.

"Nope," he said. "I've got my own company now. Swenson Safety." He flipped his wallet open, drew out a business card, and handed it to her.

"Congratulations," she said. "That's great."

"Thanks, Cat. What are you up to these days? Still working with Granny Grace?"

"Yes, but my grandmother's in rehab right now. Not the drug kind. She fell and broke her pelvis."

"Oh, that's terrible. Where is she? I'd like to stop by, bring her some flowers."

"She'd love that, Greg. She's at Swedish in Ballard."

"I'll definitely do that."

The waiter brought their smoothies, and two sips in, Greg stood up and said, "I'm healed! Look, I can walk again!" Nearby diners gazed over with amused expressions. "Order the turmeric," Greg said, pointing to his smoothie.

Cat laughed so hard, smoothie almost came out her nose.

Greg watched her regain composure, a delighted smile on his face. "It's really good to see you again, Cat. I didn't think I ever would."

She grew serious. "Yeah, I feel bad about not responding to your flowers and card, your calls." He'd reached out to her after Lee died, but she'd let the connection go.

"I totally get it," Greg said. "Really. You must have been devastated."

"It's still … hard sometimes," she admitted,

breaking his gaze to stare across the restaurant, where it appeared as if every patron sat on a Pac-Man ghost. "I only recently began dating again."

"Oh," said Greg, his voice cautious. "Anyone special?"

"Just one," she said, her gaze returning to him. "But he lives in San Francisco."

Cat thought she detected a look of hopeful relief on his face.

"Long-distance relationships are tough," he said. "But they can sometimes work."

"Yeah, I met him in New York, when I was investigating a case in Miami."

Greg smiled. "Tell me about that."

Cat related the story of the fire in Mick's studio that killed his best friend, and all that happened as she and Granny Grace worked to find out the truth when the police suspected Mick.

"You've come a long way from security-booth attendant," Greg chuckled. She'd always liked his laugh.

"Yeah, but I've been trying to access evidence from a homicide, and I'm not getting anywhere. It's stalled out my case. That's why I was in line today. For the third time."

"Maybe I can help," he said, as if weighing his decision. "I mean, if you want it. I know some of the detectives, from when I was on the force in Tacoma."

"Really?" Cat didn't know what to say. She felt intrigued but a little off-balance about seeing him again, and she liked to do things herself. But in this case, she could use the help.

"Really," Greg said. "It's not a problem."

"Thanks," Cat said. "Oh, and here's my card." She slid an Amazing Grace Detective Agency business card over to him. It listed her cell phone number.

He palmed it, dug out his wallet, and slipped it inside. "I'd like there to be another reason for me to call you, though," he said. "To be totally honest."

She didn't hesitate, her heart speaking for her for the first time in a while. "I'd like that, too."

"How about tonight?"

That felt a little fast to her, and she didn't want to break her happy hour plans with Bethany, so she said she was busy.

"Tell you what," Greg said. "I'll set this up with Homicide, but other than that, you have my card. Just call me any time."

She smiled. "I will."

When the bill came, she grabbed it before he could. "You're doing me a favor," she insisted.

He didn't fight her. "I have a feeling it won't be my first."

>>>

Grace could stand using a walker now, without unendurable pain. And that meant she could go home.

At the discharge desk, she asked to see a total for the portion of her hospital expenses that wouldn't be covered by insurance.

"Your balance is zero," said the bespectacled man behind the counter.

"Excuse me?" Grace thought she'd heard wrong. Sometimes her wishful thinking would color what was actually said in a conversation.

His specs had slid down his nose apace, but his demeanor hadn't changed. "The portion not covered by insurance was $12,213.17," he said. "That balance was already paid, by a Mr. George Connors."

"How wonderful!" If she weren't leaning on her walker, Grace would've clapped her hands together at the news.

"Well, when did he make those arrangements?"

The clerk clicked through a few screens. "It looks like … the night you were brought in."

"Thank you so much," she said.

"Don't thank me," he said. "Thank this Mr. Connors."

"I certainly will."

Mick picked her up from the rehab center in Siddhartha. He didn't have a car of his own in Seattle yet, having left his old Fiat back in Miami with Rose de la Crem. Grace knew it was part of the deal in exchange for Rose managing his four-family flat. But Mick got around Seattle fine using public transportation.

She told him about George's gesture.

"Well, it's only right," said Mick, visibly less swayed by the generosity. "I mean, technically, you could sue him."

"Oh, Mickey, I hate that kind of talk. People are so litigious these days. Look what happens when you leave it up to personal responsibility."

"In this case," he said.

"Why are you so foul?" she asked, picking up on his mood. "You and Cecily still at odds?"

"You could say that, seeing as how she hates me and never wants to see me again."

"Oh, Mick. I'm so sorry! I thought she'd come around by now. Maybe I should—"

"—*You* shouldn't do anything. You're the one who got me into this mess in the first place."

"Well, how do you like that? I'm not even home yet, and I'm getting blamed for the state of *your* love life."

"You did set me up with her."

"At least she didn't knock you down and break a major bone in your body."

That silenced her brother.

In the quiet, Grace admired the day. Though overcast, the sky glowed orange where the sun backlit the clouds. She'd been cooped up in rehab for more than a week. Freedom felt so sweet.

She began to make plans. While in rehab, she'd read as much as she could about how to heal the body, especially in old age. Already she'd been in contact with that studio where she danced Nia. The teacher said she could come to class and chair-dance until she was ready to dance on two feet again. Grace couldn't wait.

"Where's Cat this fine day?" she asked, hoping Mick would change his tune.

"Working on the case, I guess," he said.

"Is the house ready for the McCormick onslaught?" Cat's parents were due to arrive the next day.

"As ready as Cat and I are capable of getting it."

171

At home, Mick's mood mellowed. He seemed to anticipate that she would have trouble navigating the Victorian's narrow steps, so without Grace having to ask, he helped her to the Perfectly Pink Parlor, where he and Cat had already arranged her things. She peeked inside and shivered when she saw the hospital-style bed they'd set up for her, which didn't seem necessary, not at all.

"We thought you could stay down here for now. We'll let Mercy and Joe have your room."

Grace agreed, though she yearned for a nice respite in the Sumptuous Scarlett O'Hara. Once she was settled, Mick asked her if she wanted to see her garden.

"I'd love to," Grace said. It was only drizzling. She'd lived in Seattle for so many years that she'd grown accustomed to being outside in the rain. "And bring the whiskey, Mickey," she added. "I haven't had a drop since the accident."

She expected to see the backyard in disarray. She hadn't been there to tidy up after a stormy winter, and the spring weather they'd had over the past week surely would have brought weeds. But everything had been done: the weeds pulled, the beds mulched, the trees pruned, the pathways raked. Even the corner garden, done in Japanese style and in need of more than the usual maintenance, was spotless.

"You're welcome," said Mick. He handed her a glass, looking quite pleased with himself.

"Did you do all this by yourself?" Grace couldn't stop looking at her beautiful garden. The snowdrops were in bloom. She noticed that Mick had even trimmed back the raspberry canes she'd been meaning to get to for some time.

"Of course," said Mick. "Cat's got her hands full with this case."

"Oh, Mickey. You've really outdone yourself." She reached out for his hand and squeezed it. "How is Cat doing, by the way? Has she kept you in the loop?"

Mick smiled. "Oh, you know your granddaughter. Likes to go off on her own. But I've got tabs on her. She's at the Seattle PD right now, trying again to get them to let her look at evidence."

Grace reflected on that. Cat must believe they had something worthwhile, either from the murder scene itself or from Nina's office.

"So, will Mercy and Joe get a chance to meet Ed?"

It was a delicately phrased question, but Grace understood Mick's meaning. "I'm not sure we've progressed to that point."

Mick nodded. "As much as your accident gave you the opportunity to meet, it's not as if the two of you have had a real date yet."

"That's right." Grace took a sip of her whiskey, enjoying the burn.

"But will you?" Mick asked. "Have a real date?"

"Yes, I think we will."

They were both quiet a few beats, and then Grace said, "But you know, I'll have the same problem you're having after a while. It's the same problem I always have."

"I know," Mick said. "I know."

"I want to believe that there's someone who will understand, but if that person is out there, I haven't

173

found him in seventy-nine years."

"Or her," he added.

Grace looked at him with surprise. Then she brightened, thinking of the new connection she enjoyed with Annie Lin. "Yes, *her*."

Her brother's face looked sad and wistful. She knew he was pining then for Cecily. Grace resolved to call up her friend as soon as she could get away from Mercy and Joe.

>>>

Cat met Bethany at a bar in Ballard called the Rusty Pelican.

"It's a slice of old Ballard," her new friend proclaimed, pointing at the desiccated king crab and dusty fishing net tacked to one wall. They accepted a pair of greasy menus.

"I'm confused," joked Bethany. "None of these cocktails use the word 'infusion.'"

"Seriously," said Cat. "All the guys at the bar have beards, and not one of them is ironic."

They kept up the gag all through happy hour, cracking themselves up by asking the waiter if they could get some healing turmeric added to their fried fish batter.

"So how are you faring in Seattle's scintillating dating scene?" asked Cat.

They were on their third round of drinks. Cat had already told Bethany all about her upcoming family visit, as well as regaled her with stories about Mick and Granny Grace, which wasn't easy since she had to filter out anything related to private investigating, not to mention dreamslipping.

"Let's just say I'm exploring my options," said Bethany. "And there are many, many options."

"Good for you. I haven't so much as petted anyone since that fiasco with the short-order cook. What's your secret?"

"Well..." said Bethany, looking unsure whether she should tell Cat.

"What is it? Come on, I'm no prude."

"Okay," said Bethany, moving closer to Cat and scrunching down in their booth so she could speak confidentially. "There's this sex-positive club. It's called The Warehouse? I guess because that's where it is, in an old warehouse. It's been there like fifteen years, so forever. This guy took me there on a date last night. He's a member. I'm thinking of going back, but you can't get in unless you join or are a guest of a member."

"Whoa," said Cat. "What was it like?"

"They had different rooms for different things you could be into, you know, like a rope room, where this woman was suspended from the ceiling, and another place where they were basically wrapping people up like mummies."

"That's a sex thing?"

"Well, not really. I don't know. People get off on it, I guess."

"People get off on a lot of different things," said Cat.

She must have been deep in thought about the case, as Bethany snapped her fingers in front of Cat's

175

face.

Bethany giggled. "Where'd you go? Thinking about your own fetish?"

Cat smiled. "My fetish is turmeric. Definitely turmeric. As an infusion. In everything."

Chapter Thirteen

Greg was true to his word and scored a meeting between Cat and the lead detective on the Nina Howell homicide case.

Detective David Spencer greeted her politely, though it was clear from the look on his face when they met that he'd expected someone older, and possibly male.

"Amazing Grace Detective Agency," he said aloud, reading it off the card she'd handed him. "Not very Seattle of you, is it? I mean, we have fewer churches than any other city, except maybe San Francisco."

"It's named after the founder, my grandmother," Cat said. "Amazing Grace is her legal name."

"Interesting," he said, in a way that showed it really wasn't. He motioned for her to sit in a chair next to his desk, which was out in the open room with a lot of other desks, not in an office. She said something to that effect, and he shrugged.

"Probably just their way of making sure we're working on cases, not holed up in our offices looking at porn."

Cat angled her eyes at him, trying to judge if this inappropriate remark would be a precursor to sexual harassment. She couldn't tell. He didn't seem overly interested in her. If anything, he seemed distracted.

"So you want to look at the evidence, eh?" He glanced at her formal request, which she'd had to submit on paper.

"Yes," she said. "From Nina Howell's office."

"But not the crime scene?"

"Well," Cat said. "I'd like to see that, too, but I thought I'd start with the low-hanging fruit, maybe work my way up."

"Not much the crime-scene stuff will tell you without forensics."

"That's true," Cat said, "unless you found personal items in the hotel room...."

She'd hoped he'd divulge information, but his bland expression remained intact.

"What are you looking for?" he asked, his gaze shifting from the request form to her face. She suddenly felt as if she were being interrogated.

"I won't be sure until I find it," Cat said, holding eye contact with him.

He continued to stare at her as if this were a contest. "What's your angle?" he asked.

"I don't have one."

"But you must. You're working for the spouse."

"You've talked with her, I'm sure," said Cat. She wasn't sure whether or not Robin told the police about her Sam Waters theory. If so, they didn't seem to be following up on it.

"Yeah, we talked to her." Spencer crossed one leg over the other. "Pretty much a wreck. Kind of useless when it comes to our investigation."

"So you're not looking at her for this?"

"We're about to clear her."

Cat thought about their reasoning, based on what she knew of the crime scene. "Nina was murdered by someone physically stronger than Robin. It couldn't have been her."

His silence told her she was right.

"Why'd she hire you?" he asked.

Cat smiled. "I guess she didn't think the Seattle PD would catch Nina's killer."

Spencer seemed unamused. "It seems odd to hire a PI so soon. More likely with cold cases."

"Robin and Nina were friends of my grandmother's."

His posture relaxed, the information seeming to put him at ease.

"Who are your suspects?" Cat asked.

No answer.

"If you're not going to tell me anything," she said with a sigh, "maybe you should just take me to the evidence."

"All right," he said. "If *you're* not going to tell *me* anything, maybe I should."

At that, he launched himself out of his chair and walked toward a stairwell. Cat followed.

>>>

She hadn't realized the detective would monitor her as she made her way through the two boxes from Nina's office. In the first one, she found a gym bag full of workout clothes: jog shorts, yoga pants, a spandex top. All color-coordinated from Lululemon, a spendy designer label. Two iPods, plus an armband to hold a phone in place during a workout. Racquetballs and a racket. Cat thought about Sam at the SAC, playing racquetball. But then the gyms hadn't matched up.

Also in the first box: A scale model of the St. Louis Arch. So familiar to Cat, she nearly dropped it when she saw what it was.

"Does that mean something?" asked Spencer, who'd been sitting on the other side of the table, his fingers steepled.

"It does to me," Cat said, explaining that she grew up in St. Louis.

But since the Arch was an elegant monument designed by renowned architect Eero Saarinen, it made sense for Nina to have it. Maybe she'd gone there as a kid; maybe it made an impression on her. Cat remembered the exhibit at the St. Louis Science Center about the Arch, a little station for kids to put their own version together using blocks. She recalled the geometric name, *catenary arch*.

At the bottom of the box was a thank-you card, not yet addressed. Inside was an inscription: THANK YOU FOR HELPING ME SAVE MY OWN LIFE. The sentiment, now seeming to express some tragic irony, made tears come to Cat's eyes.

Spencer's voice was softer this time. "The thank-you note. Yeah, it struck some of us that way, too." He cleared his throat. "It's not often you come across something like that in the middle of a murder investigation."

The cover of the note was a generic blue with the words THANK YOU in white. Nina had not yet signed it, as if undecided whether or not to send it. Cat set it aside, to be copied later.

"Any idea who that was for?" asked Spencer.

"No," said Cat. "Have you asked Robin?"

"We did," he said. "She broke down crying, saying she thought Nina had planned to give it to *her*."

"Right," said Cat.

"You don't think so?"

"I don't know. It just doesn't seem like something you give your wife. Are you married?"

He nodded just as Cat spied his ring.

"Would you send a card like that to your wife?"

"No. But I'm a man. I don't know what two women do for each other. And I mean that in more ways than one."

Cat let the comment pass. "It's not romantic. Even you'd send something red, or with flowers … something that echoed the intimate aspect of your relationship."

She picked up the card again. "This seems … almost … professional." A possibility hit her as she said that out loud, and she decided to keep it from Spencer.

But his curiosity was already piqued. "You mean career-wise? Maybe somebody mentored her, or helped her out with a job. There was that period of time she took a break…"

Cat let Spencer spin his own theory while keeping quiet about her own. *Thank you for helping me save my own life.* She thought about Nina escaping an abusive father, the list of addresses, and the Photoshopped obituary. There had to be a therapist in the mix, she reasoned, someone helping her deal with the past, maybe even giving her exercises to do to release her pain. Nina

181

seemed to be the type who would get herself help if she needed it, and she certainly could afford one. That type of thank-you would be just right for a therapist, who couldn't directly save Nina's life—the work would be all hers to do. But a therapist could have helped her a great deal.

In the second box, Cat found what appeared to be a collection of things you'd find on the street: a wooden tourist nickel, a broken phone case bearing a tire tread, a strip from a Mylar balloon. Nina must have picked them up on her walks or jogs. The creative in her kept them, maybe for design inspiration.

Then Cat came across a plastic bag full of jewelry, all tasteful, classic pieces—gold hoops, pearl studs, diamond teardrops. A gold tennis bracelet. Interlocking silver rings. But lumped in with the rest was a velvet collar.

The police must have thought it belonged to a pet. The ID tag read DANDELION. But it was large enough to fit Nina, who was petite. Cat tried to control her reaction in view of the detective, but her mind flashed on the strange dreams she'd been slipping into, the woman named Dandelion wanting her lover to hurt her.

"You see something?" asked Spencer.

"No—" Cat faked. "It's just—I used to have a dog. She had a collar like this one."

"Right. Why don't you just 'fess up? I can see you're thinking something."

Cat was quiet.

"I could book you for withholding evidence."

"I'm investigating Sam Waters," Cat said.

"I figured as much," said the detective. "I mean, you do work for Robin Howell. What else would that woman want you to do? She's been after us to arrest him since day one."

"But you've got nothing on him."

"Not a damn thing. As far as we're concerned, those two never met."

Cat reflected on what she knew, how much of it came from her dreamslipping. None of it would be admissible in court.

"Welcome to my world," Cat said, rolling her eyes.

Spencer breathed out a sigh of relief. But he wasn't letting her off easy. He stood up, his hands on his hips. "The pet collar?"

"I don't know," Cat said. "I thought it could mean something, since Nina and Robin didn't have a pet. But then again, maybe Nina picked it up on one of her runs. Your people bagged it with the jewelry, but maybe it belonged with this junk." She motioned toward the wooden nickel and other street finds.

>>>

Grace heard the doorbell ring. The only one at home, she hoisted herself up from the chaise lounge where she'd been resting and, using her walker, made her way to the front door.

"Greg Swenson!" she exclaimed, maneuvering the door around her walker. "It's so nice to see you again."

She reached out to hug him. "But I'm afraid Cat's

not here right now."

He recovered quickly from the obvious disappointment, smiling brightly and producing a bouquet of flowers he'd had tucked behind his back. "That's okay," he said. "I'm here to see you anyway."

"Oh, how nice," she said, "I love sunflowers. They're not even in season yet! Where did you get them?"

"I know people," he chuckled.

"Come in," she said. "Follow me back to the kitchen. We'll put them in water."

He followed, taking over for her to retrieve a very tall vase off a high section of cupboards. He filled it with water and the sunflowers and set it on the table.

"It's so cheerful," Grace beamed.

They made small talk for a while, catching up on their lives. Cat had mentioned to her that he might visit her in rehab, just an offhanded comment. When Grace had tried to make something of it, Cat squelched the discussion. But here he was, in her kitchen again after a year and a half.

"The last time you were here, Greg," Grace said, "we broke bread with Jim Plantation."

"I remember," said Greg. "Everyone was here. Ruthie, my sister, me…"

"My friends Simon and Dave, too. And Cat, of course."

"Of course," he said, meeting her gaze, and it was as if Grace could see his heart in his eyes.

"What is it with my granddaughter and strong men with facial scars?" Grace said, knowing she shouldn't but feeling mischievous.

Greg looked as if something registered. "His ear," he said, as if remembering. "That's right."

"She's had some time to recover," said Grace. "And she's young. She's healing well."

Greg smiled awkwardly. "I'm glad, but not for my own sake."

"I know." Grace put her hand on his. "Would you like some tea?"

"Yes," he said, getting up. "But let me make it."

>>>

When Cat burst through the door late that night, she found her grandmother still awake, reading in the Daring Damask Den.

"What are you doing up?"

"Oh, I got to reading this book," she said. "Nina gave it to me. It's about the story behind the Space Needle. Did you know the idea came when two guys were sitting in a bar? One of them drew it on a napkin."

"Hmm…" said Cat. She set her things down and plopped into a wingback chair.

"Nina inscribed the book," said Granny Grace, flipping back to the front matter. "It really caught my heart to read it again. Listen. 'To darling Grace, whose spirit could build a thousand monuments.'"

Cat smiled. "She sure had your number."

"And Greg Swenson has yours. He came by today."

Grace thought she saw her granddaughter stifle

an involuntary grin. "Yeah, he said he planned to pay you a visit at Swedish. But you left before he could."

"We had a lovely talk. Did you know he and Sherrie were both born and raised in Belleville? That's just across the river from where you grew up."

"Yes, I did know that," Cat said. "Remember? I found Sherrie's high school class ring when I worked that case."

"Isn't your new friend Bethany from St. Louis, too?"

Cat nodded.

"It's so interesting how you move to Seattle and unwittingly surround yourself with people from home. It's like the place is a magnet for you."

"Well, the Arch looks like one," said Cat, yawning. "A gigantic magnet sitting on the edge of the Mississippi."

>>>

After Granny Grace had shuffled off to bed using her walker, Cat received a text from Jacob in San Francisco. *Missing you*, it read. *Visit soon?*

She replied. *Me there or you here?*

You here, he said.

She sent him a smiley face back.

In my bed, he continued. *In my head.*

Her phone screen showed a bouncing ellipses sign, which meant Jacob was tapping his keyboard. She held her breath, waiting for his next text.

And in my heart, he wrote.

That melted her. But how should she respond? She panicked, knowing that her delay might be causing him to hold his own breath.

She decided on the "<" followed by a "3," which would morph into a heart symbol. Not exactly "I love you," but he hadn't said it either.

It worked. He responded with the same, followed by *When?*

I don't know, she wrote, including another smiley face. *In the middle of a huge case. Plus family visiting.*

Yikes.

She sent him an emoticon of a smiley face with steam coming out of its ears.

LOL, sorry.

Me, too. Week after next?

Sure.

Chapter Fourteen

Cat dumped the entire stick of butter into a pan to melt. Mick stirred a bowl of flour and other ingredients with the same look of reverence on his face as when he mixed paint.

"That's enough butter to moisten the Mojave," said Granny Grace.

"The word 'moisten' should be excised from the English language," Cat replied. "It's just ... icky."

"Tell that to the hosts of the Moisture Festival," said Granny Grace.

Cat laughed as she stirred the butter, which dissolved into a thin sheen at the bottom of her grandmother's copper pot.

"Hey, I was thinking of going to that," Mick added.

"You should," said Granny Grace, rising up and leaning into her walker. Cat and Mick had been navigating around the metal contraption all afternoon. Thankfully, the Terra-Cotta Cocina was spacious, with enough room between the table, island, and cooking area for her grandmother to come through and take part in the preparation.

"Only Seattle would have a festival dedicated to *moisture*," said Cat, scrinching her nose up. "God. I can barely even say that word."

"It's a really good show, with acrobatics, performance art, and burlesque," said her grandmother.

"You both should go."

"I hear the burlesque includes a trapeze act," said Mick.

"Yeah, that's what I want to do, go with my great-uncle to a nudie circus show called 'Moisture.'"

Mick laughed. "Maybe we should take your parents with us."

"Because there's nothing my straightlaced Catholic mother likes more than a little moisture."

"What's that smell?" asked her grandmother.

Cat yanked open the oven door, and a cloud of smoke billowed out. Her casserole had bubbled over the edge of the dish and onto the heating coil at the bottom. The smoke detector blared. Granny Grace covered her ears, Mick jumped up to open the door to the outside deck, and Cat turned on the stove vent.

"There goes dinner," Cat said. She bit her tongue to keep from chastising her great-uncle, who'd chosen too small a dish for the casserole, and hadn't covered it like Cat asked. She glanced at the stove clock. "And look what time it is! You should probably go pick them up."

"I'll get Thai food on the way home," Mick muttered, grabbing his keys.

In his wake, Cat slumped at the counter, exhausted. Her grandmother sat at the kitchen table, her walker by her side.

"Are you ready for this?" asked Granny Grace.

"Are you?"

Neither answered the question.

>>>

189

Mick arrived home with Cat's parents more than an hour later. After greetings at the door, Cat noticed Mick had picked up groceries instead of Thai food.

"What's all this?" Cat asked her mother, who lugged the bags into the kitchen and began putting them away while Cat's father took their luggage upstairs.

"Oh, just a few provisions I thought we'd need while we're here."

Cat picked up an economy-sized jar of apple sauce. "Mom, this could last you, like, *a whole year*. You're not staying longer than two weeks ... are you?"

Her mother grabbed the jar out of her hands. "It's a much better deal to buy in bulk. Here, chop this broccoli."

Cat eyed Granny Grace, who'd just come through the doorway to the kitchen. Her knuckles gripped the walker tightly, as if she were bearing down to keep from saying what was on her mind.

"I didn't realize you could still buy these," Granny Grace said, her voice in a forced, neutral cadence. She sat down at the table and picked up a jumbo box of dehydrated potato flakes.

Mick, who'd followed her into the kitchen, grabbed the box out of her hands. "Hallelujah! I love spuds."

Cat's mother, Mercy, handed him a measuring cup. "Good, because we're having some for dinner. Here, set me up with the right amount."

Cat watched Granny Grace, who seemed to be struggling with herself.

"Darling," her grandmother said, "it's been so long since you and I were in the kitchen together."

Mercy stopped in her flurry of activity and turned. She seemed to be appraising Granny Grace as if for the first time since she arrived. "We've hardly ever been in the kitchen together." She smiled, and Cat had a hard time reading whether the smile was genuine or not. "You weren't exactly the milk-and-cookies type."

"Speaking of milk," Mick inserted, "are we using this in the mashed potatoes?" He held up a commercial carton of cow's milk. "Please say yes."

Granny Grace shot a panicked look at Cat, who felt called to come to her aid. "You know, Mom, there's already some hemp milk in the fridge. It's very creamy, just like cow's."

"Hemp!" Mercy exclaimed. "Is that one of those marijuana edibles I've been reading about? You Seattleites and your pot. I've heard it's really easy to overdose."

Cat reflected on how her mother always managed to pick up on some actual fact, yet apply it to her rather irrational fears. "You're right about the edibles, Mom. But hemp milk doesn't have any cannabis. It's just milk."

"What's this about cannabis?" said Cat's father, who'd just entered the room. "So the party's already started. Yippee!"

"It's just hemp *milk*, Dad," said Cat. She marched to the fridge, took out the carton and poured him a glass. "Here, see for yourself."

Her father swirled the glass as if at a wine tasting. "Creamy consistency, thicker than two percent. Not as bright in hue as your cow's milk, mind you. A bit dingy, in fact. But maybe rustic is the better word." He bent his face over the glass and inhaled. "Not much of a bouquet either, but at least it doesn't smell like a bong."

"Oh, for goodness' sake, Joe," said Granny Grace. "Just try it."

He took a sip, swished it around, and swallowed.

They watched as his face began to twitch, his eyelids droop. "Dude," he said to Mick, "This is groovy. Best milk I've ever had."

"Very funny," said Mercy, shaking her head. "And to think, you were never even a hippie."

She took the glass from him and gave it her serious consideration. Then she shrugged. "Here goes nothing!" She downed the whole glass.

"It's quite tasty," she pronounced. "Let's use this instead. In the spirit of compromise."

>>>

Cat awoke early the next morning to the sound of someone banging pots and pans around in the kitchen.

She pulled on her robe and stumbled down the hallway to the Terra-Cotta Cocina, where she found her grandmother, who appeared to be baking cookies.

"What. Are. You. Doing?"

"Giving my daughter what she's always wanted."

Cat rubbed her eyes as she noticed that her grandmother was out of her usual stylish clothes and had dressed herself like, well, like a schoolmarm. Her hair was up in a tight bun, her blouse was buttoned up to her chin, with a ribbon tied at her neck, and her long skirt brushed the top of—Cat gasped when she saw them—orthopedic shoes.

"Oh, Granny Grace," Cat said. "Is this really necessary?"

"Yes," she said, sliding a tray of cookies onto the kitchen island to cool.

"And now, for the pancakes."

The aroma of fresh-baked cookies made Cat's mouth water and her stomach rumble. She reached to filch a cookie, and her grandmother smacked her with a wooden spoon. "You'll spoil your breakfast!"

"But Gran—"

"You can wait. The pancakes will be done in no time." She cracked a few eggs into a bowl and used the wooden spoon to stir the mixture, balancing herself on her walker as she cooked.

"Should you be doing so much so soon?"

Her grandmother shrugged. "I'm recovering faster than you all think. For example, that ridiculous bed in the Pink Parlor—I don't need it!"

Mercy walked in. "What don't you need, Mother?"

"Good morning, dear!" beamed Granny Grace.

Mercy walked over to the counter and picked up a cookie. She smelled it. And set it back down.

"So, what exactly are we doing here?" she asked, her hands on her hips.

Cat tried her best to appear invisible, but it didn't work. Why couldn't she have inherited a superpower like that?

Granny Grace took her time flipping over the four pancakes in her skillet. "What we are doing here," she said, licking batter off her finger, "is giving you the image of motherhood you always craved. Because I certainly never fit the bill."

"Oh, Mother. Must you always be so dramatic?"

"Yes," she said. "It's time you had a chance to contrast what you had against what you think you should have had. So here I am. Your milk-and-cookies version."

"What's this?" asked a voice at the doorway. Cat turned to see her father. "Pot for dinner and cookies for breakfast—wow, you Seattleites really know how to live."

"We're having *pancakes* for breakfast," Granny Grace corrected. "The cookies are for later." She deftly shifted the flapjacks from the skillet to a plate, and soon the stack was pretty high. "Why don't you all set the table?"

"Mother, you didn't need to do this," said Mercy. "I mean, what is this supposed to prove? You want me to say that I'm glad you had more fashion sense than the average mom? That I was better off learning the various uses of Tibetan prayer flags than I would have been making mud pies?"

"I was always in favor of mud pies," her grandmother said.

"Are we really doing this right now?" whined Cat. "Because my stomach and those pancakes both suggest we table this discussion."

"Well, in order to make mud pies, you'd need a backyard…" said Mercy, banging a plate down onto the table.

"Okay, so I guess we're doing this," said Cat.

"It's breakfast and a show," said her father, who busied himself setting out silverware.

"…Not some walk-up tenement, or a gypsy caravan bus, or an ashram," continued Mercy.

"There was plenty of mud to be had at that ashram," said Granny Grace.

"Oh, sure, but there weren't any other kids to play with. Because no one else was selfish enough to drag their children there!"

The kitchen became still after that comment. Cat was afraid to breathe. Next to her at the table, her father swallowed hard, and sighed.

Granny Grace set the enormous stack of pancakes down with a clatter. "I gave you a childhood of diversity, of unique experience. You were loved. You were taught more than most people learn in a lifetime. I'm just sorry you think of the whole thing as my colossal failure. But I refuse to buy into your story, Mercy. It isn't mine. And it shouldn't be yours, either. It's not serving you in any way."

At that, she limped out of the room.

Chapter Fifteen

Grace didn't want to be in the house anymore. She changed out of her ridiculous clothes and put on a beautiful Nia outfit she'd ordered online while in rehab. The pants were deep maroon, the legs flared bells that would twirl as she danced. That is, once she got back to a point where she could dance on her feet. Today she'd be chair-dancing. The top looked sari-inspired, with drapes of maroon and orange, and a gold coin at the base of each strap.

She felt her aching, angry heart underneath the drapes of fabric. Sitting on the edge of her completely unnecessary hospital bed, she took a moment to meditate, clearing the negative energy and replacing it with the wispy smoke of peace.

Then she took herself by walker to the Nia studio in her neighborhood, where her wonderful teacher promised she could begin to heal her own body. Maybe she could heal her own heart there, too. This was something she knew how to do. She'd had a lot of practice.

>>>

In Granny Grace's absence, Cat tried to bring the visit back to normalcy. She and Mick took her parents to the Asian Art Museum after breakfast, but Cat begged off in the afternoon, needing to get back to the case.

Her first order of business was to see Robin.

The woman answered the door only after three doorbell rings and a text message from Cat. Her eyes red-rimmed and her face puffy, Robin ushered Cat into the living room, where Jin Mae played on the floor with a set of blocks.

"I feel like I'm in hell," Robin whispered, holding her hands over Jin Mae's ears to shield her daughter from the expletive. A tear slid down her face.

"I need to ask you a few questions," Cat said.

"Have you found anything on Sam? I just—really need—that man to be brought to justice." She clenched her hands into fists at her side.

"I'm working on a few things," Cat said. "I need to know if Nina ever saw a therapist."

"Oh," said Robin. "Yes, she did. But that was a while back, before she and I got married."

"Do you remember the therapist's name?"

Robin appeared to think it over. "I can't remember. He doesn't live here in Seattle. Back in Waco. They started when Nina was at Baylor and then continued by phone for a while after she'd moved out here."

"I need a name," said Cat.

Robin made a fist and tapped her forehead, as if trying to summon the name. "Wait, I know how we can find out," she said. "She had sessions with him every once in a great while, when she needed them. I remember she always mailed him a paper check. Kind of old-school."

"Can you get a copy of the canceled image from

your bank account?"

"Yeah, I think she had a phone session with him a couple of months ago and must have sent him a check for that. Let me see if I can print out the image."

Robin went upstairs, leaving Cat with Jin Mae. Cat turned her attention to the girl's blocks. They were painted in bright primary colors, and most were cube-shaped. She noticed a pile of triangular blocks and realized what they were for. Dropping to the floor, she scooped them up.

"Jin Mae, want to help me make something cool?"

The girl nodded. Together they created feet for each side, placing smaller and smaller triangle wedges. Cat made sure they angled to create a curve, one foot reaching to the other. She remembered the video she'd seen probably dozens of times, that exciting moment when they lowered the keystone into place, creating the Arch. She found the keystone block, a canary yellow, and with Jin Mae's help, used it to anchor the two sides of the arch they'd built.

"That's Nina's favorite architectural structure," said Robin, who'd come back downstairs. "How did you know?"

"She had a scale model of it in her office."

Robin nodded.

"It's a funny coincidence," Cat said, "but I'm from St. Louis."

"Here's the name," Robin said, ignoring Cat's St. Louis comment and handing her a printout of the check image.

The check was made out to ELI BERKMAN, PHD.

"Thanks," Cat said. "There's one more thing. Does the name Dandelion mean anything to you?"

>>>

Grace didn't want to go home after her Nia class, so she went to a coffee shop. It was just a little out of the way, she reasoned. But once there, she realized she'd gotten a little ahead of herself, especially after Nia. As much as the class had been gentle and healing, she thought with the long walk maybe she'd taken on too much too quickly.

She messaged Cecily and asked her help in getting home, but it would take her a few minutes to get there. So Grace picked up her phone and checked her app to see if Annie Lin was available for a chat.

Hi, my Grace, the woman answered. *How are you feeling?*

Grace had grown fond of Annie's use of the possessive before her name, "my Grace." *Just did a Nia class*, she answered. *Mostly using a chair.*

I bet you rocked that chair.

Are you saying I need a rocking chair? Grace giggled, attracting a quick glance from the hipsters next to her, a cute young couple both in jeggings and knit caps.

Not at all. More likely a trampoline.

Grace smiled, this time controlling her laugh. *Not for at least a year, or this broken bowl I'm sitting in will never heal.*

It might be worth it to see you on trampoline. I'd like to paint the way you'd look suspended in the air for a moment, your face full of joy.

Grace caught herself breathing harder, her pulse picking up. She hesitated, unsure what to write back. Nothing she could say would equal the beauty of what Annie had just conveyed, she feared. She couldn't remember the last time she felt so recognized, so *seen* by someone. And here they were thousands of miles apart.

Sorry, said Annie. *I hope that didn't freak you out.*

Don't apologize. It's lovely. I'm —

Grace accidentally hit return before finishing her last thought. So she tried again. *I'm moved.*

I wish, came the reply. Just that. *I wish.*

Grace saw Cecily pop into the coffee shop.

Me, too, she replied, wondering if it was too much. Maybe it was more than she could really do.

There was Cecily, fresh-faced and ready to rescue her.

"Will you have a coffee?" Grace asked. "I'm buying."

She tried to stand up, but Cecily stopped her. "Stay right there and rest, silly woman. I can get my own coffee."

"Oh, all right," Grace demurred.

When she returned, Cecily asked, "Isn't your daughter supposed to be in town? Why are you off on your own?"

Grace had meant to be the one asking questions, but she realized she was glad for Cecily's sympathetic presence when tears sprang to her eyes at the thought of Mercy.

"I lost my patience," Grace said, and she spilled the whole story.

"Oh, my," said Cecily. "That is some ancient baggage you're both carrying around."

"You don't know the half of it." Grace shared her grief at having had such a strained relationship with her own daughter all these years, practically for Cat's entire upbringing.

"Well, of course you were right to call her on the woe-is-me narrative," said Cecily. She crossed her arms in front of her. "But I have to say, I think you're missing the main issue."

"And what's that?"

"It's not that Mercy wanted a different kind of mother. No, not really. I think it's that she thought she was playing second fiddle to her mother's adventures."

Grace turned that over in her mind. Doing so made her heart ache.

"Oh, what a mess I've made," she said.

Cecily squeezed her hand. "But if I know you, Grace, you'll find a way to connect with your daughter again."

"Speaking of connection," said Grace, "what exactly happened between you and my brother?"

Cecily pulled her hand away from Grace's. "I'm not sure that's something we should discuss in public." She glanced at the people sitting near them. "I brought the car if you want to go for a drive. There's something I've been meaning to ask you anyway."

Cecily drove a hybrid car with an engine so quiet that pedestrians wouldn't hear her turning a corner. Grace watched as Cecily navigated the city streets, taking care in the turns. She took Grace to an overlook in

Ballard, a neighborhood that had once prided itself on being a "quaint little drinking village with a fishing problem" but had lately begun to lose its character to the bulldozers and a barrage of mixed-use apartment complexes.

From the overlook, which was deserted, they could see the entire Olympic mountain range in the distance, with Puget Sound spilling out wide below. A cloud bank obscured most of the range, but Grace spotted a few snowcaps. A container ship made its slow path northward on the Sound, and a flotilla of sailboats plied the waters near the jetty at Golden Gardens, where seals barked.

"Do you remember that time I stayed with you last year?" asked Cecily. "When I had my apartment painted?"

"Yes."

"I was struggling with my art back then, dealing with some kind of block that was slowing me down even though I'd received that commission and could basically paint full-time for the first time in my life."

"I remember," said Grace. She had a feeling she knew where Cecily was headed with this, and it made her breath quicken.

"One of those nights at your place, I had this dream. It was a doozy, full of symbolism from my childhood, and my hideous mother making an appearance at one point."

Grace remained quiet.

"I mean, fuck. She locked me in the trunk of her car when I was ten. I relived it in that damn dream."

Grace remembered the dream, one she'd inadvertently slipped into. The trunk lid, thankfully, became the escape hatch on an airplane.

Cecily had been gazing out at the beautiful view, but she turned to Grace and touched her arm. "You helped me see that I had a deep-seated fear of success. I thought at the time that you were incredibly wise, but now I'm beginning to think there's more. Because I *felt* you in that dream, Grace."

"Cecily…" Grace did not know what to say.

"Same as I felt your brother. Then he tells me he's psychic. That a-hole spits back my dream to me as if it were his." Cecily's voice rose, cracking on the last word.

She swallowed hard and went on. "So I just want to know what's going on with the two of you. I want to hear it in your own words. The truth."

Grace took a deep breath. "We're what I like to call 'dreamslippers.' We both have an ability to slip into other people's dreams…"

Grace told Cecily everything.

>>>

"I want you to tell me your real name," he said. She'd known this was coming. She wanted to tell him, wanted to let the two syllables slip off the end of her tongue, just like that. Nee-nah.

But there was the bird to consider. Her beak so sharp.

"Real name, real game," she chanted, pulling away from him.

"I want to know you in real life," he said. "I want you to be mine."

203

"Mine, pine," she chanted.

She was his here, in the safe space. All the others had fallen away. They knew she belonged to him.

The collaring ceremony sealed it. The tag said, "Dandelion," not Nina. Never Nina.

Cat woke with a start. There it was again, and this time she believed it had to be Nina's dream. But the implausibility—not to mention creep factor—that she was slipping into a dead woman's dreams made her question it.

Cat considered whether or not they could be Robin's dreams. But Robin knew nothing about the name Dandelion, did not have any significant reference to it. *Her beak so sharp.* Maybe the bird in the dream was Robin. Cat fell back to sleep, considering that.

They brought her to him, where she knew the chains waited, a gigantic W painted on the wall behind them. The members cheered all around her.

Her head covered in a black velvet bag. The escorts guiding her, since she could not see. Her hands tied behind her back. On her feet were the heels he'd selected for her to wear.

Finally she stood before him. The velvet bag was lifted off her head.

But it wasn't her masked man.

It was Robin. The wife she could not leave.

Again, Cat awakened abruptly. The wall of chains marked with a W, the members cheering. Cat thought of the club Bethany had been to. What was its name? The

Warehouse.

She reached over for her phone and searched for the name. Bingo.

That must be where Nina and Sam met.

Chapter Sixteen

Mick reacted with surprise when Cecily called him. He greeted her with a cautious "Hello?" even though his phone identified the number as hers.

"Mick?" she asked. "Is that you?"

"Yeah. Is this Cecily?"

"Yes. Well, now that we've uncovered the obvious here, I'd like to propose we meet for coffee. And maybe a walk."

"Y-yeah," he sputtered. "Of course. I'm glad you … asked. I'm glad you called."

They agreed to meet within walking distance of both their places at a café called Toast, which served the same, with tea. It made Mick wonder, why not call it Tea and Toast? But then he remembered the current trend for one-word restaurant names. Lark. Poppy. Trellis.

He stopped on the way in to watch the café awning flap in the wind, thinking of a painting he was working on and how that flipped-over fabric pattern would look superimposed on top of the field of gold he'd so far put down. He found Cecily at the back of the place, in a half booth. He took the chair opposite her.

"Do you want toast first?" she asked.

They both laughed, and then he went up to the counter and ordered an organic, whole-grain rye toast with turmeric-spiced apple jam.

When he returned, she smiled. "How have you been? Enjoying your visit with family?"

So they were to make small talk, at least for now. He glanced at the hipsters sitting to either side of them, who wore earbuds plugged into laptops but could probably hear them anyway.

"It's been nice," Mick said. "Mercy's been a great source of Midwestern cuisine."

"I bet," said Cecily. "I know it's been a bit challenging for your sister."

The barista brought his tea and toast. He gobbled them down, finding the combination satisfying.

"I see you liked it," Cecily said, gesturing toward his empty plate.

"Yes, but I think that's the most I've ever paid for a slice of bread."

She laughed, the skin around her eyes crinkling in a way he found sexy.

Cecily looked great, fresh and pretty in a blousy yellow top. But he didn't know where this was headed, and he'd never been particularly good at small talk anyway. Pris had told him she talked with Cecily but wouldn't give him details, saying only that he should wait for her to come to him when she was ready.

"Should we walk?" she asked. "We could take in the view from Counterbalance Park."

The park was named after the trolley-car counterbalance that used to sit atop Queen Anne Hill, allowing the trolley to climb the steep incline to the peak. The park afforded a world-class view of Seattle: the Space Needle and the taller skyscrapers beyond, with Puget Sound stretching out at its feet, and on a clear day, mountain peaks all around. The sky was overcast, so none were visible. But Mick didn't mind. He was beginning to get a feel for the city, enjoying its ever-present rain as a kind of jovial sloshiness, the cry of seagulls always overhead.

"You have to forgive me," Cecily said as they both took in the view. "Your big dream reveal totally freaked me out."

"I know. I'm not very good at these things."

"Oh, you were … you tried." She turned to him, touched his arm. "I don't know that there was any better way to go about it."

He looked into her blue eyes, letting himself hope again.

She returned her gaze to the view. "Mind you, I'm still struggling with all of this. Your sister explained some things to me … and I've had my own weird dream experience with her. I swear, has everyone in your family been up in my dreams? Damn, Mick. It's a lot to absorb."

"I get it," he said. "You're the only one I've ever told."

She looked at him, touched him again. Instinctually, he opened his arms, and she went into them. He hugged her. It felt right.

>>>

Grace walked into the kitchen, where Mercy stood washing vegetables at the sink.

"Mercy," she began. "I wonder if you could sit down with me a minute."

Her daughter turned, a paring knife in one hand.

"That depends. Will there be another performance? Another dramatic exit?"

Grace thought of a saucy retort but held her tongue. "Please," she said, motioning to the bench at the kitchen table. "Talk with me."

Mercy sat. Grace reached for her hand. Her daughter didn't move away from her, but she didn't return the warmth, either.

"I want you to know that you were always my first priority, even if I didn't look like a typical mother. Everything I did, I did for you."

"You were always having so much fun with everyone," Mercy said, tears welling up in her eyes. "I didn't feel I was enough for you."

"Oh, I can make anything look like fun," Grace said. "But so much of it was very hard. It was a different time. Much more difficult to be a single mother back in the fifties and sixties."

"I know, Mother. I know. I tell myself that all the time. I don't mean to hold onto this. It's just—" Mercy stopped.

"What is it?"

She gazed at the painting above the kitchen table, an abstract in orange and yellow that made Grace feel as if she had a source of sunshine on her wall.

"I think there's more to this," Mercy said. "I've always felt … that what you tell me about my … father … isn't true."

Grace did not see this one coming. She felt herself spiraling and wasn't sure what to say. There was no way she could ever tell her daughter the truth.

"But it is," she protested. "You know the story."

"Yes, yes. That you never knew his name, that you met him at a bar when you ran away from home, that you had no way to get in touch with him. It's just … I've always had the feeling there's something you're not telling me."

Grace mustered as much conviction as she could. "Mercy, my dear, there's nothing else. If I knew his name, or even where he was from or what he did, I'd tell you. But I don't. I'm so sorry, honey."

>>>

Cat walked in on her mother and grandmother at the kitchen table, holding each other's hands. She was about to leave them to their moment when her grandmother spoke.

"Hello, Cat. How are you, dear? I feel I've been neglecting you—and our case."

"I'll leave the two of you PIs to talk shop," said Mercy. "Besides, your father wants to see if he can catch one of those fish they're throwing down at Pike Place Market." She exited the room.

"Sit down, Cat, and tell me what I've missed."

"What was that all about?" Cat asked. She felt wary. "Everything all right between the two of you?"

Granny Grace nodded. "I think we're better now."

Cat sat down and briefed her grandmother on what she'd found in the Seattle PD's evidence boxes and learned from Robin herself.

"Good work, Cat."

"There's more," Cat said. "I'm sort of—I don't even know how to describe it. I might be picking up fragments of dreams *from the past*. Unless ghosts can dream, in which case I'm slipping into ghost Nina's dreams."

"What? Tell me everything."

When Cat finished explaining, Granny Grace clapped her hands. "I just knew it! You're progressing in your ability in ways Mick and I never could. This is so exciting."

Cat brushed off the praise. "You don't think this is just my imagination?"

"No, I mean, the way you describe them, it sounds like you're a receiver for the dreams Nina had when she was alive. Maybe dreams continue to exist in a sort of ether. It would make sense even from a quantum-physics perspective, thinking outside the time continuum."

Cat followed the thread of her grandmother's logic. "Right. If we assume time and space are, like, curved, the dreams are out there all the time. I could slip into anyone's dream, from any time period."

Granny Grace continued. "But you're connected to this case, which is why you're slipping into these dreams. You're connected to Nina, even though she's dead. Just like you had Lee's dreams across all those miles."

"Yeah, and how Mick slipped into Candy's dream."

"Yes," her grandmother said. "Just like that."

They were silent a moment.

Then Cat spoke. "The content suggests Sam and Nina were having a consensual affair."

"Yes," said Granny Grace. "Unless you want to believe that Nina was not in her right mind to enter into a submissive relationship."

"Which would likely be Robin's take," Cat said. "But I don't buy it. The Nina in my head in these dreams —she knew what she wanted. She seemed ... healthy."

Cat told her grandmother about The Warehouse. "I think I need to go there, undercover."

Granny Grace smiled deviously. "Well, my little dreamslipper. Would you like some company in that endeavor? Because that's one experience your otherwise well-seasoned grandmother has never had."

Cat laughed. "Oh, my God, Gran. You're serious, aren't you?"

"Yes."

Cat pointed at her walker, there by the side of the table. "With that and everything."

"Why not? I'll fit right in. I'm a well-established fetish icon just waiting for some fans."

Chapter Seventeen

They decided to go undercover separately so they could explore different aspects of The Warehouse without looking too suspicious, or to Cat's point, weird, attending a place like that as granddaughter and grandmother. So Cat took the bus, and Mick dropped off her grandmother in Siddhartha.

First, they had to sit through orientation. After confiscating their cell phones, a bearded gentleman around Cat's age escorted them to a small auditorium, with stadium-style rows curved around a tiny stage. There, another staff member of indeterminate gender sat cross-legged and began to speak.

"Good afternoon. I am Sasha. My gender is fluid, and I prefer the pronoun 'ze.' If you're unfamiliar with this, I'll demonstrate. You can say, 'Sasha gave us our orientation. Ze was very clear about The Warehouse's rules.' You can also use the pronoun 'zers' to show possession—though I prefer to be collared." Sasha laughed at zer joke. "Any questions?"

Cat looked around the room. Near her were several young men who'd come together, all dressed similarly in tight hipster jeans and tiny T-shirts. On the other side of them was a middle-aged woman who'd grown out her gray and wore it in Bettie Page style, with chunky bangs and a pageboy curve to the ends. Granny Grace sat on the opposite side. She winked at Cat.

No one had questions. Ze outlined The

Warehouse's history, mission, values, and rules.

As Sasha explained how The Warehouse community was about "open dialogue on all forms of sexual expression," Cat tried to picture Nina sitting there getting the same spiel. She could see how this would appeal to the woman's personality. Lots and lots of rules creating a safe space where she could let go and explore at will.

Sasha spent a great deal of time discussing consent. "'No' really does mean no," ze said. "If someone is talking to you, and you don't want to talk to that person, you say no, thanks, and walk away. You can also change your mind at any time, revoking consent. If someone is smacking you in the face and you no longer want that, even if you filled out a form explicitly asking zer to smack you in the face, and let's say you even specified the duration of the face-smacking, and that time isn't yet up, but you've changed your mind, then you say no, and ze must stop."

Cat found all of this fascinating. The pronouns, of course, which she'd encountered once before in a gender studies class but had never witnessed anyone actually use. But most of all the ironclad application of consent. While she could see it taking some of the romance out of the situation, the clarity appealed to her immensely. She flashed on her awkward sexting with Paul Dorian. Meeting someone at The Warehouse seemed a much better bet.

After Sasha gave a slide show of some of the play scenes and parties so they would know what to expect, ze opened it up for questions.

One young man raised his hand. "I understand that privacy is really strict here, and cell phones are not allowed. But what about Google Glass?"

Cat thought that was a good question.

Sasha didn't miss a beat. "That's not allowed. We do everything we can to make sure no image-capture devices get past the front door."

Everyone in the orientation signed up as members.

At home later, Granny Grace asked Cat what she thought, and she shared her insight into Nina's possible motivation for going there.

"Sounds right, but what about Sam?"

Cat thought of what Bethany said about him, that he hadn't presented a serious flirtation because he wanted something more than she represented to him. "I think the man in my dreams was playing for keeps."

"I see what you did there," said Granny Grace. "Nice play on the idea of possession."

"Ze was right."

>>>

First they needed to buy outfits that would allow them to fit in well at The Warehouse. Grace brought this up with some delicacy to her granddaughter, who agreed but wasn't excited about the prospect of shopping for BDSM wear together.

"This is right up there with going to the Moisture Festival with Uncle Mick," said Cat. "I mean, gross."

"Oh, I used to throw these 'dirty lady' parties

here in the house," Grace countered. "Back then you couldn't just walk into a store and buy a dildo like you can now."

The two of them were putting on their jackets and grabbing their purses in the foyer when Mercy came downstairs.

"Where are you headed?" she asked. Grace could see the hopeful look in her eyes.

"We have to sort of go undercover for the case," said Cat. "So you can't come along."

Mercy looked crestfallen. "You're going undercover right now?"

Grace broke in. "Not exactly. We're shopping for disguises."

Mercy laughed. "I feel like I'm in a TV show. Or back about thirty years. Mother, do you remember when you went undercover with the Rockettes? I loved playing dress-up with those boas you'd bring home."

Grace felt touched by Mercy's rare attempt to wax nostalgic about her childhood. "Why don't you join us?" she asked, ignoring Cat's warning glance.

"Really? I won't be in your way?"

Cat tried to protest. "I don't think that's a good —"

"—Of course not!" interrupted Grace. "You'll get a kick out of this. Cat's taking us to an adult toy store."

"You mean, as in fuzzy handcuffs and negligees and all that?"

"Nobody calls them negligees anymore," Cat corrected. "Not since, like, the seventies."

"That sounds fun," Mercy said, grabbing her own

coat and purse.

"Kill me now," Cat muttered as they walked out the door.

Rather than risk running into Sam at Leather Underground, they opted for a woman-owned shop Cat had found in an Internet search. Grace appreciated the innuendo in the name Tender Buttons as much as the literary connotation, since it came from a Gertrude Stein memoir.

A middle-aged proprietress showed them around the store, extolling the virtues of the "figure-flattering, realistic range in sizing" of their fetish wear and the dizzying array of clitoral stimulators. Grace was very impressed. In contrast to the male-oriented porn shops she'd entered in the past, where she felt more alienated than turned on, this place was warm and inviting. Mercy and Cat hung back, but Grace dove in, pulling out a red velvet bustier for Cat. She held it up to her granddaughter.

"Granny Grace, please," whined Cat, putting the bustier back on the rack. "I don't need your help."

"Are you all related?" asked the owner. "I love it when mothers and daughters come in here together."

"You've got three generations right here," said Mercy. "I'm the one in the middle."

"Wonderful!" said the owner. Then, turning to Mercy, she said, "We just had these new corsets delivered this morning, and there's a pale blue silk that would really work well with your lovely silver hair."

"Oh, nothing for me," Mercy begged off. "I'm just here for the entertainment value."

"Do you want to take a look anyway? It's just so perfect for your features."

Grace saw Mercy blush. "Why not?" she encouraged her daughter. "When's the last time you and Joe did something to spice up your love life?"

Mercy considered it. "Well ... okay."

Cat had already retreated to a far corner of the store, where she seemed to be conducting a thorough review of the whips and other implements. Grace perused a clothing rack, a green corset catching her eye. She'd never tried one on before, though she'd admired them on other women during burlesque shows. Her sexual coming-of-age had been delayed by motherhood too early, and then when she finally did branch out, it was the seventies, so women were more likely to go braless than don a corset.

The owner returned with a package wrapped in tissue paper, which she removed, unveiling a silk brocade corset in slate blue with silver trim. She was right, thought Grace. It would look perfect on Mercy.

"Can I get the dressing rooms started for you?" she asked, offering to take the green corset from Grace. She set their garments in the rooms, sumptuous little caves done up in boudoir style. The phone rang, and the owner went to answer it, leaving the three of them to talk without an audience.

"I don't get this Catholic schoolgirl thing," Cat said, holding up the shortest kilt Grace had ever seen. "I was forced to wear these things from grade school on, and I don't think they're sexy at all."

"Well, what *are* you going to wear?" asked Grace.

Then she noticed Cat held a collar—and leash—in one hand. "I see you've got your gear."

"I don't know," Cat said, blushing. "It called to me... But it's probably just the case." She said the last part in a whisper so Mercy wouldn't hear, but her mother spotted the collar in her hand anyway.

"A collar?" asked Mercy. "Like you're someone's pet? I don't think I like you wearing that."

"Then you shouldn't have named me 'Cat,'" she replied, laughing.

"Very funny," Mercy said. "But I'm serious. I didn't"—she looked at Grace and revised her statement—"*we* didn't raise you to be a strong, independent woman just so you could give your power away to some man."

"It's just a costume," Cat said. "It doesn't mean anything."

"Well, can't you pick something else? I know how these things work. I've read all about that *Fifty Shades of Grey*. A collar and leash means he owns you."

Grace studied Cat's face. Her cheeks had colored, and she was pursing her lips. Grace had a thought about Nina. "Mercy, we can't tell you about the case," she said, "but sometimes going undercover means putting yourself in your victim's shoes. Cat's trying to do that here, and I find it admirable."

"Your cases worry me," said Mercy, her tone softer.

"I know," Grace said. "But Cat can handle this. I know she can."

"This would set off that collar nicely," said the

owner, who'd just hung up the phone. She offered Cat a black waist cincher.

"Oh, I don't know," said Cat, gesturing to her chest. "I think I need these covered."

The owner pulled up the same red bustier that Grace had offered earlier. "How about this?"

"Perfect," said Cat, and Grace gave her a look, which Cat seemed to pretend not to see.

The three women took their outfits into the dressing rooms.

"Give me a holler when you want your corsets laced up," said the owner. "That's not something you can do on your own, trust me."

After about a minute, Mercy whispered through the curtain between her and Grace. "Help me, Mother! I think I'm trapped in this thing!"

Grace was struggling with her own outfit, as there were crisscross ties on both the front and back, and she didn't know what to try to deal with first to get the thing to hang on her body long enough for the owner to lace her up. Especially while navigating around her walker. "Okay, hang on…" she said. She pinned the corset underneath her arms and moved the curtain aside.

There was Mercy, with the corset laces wrapped around and around her waist, as if they were a belt, and then up over her shoulders, as she'd tried to fashion spaghetti straps out of them. "I can't get this knot undone," Mercy said, tugging at a bundle of laces that she'd managed to work into a spider's nest of a knot.

Grace burst out laughing. She couldn't help it.

"What?" Mercy defended. "Like I'm supposed to

know how any of this works?"

Cat popped her head out of the dressing room, and Grace noticed she'd put on the collar and leash.

"OMG, Mom," she said. "Seriously, have you not ever seen a corset before?"

The owner came running at that moment to help Mercy put things to right, and Grace tried to get her giggling under control.

And she did when she turned over the price tag on her lovely corset. She slid the velvet curtain aside and peered out at the store. "Excuse me," she asked the proprietress, who hovered near the dressing rooms. "Is this a typo?"

"I'm afraid not." The woman smiled graciously. "They're handmade, by a local seamstress," she added, as if to justify the price.

Grace and Cat would expense their disguises to the Howell account, but Mercy would have to foot the bill herself. At least Joe came from an era in which there were still pensions, Grace thought, closing the curtain and turning back to the mirror to admire herself in the stunning emerald silk. Still, they were on what people euphemistically called "a fixed income."

"Mother, did you get a load of these prices?" asked Mercy as if on cue.

"Yes, just now," said Grace.

"I understand if you'd rather not—"

Mercy just then whipped the curtain away from Grace's doorway and posed herself against the jamb. "I look like a pinup girl!" she exclaimed. "This thing is amazing. I have to have it."

As they headed to the cash register, Mercy said she wanted to look around some more. After perusing the toy section, she added a gigantic purple dildo to her purchases.

"Look, there's a rabbit at the end," she showed them. She pressed a button at the base of the device, which made the rabbit twirl, its ears flapping in rhythmic waves, pulsing lights in neon colors flashing as it turned.

Grace laughed. "It's like a sexual experience and a laser light show wrapped in one."

"Aren't all laser light shows basically sexual experiences?" Mercy replied.

Cat groaned. "I'm not going shopping with you two ever again."

>>>

Looking at The Warehouse calendar, which was chock full of events every night of the week and more, including a "Nooner" party in the middle of the week day, Cat wasn't sure which one Sam would attend.

Not that it mattered. It might be easier to get information about him and Nina if he wasn't there.

Cat and Granny Grace settled on the Black Light BDSM Party.

Cat's parents were reading in the Daring Damask Den, so the two tried to quietly slip past them and out the door. They both hid their corsets underneath black sack dresses, but their faces were done up in more makeup than Cat had ever worn in her life, including the time she dressed up as a clown to entertain kids in the hospital.

"Woo-hoo!" yelled Joe. "You two look like you're ready for the stage!"

"I told you, dear, they're going to a sex club," said Mercy, peering over the top of her *Seattle Times*. "It's undercover work."

"Are you sure you can walk in those things?" Joe gestured toward Cat's footwear: three-inch heels that made her tower over her grandmother, who leaned into her walker and had opted for sensible flats.

"She's been practicing," Granny Grace interjected. "And the yoga helps."

"She's young," said Mercy. "No bunions yet."

"What's with all the white?" Joe asked, motioning toward the magnolias Granny Grace had tucked into her hair. What he didn't see is that they were tucked into her cleavage as well.

"That's for the black lights," Granny Grace explained.

"That sounds perfect for the Rabbit," Mercy said. "Want to take him along?"

Cat shook her head. "Absolutely not. Now that we're done assessing our looks, can we go?" Cat felt nervous, and her parents' scrutiny made everything more intense.

"Lead the way," said Granny Grace.

They decided to go together this time, and it wasn't as if they stood out as odd. In the parking lot were a flurry of caped, trench-coated folks in heels, but as soon as they were inside, the outerwear was shed.

Cat had never seen so many bare butts.

The thing seemed to be chaps without jeans

underneath them, or else garters and stockings sans panties. With her breasts and privates covered, she suddenly felt overdressed.

"I think we should split up," Granny Grace offered. "Meet me back here in an hour for a check-in?"

Cat agreed. She hesitated for a moment, watching her fearless grandmother limp her walker into a throng of thongs as if she belonged there already.

Cat walked down a corridor and stepped into one room, careful in her heels, where a band played. Several people were getting freaky on the dance floor, and this sex wasn't just simulated. Under the black lights, her red bustier looked muddy brown, but the stripes in her stockings glowed, as did her lipstick, her collar, and her fingernails, which were also white. She'd felt too self-conscious about the leash dangling down her back, so she'd left that at home.

She inched over to a woman standing off to one side. Over the band noise, she yelled to her, "I'm looking for a green-eyed man in a mask. Have you seen him?"

The woman shrugged, shook her head.

It was clearly too loud to ask questions in there, so Cat left that room and went to another, without black lights. Here she had her choice of a "feather tent" or pedestals, where naked human statues were being hand-painted by their artists. Cat opted for the feather tent.

Inside she found a handsome man, the type who carried his extra thirty pounds well, in a suit, sitting at a throne surrounded by hundreds of peacock and ostrich plumes. She watched him stroke feathers over a man and two women. Each offered parts of their bodies to this

224

man, and he would in turn stroke them there with the feathers.

Cat felt her throat grow dry but other parts of her get wet.

She had the sense that the feathering man had taken note of her the minute she walked in and that he continued to note her presence as he stroked the others. Several times he locked eyes with her, and Cat felt as if he were homing in on something inside her.

As the others receded to the edges of the tent, taking up their own feathering activities, the man moved toward Cat. "Would you like me to feather your hand?" he asked.

Slowly she extended her hand toward him, offering her bare palm. He grazed it with a peacock feather, just lightly. The sensation gave her shivers. He moved the feather up her arm, caressing the inside of her elbow. Then across her clavicle, her neck, ears. Cleavage. Cat breathed heavily now.

"Do you want me to move down?"

Cat's nod must have been too subtle.

"Say it," he said. "Tell me what you want."

"I want you to move down," she whispered.

He did.

"I could do much more than this if you want," he said after a time, and the offer broke her aroused reverie.

She backed away from his feathers. "Actually," she said, gulping for air, trying to regroup, "I wonder if you could tell me about a couple who comes here regularly. He's a green-eyed man in a mask. The dom, I think. And she's a petite blonde, very ... with it."

The man regarded her with swelling disappointment in his eyes. But he shook it off. "You must be new here. The blonde—I think he called her Dandelion—she's no longer with us."

His answer surprised Cat. "Do you know her real name?"

He laughed, giving Cat a curious once-over. "No. Do you?"

Cat smiled. "I might've met her in real life."

"All I know is a few of the BDSM regulars, the middle-agers, not the young 'uns like you, they held a memorial for her. Her dom, Mr. Master, did the honors. I was there, paid my respects." He sniffed. "It was kind of beautiful. I think he loved her."

"Wow," said Cat. "I didn't think this place was about … romance. I thought it was just where people went to get off."

The man touched the tip of his feather to Cat's chin. "Then you don't know much about this place…" he paused, letting the feather trace her neck and down into her décolletage. "Or about getting off."

Cat blushed, feeling distracted. She stepped back, away from his feather, and he pulled away. He slipped the feather into a nearby vase, stuck his hands into his pants pockets.

"Tell me about the memorial."

He sighed. "We don't have them too often, but when we do, it stands out. They allowed candles, not those damn battery-operated ones we usually have to use. Mr. Master wore a tux."

The man's eyes watered. "He gave this speech

about how he'd held back, afraid to be who he really was with a woman who accepted him. He said it was too late, that he'd missed his chance."

Cat felt her eyes mist, too. But she focused on the details of the case. "Did he have something there to remind him of her, clothing, maybe?"

"What? Oh, yeah. He laid them out on a massage table, an outfit he would have given her, except this one was black."

"Was there sex in this ... scene? Or was it strictly a memorial?"

The man smiled. "You're a cynical one, aren't you? So here's the thing. He's the dom, right? Well, for this scene, he asked several of his fellow doms to whip him. I'm telling you, this guy is no switch. They whipped him, and he cried. It was as if he needed them to sanction his pain. And the doms—you could tell they were whipping him out of mercy, not pleasure."

Cat spent the rest of the hour confirming the man's account of Mr. Master and Dandelion with other members as well as a few of the staff policing the event in Day-Glo orange reflective vests. Everyone consistently painted them a couple who'd joined independently, but once Dandelion had gone through her collaring ceremony, they played scenes only with each other. Mr. Master hadn't been back to The Warehouse since the memorial.

Chapter Eighteen

The music was too loud for her taste, and Grace saw Cat go into the room housing the tent, so she pushed further into an area where four people were suspended from the ceiling.

She'd seen trapeze burlesque, and she had some idea that sex-while-suspended was a feature of BDSM play, but she'd never witnessed it, not in porn, which she avoided since so much of it was based on male fantasy, and certainly not in person.

The one closest to her had been hog-tied and suspended from the back. This left her mouth, her breasts, and her nether regions exposed. A man and a woman took turns whipping her and entering her, the man with his body and the woman with a strap-on version of the same. The suspended woman seemed to enjoy all of this immensely; rather than cries of pain or defense, she made pleasure noises and kept asking for more.

None of this did anything for Grace. She felt no arousal whatsoever, only curiosity. She had the impression of herself as an anthropological explorer, making note of the wide range of human sexual expression.

It was while mulling this over that she saw Ed.

Yes, that Ed. The one from the hospital. The one who'd dreamed of nothing saucier than a ninja clown, fully clothed and not fetishized in the least.

Grace ducked behind a wide pillar just in time. She really didn't want to surprise him like this. She also wanted the chance to observe him without his knowing.

He wore black leather pants, filling them out rather well, she noted. His chest was bare, and while he of course exhibited the kind of slack that naturally accompanies old age, he held his own there as well. He swatted the buttocks of a gray-haired woman suspended above him, her cheeks turning red from his paddle. She carried on as if she were riding a roller coaster, screaming and laughing in turns.

Ed laughed, too. Sweat broke out on his forehead. He called the woman "baby" and asked if she'd had enough. She hadn't, so he motioned for another man to step in.

Too soon, Ed turned and walked directly in Grace's direction. She realized he'd spot her easily due to the walker. She tried to pivot the metal contraption and head in the opposite direction, but it caught on a row of thick wiring on the ground, and she nearly lost her balance.

"Easy there," said his voice behind her, his hands steadying her. She smiled at Ed just as he looked into her face and realized who she was.

"Grace!" he said. "What in God's name are you doing here?"

"I could ask you the same," she said.

His face colored. He sighed. "Well, it was bound to come out soon enough. I'd hoped to bring you here someday … eventually…"

The two of them stood a moment, Grace feeling

awkward and confused.

"Isn't this kismet?" he tried. "We're both into the same thing."

"I'm not—" Grace started but stopped. She motioned for him to follow her to the side of the room, to an alcove. "I'm undercover," she said. "Remember? I'm a PI."

Disappointment mixed with fascination broke across his face. "Of course," he said. He tucked the paddle still in his hand into his back pocket, out of sight. "I guess I'm outed then. I hope it doesn't … change things for us."

"I don't know," Grace said. She felt herself too shocked to make a decision in the moment, but she knew she could never imagine herself suspended from the ceiling, exposed to Ed's paddle.

He studied her face. "You regard me differently now, don't you?"

"I-I just didn't expect … to see you here."

He smiled. "I've been coming here for a while. Don't worry—this isn't how I broke my hip."

Grace laughed, relieved for the humor.

"I loved my wife; we were together for thirty years. But we never had a passionate connection. You know what it was like when we were young. Sarah and I had never slept with anyone else. We married as virgins. So a while after she passed, I began to explore. There's so much freedom here. I realized I'd been suppressing my urges my whole life."

Grace placed her hand on his arm. "That's so wonderful for you, Ed."

He touched the side of her face. "You're such a beautiful woman." He bent down to kiss her, letting his lips hold hers for a few seconds.

Grace couldn't get the image of him paddling that woman out of her mind.

Ed backed away. "You don't want me this way, do you." It wasn't a question.

He sighed, pulling away from her. "I spent too much of my life denying who I am. As tempting as it is to chuck it all to be with you, I have to say good-bye. I'm sorry, Grace."

With that, he was gone.

>>>

Cat headed to their rendezvous point a little early, not expecting her grandmother to be there already, but she was. Her walker beside her, Granny Grace sat on a bench, dabbing at her eyes with a black handkerchief.

"What happened?" she asked, sitting down beside her. "Are you feeling okay? I worried this would be too much—"

"It's not my hip," said Granny Grace. "It's my heart."

Cat was thoroughly confused.

"Did you get the information you needed? I think I'd like to go home now."

Cat wanted to return to the club, but the truth was, she had all she needed for now. She'd talked to two others who confirmed the details the feather man told her about Nina and Sam, a.k.a. Dandelion and Mr. Master.

231

She put her arm around her grandmother. "We can go now."

"Oh, Cat," said Granny Grace, throwing her arms around her.

Just then a woman Cat recognized emerged from a curtained area and saw their embrace. She broke from her partner—a guy in a puppy costume—and wandered over. It was Bethany.

"Uh, hi, Cat," she said, giving Granny Grace a curious glance. "So, is this how you roll? GILFs?"

Cat separated herself from her grandmother just as she'd deciphered the acronym, a variation on "Moms I'd Like to Fuck." "Ah, no," Cat replied. "No judgment on those who do, but this really is my grandmother. We just came here together, and she's a bit upset..." Unsure what to do next, Cat realized introductions were in order. "Amazing Grace, meet—"

"—Mistress Mary," said Bethany, giving Cat a sideways wink.

Mistress Mary turned to the guy dressed as Fido, who dropped down on all fours. "This is Doggington," she said with a laugh. He barked.

Granny Grace seemed unusually stressed. While she politely shook hands with Mistress Mary, she regarded Doggington with apprehension.

"It was good running into you, Mistress Mary," said Cat, "and nice meeting you, um, Doggington. But we need to go."

Cat turned back once before leaving and saw Mistress Mary trying to catch her eye. *Text me*, Mary mouthed, while making text gestures on an imaginary cell phone. Doggington snapped at her hands, and she reached down and scratched behind his ear.

>>>

In the car on the way home, Grace felt her age as acutely as she had that first day in the hospital after the fall on the ice.

"You want to tell me what happened in there?" Cat asked. She seemed to drive carefully, a worry mark across her forehead.

"Ed Maxwell is a dom," she answered, as if that explained everything.

"Ed who?" Cat asked. After a beat, she followed up with, "Is that the guy you met in rehab?"

"Yes."

"Oh. You, um, saw him at The Warehouse?"

"Yes."

"That's awkward."

Grace did not respond. She wasn't a fan of that phrase anyway, as it seemed to be applied to a great many situations these days, as if the youth of today feared nothing more than the social faux pas.

"You know, Gran," Cat said, her tone taking on a know-it-all quality, "you pooh-poohed my online-dating habits, but if you and Ed had met that way, you'd already know he was into spanking his dates."

Again, Grace remained silent.

"I take it you don't think you could go there," Cat added. "Not that it's any of my business. I mean, ew. I'm already way more aware of your sex life than any granddaughter should ever be in, like, the history of the world. But if you were down for the dirty, you'd be super happy to find out Ed's been secretly picturing you with a ball gag in your mouth."

Grace busted up laughing, and so did Cat.

"Oh, God," Grace said. "Why couldn't he have had a bondage dream while we were cooped up together in rehab?"

"Yeah, or maybe if he'd have introduced himself with his club name when you first met. Did he say what it is?"

"No, he didn't. But I'd pay money for it to be the Gray Blade."

>>>

Once the hilarity and pathos died down and they were out of their boudoir togs and lounging in the Daring Damask Den alone, the rest of the household having shuffled off to bed, Cat and Granny Grace took stock of the case.

"I'm glad you at least got something useful out of this," said her grandmother. She'd already complimented Cat on a job well done for sniffing out the club members' accounts of Sam and Nina.

"Yeah, but where does this leave us? It's looking like my first hunch is correct, that Sam is innocent. The Seattle PD totally missed the fact that these two were having a secret love affair, so that's a point in our corner. But we're no closer to catching the real killer than they are."

234

Cat watched as Granny Grace got up, walked over to the liquor cabinet, and poured short tumblers of whiskey for the two of them. Cat's jaw dropped.

"Gran," she said, "did you see what you just did?"

Her grandmother walked back over and handed her the whiskey. "Yeah, I set us both up with a much-needed nightcap."

"*Without your walker.*" Cat gestured to where she'd left it, to one side of her armchair by the fireplace.

Granny Grace looked at the walker, then down at her own feet, and then back at Cat. "What do you know? I guess I did." She held up the tumbler of whiskey. "You're a powerful motivator, aren't you, honey," she said to it. "Actually, though, I should credit that dance class I've discovered. It's called Nia, and you've just got to try it—"

"—Getting back to the case," Cat said as Granny Grace sat down, "do you have any idea who really killed Nina?"

Cat stared at her grandmother as the seasoned PI mulled over the threads of the case. She waited as Granny Grace took a sip of whiskey, sighed, pursed her lips, and then sighed again.

"That stuff about Nina's father still bothers me," she finally said.

"It bothers me, too," Cat said. "But we're trying to catch Nina's murderer. We can't do anything about what her father may or may not have done to her as a child. And logically speaking, both spouses are the next likely suspects."

235

"If either of them knew about the love affair, there's the motive."

Cat nodded. "The Seattle PD didn't know about that when they cleared Robin."

"It's a pity you blew your dreamslipping cover at Sam's," Granny Grace said. "I'd like to know more about Cassidy's headspace."

"What about Robin's? It would be a cinch to arrange a sleepover there. I'll just set up a project that goes late into the evening."

"I like it," said her grandmother. "But I wonder if you could try remote-dreamslipping with Cassidy as well."

"I guess I can try," said Cat. "Though I don't feel much connection with her. I feel the opposite, actually. I could also just talk with Sam. Maybe if I come clean about investigating him—like he hasn't figured it out already—and make sure he knows I think he's innocent…"

"He could give us more insight into Cassidy," finished her grandmother. "If she got wind of his affair and killed Nina, I suspect he'll cooperate."

"True." Cat took a bold sip of her whiskey, enjoying the subtle burn as it slid down her throat. She needed to ask her grandmother another question but didn't know how to go about it.

"What's on your mind, dear?"

"How are your … rehab bills? You must've racked up a ton over the time you were there."

Her grandmother clapped her hands together. "Oh, Cat. I forgot to tell you! George Connors paid them.

That reminds me, I've been meaning to call him up to thank him in person…"

"That renews my faith in humanity," Cat said, feeling relieved. She wouldn't have thought the guy capable of such a gesture.

"We also got a check from Henrietta," her grandmother said.

"Henrietta?" Cat drew a blank.

"The woman you refer to as 'the crow lady.'"

"Oh. Right."

"That case is closed, though it wasn't the outcome she wanted. We never did nail any of her neighbors for misconduct."

"We would have in St. Louis," said Cat, giggling. "The neighbors back home have guns, and they're not afraid to use them. We'd have a murder on our hands—a murder of crows!"

Her grandmother groaned.

"We still need to follow up on that therapist lead," Cat offered. "Maybe he can tell us whether or not Nina felt threatened, by Robin or anyone else."

"Including her father," said Grace.

After a quiet moment, Cat said, "Robin's not going to like that we think Sam is innocent."

"No," Granny Grace agreed. "She won't. She's our client, and she's paying us to investigate him."

"But what if she's the killer?"

>>>

As it happened, Cat didn't need to seek out Sam Waters.

237

He came to her.

Sitting with her laptop at a coffee shop near her grandmother's house, her earbuds plugged in, she did a double-take when Sam walked in. How interesting, she thought. It couldn't be a coincidence. Maybe the stalker had become the stalked after all. If he noticed her, he pretended not to, so she kept up the ruse, watching as he went to the counter and ordered a coffee to go.

As he came back down the aisle past her, she turned her head and met his gaze. Again, he seemed to pretend to notice her for the first time.

"Hey," he said. "I know you."

She took out her earbuds. "Hi, Sam," she said, sticking out her hand to shake his. "I was just thinking about you."

He seemed flustered by this even as he returned the handshake. "That's an odd thing to say."

"Would you like to sit down?" she asked, motioning to the chair opposite.

He looked around, seeming wary, but took the chair.

"I'm surprised it took you this long to find me," said Cat. "I mean, you don't expect me to buy this casual-coincidence act, do you?"

"I guess not any more than I bought your phony story about growing up in my house."

Cat smiled. "You know, I was actually a big fan of yours, Mr. Waters. I used to listen to you all the time."

"Was that research for your case?" His look challenged her.

So he'd done his homework on her, discovered

that she was a PI.

"No," she said. "I was a genuine fan."

He seemed put off balance by this. "Is that supposed to be flattering? Even though you're speaking in past tense?"

"Nope. It's just the truth. I didn't want to think you were guilty when we took this case, but I had to assume you were. And now, let's just say I've been too distracted by the need to catch a killer to listen to your political insights."

He glanced around at the crowded coffee shop. "Could we go somewhere more private to discuss this?"

"Sure," Cat said. "There's a school playground not far from here."

They walked the busy neighborhood in silence, people milling around them as they passed restaurants and shops. Cat led him down a side street toward an elementary school playground. She still felt an edge of wariness with him, so she made sure she was within sightline of several homes and shops, though their conversation would be private. She also sent a quick text to her grandmother. *With Sam at school playground.* She sat down on a bench, and he sat a healthy distance from her.

"You're investigating me for Nina Howell's death," he said.

"Yes," said Cat. "But we're working on a new theory now."

"I heard you were at The Warehouse, asking questions about me. About Nina. Us." Sam seemed to be in pain, wincing as he talked.

"Yes, I was. My partner and I both, actually."

"And you're dropping me as a suspect based on that?"

Cat was quiet. It hadn't been just that. The dreams she'd slipped into had helped, too. That and the method of killing itself. And her gut, her instinct. She didn't think he was the one, but logically, she supposed he couldn't be eliminated entirely.

"Well, we haven't completely ruled you out."

"I didn't know her real name until I read about her murder in the news, saw her photo," he said, choking up.

Cat gave him a moment to recover, but he didn't. "I'm sorry," she said.

"Nina," he said, crying openly. "To know who she really was, I had to lose her."

Cat remembered the dream she'd picked up that night sleeping outside Sam's house, when he kept yelling "Nina." She offered him the napkin she had wrapped around her coffee cup. "Were you planning to take the relationship ... outside?"

Sam wiped his eyes, inhaled deeply, and then sighed. "We talked about it. But we deliberately kept our identities from each other, only meeting at The Warehouse."

"Neither of you in happy marriages."

Sam clenched his fist. "We didn't discuss our outside lives at first. But pretty quickly, we were playing only with each other in The Warehouse. We became ... more. Lovers. Friends. We talked. Dandelion told me the best thing she could say about her wife was that she was safe."

Cat pondered that. It made sense, in a way. If Nina's father had been abusive, she'd want to escape into the polar opposite of that, which for Nina had been less about being gay and more about the temperament of her partner.

"Did ... Dandelion ever talk about her childhood?"

Sam nodded. "Yes. It was a concern of hers, at first, that she was attracted to BDSM because she was broken or damaged. You know, she internalized all that nanny-feminazi crap."

Cat gave him a look.

"Sorry," he said. "It's not all feminists. Just the ones who seem to hate sex."

Cat stared at him. "But, ultimately, Nina rejected that, didn't she?"

"The Warehouse sponsored this workshop with feminists, counselors, sex experts. They presented research that shows that the percentage of past abuse victims is the same in the BDSM community as it is in the general population. So there's no correlation. People don't seek out BDSM practices to carry out some childhood programming. That's just an insulting assertion, if you ask me. If anything, BDSM is a powerful way for them to enforce consent."

Even though he'd lapsed into his radio voice, the whole thing clicked for Cat in that moment. In exploring the fetish lifestyle, Nina had found a path toward her natural sexual expression, but in a way that created the safety she'd felt in marrying Robin. It had less to do with Robin being a woman and more to do with her

241

personality. Nina was the breadwinner, the strong one in the relationship, the one who could easily leave. Robin was the nurturer, stable, steady, and nonthreatening, as well as dependent on Nina. Maybe too much.

"What was your safe word?" Cat asked.

Sam swallowed hard. "That's the thing. At first I thought it was a common noun, the name of the bird. It was 'Robin.'"

Chapter Nineteen

Grace fell asleep that night thinking of Annie Lin. She hadn't heard from her since the exchange about the trampoline, and she wondered what it all meant and where they stood. Having Ed unequivocally state his needs had rattled her, too, and in a good way. She thought about what he'd said. *I spent too much of my life denying who I am.*

She'd never been one to deny herself sexual experiences, with dalliances and liaisons stretching from coast to coast. Some of those had included women over the years, though not as often, to a ratio of about one woman to every eight men. And yes, in the seventies there'd been the whole swingers scene, along with the occasional ménage à trois.

But romance was something else. Love was something else. To really mean something to another person, to be always in that person's thoughts. To have them see you the way Annie seemed to see her. Maybe she'd spent too much of her life denying herself that.

Grace floated on a cloud above a pond full of koi. Butterflies flitted in and out of her view. But this wasn't her dream. It had been a while since she'd slipped into anyone else's, but she could tell it wasn't hers. The koi pond drew closer, and in its reflection, she saw not her own face, but Annie's.

Laughing, the woman reached down into the pond and grabbed a koi. It slithered between her hands, slickening them with slime. But she held firm.

The koi turned into car keys, the cloud a car seat. She stuck the keys into the ignition, and when she started the car, it exploded, the light blinding her. She floated again, but this time she seemed to move forward. She found that if she flapped her arms like a bird, she could go faster. She soared, learning how to fly, completing arcs in the sky. In the distance she saw water, a tall structure. The Space Needle. "Grace," she said, "I wish we could join our hearts. Do you feel me, too?"

Grace woke drenched in sweat, which hadn't happened to her in years, not since menopause. Her heart pounded. Blinking in the dark of her bedroom with its romantic red décor, she realized that what had happened to her brother and her granddaughter had finally happened to her. After all these years, with a woman she barely knew. Their connection was strong enough to allow Grace to slip into Annie's dream even though they had an entire continent and millions of people between them.

And Annie had fallen for Grace and wanted to know if she felt the same way.

>>>

The next morning, Cat returned to her evidence board to record the changes in the case and their new working theories. As she moved around the photos and images, marking relationships and jotting notes down in whiteboard marker, she found Greg Swenson's business card, held to the board by a heart-shaped magnet.

He'd been great to help her with that Seattle PD

contact.

She didn't owe him anything, she knew that. But holding his card gave her a momentary thrill. They'd had such a nice date. She smiled, thinking of how he stood up and declared himself healed after drinking his turmeric smoothie.

It was up to her now to get in touch with Greg; he'd given her the card and made his intentions known. She thought about how easy it was to talk to him, the connection she felt with him while they were running around the Seattle area trying to keep his sister and Ruthie safe.

But this case had her firmly in its teeth.

And there was Jacob to consider. She was supposed to fly to San Fran this weekend to see him. She couldn't in good conscience start things up with someone new until she resolved her relationship with him.

She fastened the card back to the board.

>>>

Grace happily traded in her walker for a cane, choosing a lovely antique with a mother-of-pearl topper that reminded her of Seattle's "oyster light," an effect from the play of light through clouds and fog and reflected in the waters of Puget Sound.

"What a beautiful cane," Mercy said as the two of them walked to Grace's Nia class. Grace had convinced her daughter to try it and couldn't be more excited about having her there.

Grace set up her usual station, a chair on top of a

yoga mat to keep it from slipping. She could stand for short periods and move with the other dancers, but when she felt she needed to slow down, she'd sit back on the chair and move her arms and legs. Mercy stood near her. Over the course of the next hour, the two of them danced, and as they moved about the room and in and out of each other's spaces, Grace could feel the bond between herself and her daughter strengthening. Mercy smiled at Grace several times, obviously enjoying herself. In moments like this, Grace felt free and at peace with the secret of Mercy's father. But she knew it would always be there between them. Better that than for her daughter to know the truth. The truth, Grace reasoned, did not always set you free.

As they walked home, Mercy said, "I'm going to miss you, more than usual this time."

Mercy and Joe were to fly home the next day. A sting of regret hit Grace, which surprised her. After all, she'd not exactly looked forward to their visit, and things had been so tense there in the beginning.

She reached for Mercy's hand and held it. "I regret that we live so far apart."

"I never expected you to settle in the Midwest," said Mercy, sniffing back tears.

"Well, I got Mick to move here. Maybe you're next."

"I don't think Seattle's the right town for us," Mercy said. "For one thing, we'd have to move into your house in order to afford it."

Grace realized the idea actually sounded good to her. For all her roaming, and her non-family-oriented life in Seattle, she suddenly wanted to surround herself with her kin, her blood. Parting now will be so hard, she thought, just as her own tears splashed down onto the hand that held her cane.

"Oh, look at the two of us," Mercy said. "A pair of blubbering broads."

They embraced. When they got back to the old Victorian, Mercy helped Grace climb the steep steps to the front door, and Joe whisked it open as they arrived.

"I heard there were a couple of dancers tooling around out here," he said. "Thought maybe I'd let 'em in, see if they'll give me a show."

"You're incorrigible," said Mercy.

"You're right," Joe said. "I haven't a single corrige."

Mick and Cecily were there already, waiting for a double lunch date they had planned with Mercy and Joe. Grace wanted to use the time to make a few phone calls. She and Cat had divided responsibilities on the case, with Grace picking up the therapist thread, as well as the mystery of the other addresses in Texas that Cat had found on Nina's work computer. Cat would focus her developing dreamslipping skills on Cassidy and Robin, now that she'd talked to Sam.

Once the couples left, Grace went to her study and first dialed the number she had for George Connors. She'd been putting off acknowledging his gesture long enough.

"George," she said when he answered, "this is Grace—"

"From the ice rink?"

"Yes."

"Well, hello, Grace…"

His voice had a warmth in it that pricked her senses. He didn't really think they could date again, did he?

"George, I wanted to acknowledge your gesture in paying for my hosp—"

"Don't mention it," he said, cutting her off again. "It's the least I could do, and believe me, it's no trouble. I've done quite well, so paying for that was nothing, really. Pocket change. Listen, I was just thinking about you. I have tickets to the Seattle Symphony this weekend. Brahms, I think. Would you like to go?"

Grace didn't know what to say. She didn't want to date this man, not at all, but she realized she was being made to feel obligated now, as if she somehow owed him. It was a distasteful feeling altogether, and unfair. But she didn't want to make enemies right now.

"Oh, I'm sorry," she said. "Mick and I have family here from out of town. You understand."

He began to talk again, unsolicited, something about his IT business, a client or some such. After several unsuccessful attempts to disengage from the conversation, she interrupted him with , "Bye, George, I've got to run!" And hung up.

"The nerve," she said out loud.

She took a deep breath to cleanse herself of that interaction and then called up the number for Nina's therapist.

It was getting close to noon Pacific Time, but Eli Berkman's office was in Waco, where it was nearly two p.m. She got his voice mail, so she left a message.

Next she pulled out the addresses Cat found on Nina's work computer. This was really more Cat's area than hers—she preferred talking to people to researching them online—but soon she'd discovered who lived in each house and what their relationship was to Nina. One thing bothered her: None of the addresses were for Nina's mother or her family, only her father's family, including his relations through remarriage more than twenty years ago.

By then, Grace's phone rang, and she recognized the number as Eli Berkman's.

"Amazing Grace," she answered, which seemed to fluster her caller.

"Yes? Hello? I'm returning a call from someone named Grace?"

"Yes, this is she. Sorry. My first name is Amazing, and I mean that literally, not as an adjective. It confuses people sometimes."

He chuckled good-naturedly. "Oh, I've got it. Thank you. What can I do for you, Amazing?"

"'Grace' is just fine," she said. "I'm calling about a former client of yours. Nina Howell?"

"Yes," said Berkman. "Nina is my client."

Grace felt a bit perplexed by his use of the present tense. Then something dawned on her. "Have you heard the news about her?"

"News?"

Grace sighed, swallowed hard, and plunged in. "I'm sorry to have to tell you this, but Ms. Howell is dead."

249

"Oh, my God," Berkman said. There was a long pause. "You'll have to excuse me. I worked with Nina for many years. This is terrible. Just terrible."

"I'm so sorry," Grace said. "Truly. It's such a loss."

"Yes, it is."

"Would you like me to call back later?" Grace offered.

"Yes," he replied. "I mean, no. Just—you said it was in the news. Probably in Seattle, but not here. I didn't know. How did she…?"

"I'm afraid she was murdered. That's actually why I'm calling. I've been hired by her surviving spouse to investigate."

"Oh, God," said Berkman. "This is a … tragedy. She was so young still. After all her work… Excuse me a moment."

Grace waited while Berkman collected himself. She heard him blow his nose.

"You must've called me for information," Berkman said when he returned to the phone. "But the police haven't."

"I don't think they know about you."

"Well," he said. "You must be a good private investigator."

Grace let the comment go by, since it was neither compliment nor question. She surmised that Berkman wanted to know if he was dealing with someone he could trust. "I'd like to ask you a few questions, Dr. Berkman, but you must want to verify my credentials first. I'll email you everything you need; just give me your address."

After that exchange, she sent him her PI license as

well as a copy of the contract with Robin Howell but kept him on the line. In the meantime, they swapped small talk about Waco, the weather, and his work as a therapist, which he said was tough these days, clients answering their cell phones during sessions, for example. She heard him typing at his keyboard at one point and figured he was searching her online as an added precaution. She didn't want to hang up and risk that she'd lose him.

"You know, I appreciate the urgency here," Dr. Berkman said, clearing his throat. "But I'm just trying to process this news about Nina, and, and…" He stopped.

"I understand," said Grace. "It's so much to absorb."

"I'm also aware of my obligations with regard to client privilege," he said. "So I'm not even sure that I can answer your questions."

Grace didn't like where this was going. She knew that all conversations between a therapist and patient were bound by confidentiality, similar to that between a medical doctor and patient, or attorney and client. But this patient was no longer alive. "Surely privilege doesn't continue after the death of the client," Grace said.

"Well, you're wrong about that. I'm afraid it does."

"This would be in the best interest of your client," Grace realized the two of them had lapsed into the abstract language of legalese. "In Nina's best interest," she added.

"It might be. I wouldn't have any way of knowing."

Grace was silent, thinking that over. He was right,

of course. His answers might end up being in Robin's best interest, at Nina's expense, in this case. But could he also be hiding something?

"I'm very sorry," he said. "But thank you for calling, for telling me the news."

"Isn't this a gray area?" Grace persisted. "There's a reasonable exception here."

Silence for a few beats. "I-I'm afraid the best I can do is to say I'll think this over some more," he said. "I can't promise you my position will change, but I'll call you if so."

"My main question for you is whether or not Nina felt threatened by anyone," Grace said. "We just want her killer brought to justice."

"I understand, but I can't answer that, of course," said Dr. Berkman. "I'm sorry."

>>>

While Grace hit a wall with Nina's therapist, Cat navigated the tricky emotional territory of Robin's psyche.

"Why hasn't that man been arrested?" the woman demanded.

"Because so far nothing proves he killed Nina," said Cat. "We haven't found proof, and the Seattle PD don't even think the two ever crossed paths."

She wasn't sure yet if she were going to reveal the details of the affair to Robin. She didn't really know what the woman knew already. "My grandmother and I have been confused from the beginning by how sure you are that he's the one," she continued. "Is there something you haven't told us?"

"No," said Robin, meeting Cat's gaze. They sat in the living room, Robin's hands straddling either side of her armchair. Sharon Koal, from the Wyld Womyn's group, had already taken Jin Mae into her bedroom to read to her before a nap.

"Was Nina having an affair with Sam?" Cat asked.

"Not of her own volition," said Robin. "I've already told you this!" She stood up, ran her fingers through her hair, and began to pace, her clogs clunking loudly on the hardwood floor each time she stepped off the rug. "I think he had some hold over her. She loved us —me and Jin Mae. She would never…" Her voice trailed off.

"Do you think she was planning to leave you?"

"We took vows," Robin said.

"People change…" Cat said.

"Not like that!"

Cat sat, silent. Robin's pacing slowed down, and then she went back to the armchair, slumping into it. "Nina tried to deprogram her father out of her," she said quietly. "But she must have failed."

"Women internalize their abuse all the time," said Sharon, who'd entered the room from the hallway and must have heard part of their exchange.

Cat felt honestly offended by this line of thought, not to mention alarmed by the levels of denial Robin seemed to be under about her marriage to Nina. But she kept this to herself. "Tell me how that works," she said.

Sharon and Robin exchanged glances. "It's like

253

this," said Sharon, pushing up her turquoise glasses with her thumb. "We women are indoctrinated from birth to be the sexual objects of men. Even if we haven't actually been the victims of abuse, as Nina was, we internalize that role as object. Nina must have been torn between her love for Robin and the programming in herself she couldn't undo."

"But didn't she go to therapy for a long time?" asked Cat. "Wouldn't that have helped her ... deprogram, or whatever?"

Sharon scoffed. "Her therapist was a man."

Cat looked at Robin, who stared at the floor.

"Have either of you heard of The Warehouse?"

Robin returned her gaze to Cat. Sharon put her hand over her mouth.

"I see you have," said Cat. "I'm guessing neither of you have actually been there."

They both shook their heads.

"Nina was a member," Cat said. "I think she joined on her own, and she met Sam there."

"No, no, no, no, no," said Robin. "Nina wouldn't have. You're wrong. She would've told me. This is Sam's doing. He made her join."

Sharon put her arm around Robin. "It's okay, Robin. It's okay."

Robin clung to Sharon. "But it's not true."

"I know," said Sharon. To Cat, she said, "I think you should leave."

>>>

When Cat got home, she found Granny Grace in her study, her head buried in her hands.

"Robin just called," she said. "She's cancelling our contract."

"She owes us a cancellation fee," said Cat, plopping down into the chair beside her grandmother's desk.

"Yes. There is at least that."

"But that's not why you're upset?" Cat said. "I mean, we thought she might."

"I hit a dead end with the therapist."

Cat waited. This still didn't seem like enough to get her grandmother down. There had to be more.

"I don't want my daughter to leave," she finally said, tears running down her face.

Cat's own eyes teared up at that. She rubbed her grandmother's back, the bones of her spine like a string of oversized pearls. "You can visit her in St. Louis," she offered.

"I know. We've been apart all these years, and now I just want all of us to be in one place. Is that crazy, or what?"

Cat laughed. "For most of my life, the two of you have been practically estranged."

Her grandmother frowned, an expression that didn't appear often on her face. "That's my fault."

"Oh, I don't know," said Cat. "My mother had something to do with it."

Granny Grace seemed about to say something, but then changed her mind and collected herself. She dabbed her eyes with a tissue and sat up straighter.

"So what's next, Dreamslipper? We've lost our client. Do you still want to catch Nina's killer?"

Chapter Twenty

Cat ran through the field as fast as she could, trying to outpace the ship hovering above her. But its beam of light caught up to her. She froze, unable to move. The beam lifted her upward, through a door and into a dark room, where she blacked out.

When she woke, one of them *stood over her. It was him. He always came for her.*

"Drink this, Nina," he said.

The liquid was dark and syrupy, but something in it burned her mouth and throat. She could feel it settle into her gut. Her eyes drooped; she could not hold them open; it was such a struggle. Then only darkness.

Cat drifted out of the dream, feeling her mouth dry. She stumbled to the kitchen and poured herself a glass of water. The house was quiet. Her father and mother had flown back home, Mick was probably sleeping at Cecily's, and Granny Grace was back in the Sumptuous Scarlett O'Hara upstairs.

Cat tried to analyze the dream, which seemed to be another dream from the past left by Nina. But what in the world…? Cat corrected herself. *Not of this world.* The dream seemed to be about alien abduction.

She had no idea what to do with that.

>>>

Mick lay down next to Cecily, trying to give off a nonthreatening vibe.

Cecily propped herself up on one elbow. "So, in order to keep out of my dreams, you're going to try to create a buffer wall or something? How does that work?"

"I'm not sure it will," Mick admitted. "Cat, Pris, and I use it with each other, in order to live in the same house together. We kind of found out accidentally, down there in Miami when we were all forced to live together, that it's a little too easy to slip into each other's dreams. In order to preserve privacy, not to mention peace, we create a buffer wall before we fall asleep each night. It's worked okay, but it's not perfect." He reflected on the strange dream of Pris's that he'd slipped into just that morning, something about a man with a paddle spanking a ninja clown.

"I guess I'll have to trust you to tell me whether it does or not," said Cecily, biting her lower lip. It was a gesture that tweaked Mick's heart, something she did when she was nervous.

He reached out and stroked his thumb across her bottom lip. "I promise I'll try to make this work, and if it doesn't, I'll tell you."

She grabbed his thumb and kissed it. "You better."

Mick settled into bed and closed his eyes. He could call up the buffer wall visually, using whatever imagery seemed to fit the best. For Cecily, he imagined roses. A thick wall of roses growing up all around her, blocking her as she slept so that her dreams would stay there, behind them.

Soon he drifted off and fell into one of his own

dreams, about an entire zombie army of Pennington James clones. It was a recurring dream that had plagued Mick since he left Miami, where Pennington James had been finally convicted of possession of child pornography after the Miami PD's initial confusion, which damaged Mick's reputation.

Mick's role in this dream seemed to be fighting each James clone as it tried to attack him. He was just about to crack open a head and spill its brains when the dream came to an abrupt halt.

"Mick, wake up. You're having a nightmare." Cecily shook him.

He opened his eyes. "Ugh. Not that again."

"You were moving your arms and legs, like you were kicking and punching somebody."

Mick sat up. "I didn't hurt you, did I?"

"No," she said. "But you've got me worried. That was like PTSD or something."

"Pennington James," Mick said, and he didn't need to explain. Cecily knew the story. She motioned for him to lie down, and when he did, she spooned him. He rebuilt the rose bower around her in his mind. When he woke again, it was morning, the sunlight streaming in around the edges of Cecily's rice-paper window blinds.

She was already up and puttering in the kitchen. He stumbled out there, intent on coffee. She looked at him, her face a question.

"It worked," he said.

>>>

Cat walked into Grace's study without invitation and plopped down in the chair beside her desk. "I had another 'dead Nina' dream," she said.

Grace bristled. She turned away from her computer screen to face Cat. "I wish you'd call them something else. I was rather fond of Nina, you know."

"Sorry," Cat said. "Is 'leftover Nina' dream better?"

"Worse."

"Do you want to hear about it, or not?"

"Call them 'dream knots,'" Grace said. "It's like they're fragmented bits of her past dreams that won't straighten out in the timeline because of the knots."

"All right," said Cat, rolling her eyes. "So anyway, about the dream. It was totally weird, not like the sexy stuff I have been getting. This was some kooky alien-abduction dream."

"Really? That has never come up before."

"I know, right?" said Cat. "Nina was super levelheaded. Some might even say she was scientific. You'd have to be crazypants to believe in alien abduction."

"Now, now…" said Grace.

"Seriously, Gran. There is zero evidence to support it. None whatsoever. Zilch."

"Well, how do you explain this dream?"

Cat gave her a blank look. "I don't know. Maybe my dreamslipping radar is off. Maybe it was some other Nina's dream."

"Did it feel like Nina Howell?"

Cat didn't hesitate. "Yes."

"Didn't her father have a UFO hobby?"

"Yes," Cat said. "But I can't believe Nina ever bought into it."

Grace pursed her lips. "It sure would be nice if her therapist would talk to us."

"You're going to start on her other Texas family, right?"

"Yes," said Grace. She had the addresses pulled up on her computer already.

"I heard from the Puget Place Hotel manager," said Cat. "No go on the staff's statements, but he did send me the MP3 footage. All twelve hours, from two different cameras. It's riveting, let me tell you. Like watching Uncle Mick paint."

"I'll trade work assignments with you if you want," said Grace.

"No, ma'am. You've been on a little vacation with your accident and everything," Cat said with a wry smile. "It's time for you to earn your part of our retainer and cancellation fee."

"Speaking of that," Grace said, "we're going to need another client soon."

Cat looked down. "Yeah. I know. Should I cancel my trip to San Fran?"

Financially speaking, Grace knew the answer should be yes. She also hoped for a solo trip to New York to visit Annie Lin, with whom she'd been chatting online every chance she got. But this long-distance thing between Cat and Jacob was unresolved, and it was keeping Cat from pursuing viable relationships in Seattle.

"I don't think that's necessary," she told Cat.

261

"All right. But I'm going to talk to Sam before I go."

As her granddaughter left the room, Grace returned to the list of Nina's relatives in the Waco area. First was her father, who'd remarried after a divorce in 1993 and lived on a farm outside of town. Grace didn't want to talk to him again, though. She wanted to talk to his wife.

After a little more digging, she had the woman's work number.

"Waco Siding," the woman answered. "Tina Jeffers speaking."

"Mrs. Jeffers, I'm a private investigator in the Seattle area, and I…" Grace heard a dial tone. Either they were disconnected, or the woman had hung up on her. Grace tried again.

This time she got the woman's voice mail. "Hello, Mrs. Jeffers," Grace said after the beep. "I believe we were just disconnected. I'm sorry to bother you like this, but I have some very important information about a relative of your husband's." She left her number.

Grace hesitated before calling the next number on the list, Nina's aunt on her father's side. She didn't want to risk another hang-up. But the alternative would be a trip to Waco, Texas, and without funding from a client, they wouldn't be able to afford it.

It was time for different tactics.

She consulted an online registry that housed the yearbooks of every high school in the U.S. She kept a membership in this service for occasions like this one. Then she ran a few more general searches online. Armed with enough information, Grace dialed Lottie Johnson's home number, and the woman picked up on the second ring.

"Hello, Mrs. Johnson," Grace said, warmly bringing on her best South Texas accent. "I'm an old high school friend of your brother's. Go, Tigers!"

"Why, hello!" Lottie said, with the overenthusiasm of a lonely person unaccustomed to getting phone calls. "I'm afraid it's a lion now, though."

"Yes, it's a pity, isn't it?" said Grace. "To lose your high school like that, to have it swallowed up into not just one but two others! The school colors aren't even the same."

"Oh, I *know*," said Lottie. "I think the red and gray are drab, don't you?"

"Yes," said Grace. "Now, you graduated well before our class, didn't you?"

"That's right," said Lottie. "I was in the class of '55, out of there before my brother Norm came in as a freshman, I'm afraid."

"Your brother was quite the looker," Grace said. "I have to admit, I had a real crush on him."

"Tall, dark, and handsome," said Lottie quietly. "That's what all my girlfriends said, though he was too young for any of them."

"Are the two of you still close?"

"We see each other occasionally..." said Lottie. Grace could hear the enthusiasm in her voice die down. "Only the big family events. You know how it is, people grow up, get busy."

"Yes, I do. Even harder when divorce enters the

picture. You know, I can't even remember the name of your brother's first wife—"

"—Susie Charles," said Lottie. "Of the old Charles family dry cleaners."

"Of course!" said Grace. "Susie. She was something, wasn't she?"

"Pretty, but never knew it," said Lottie with a sigh. "Had to have men keep telling her, but she still didn't believe it, even then."

What Lottie said reminded her of a line from a book by Dorothy Allison. "'Beauty is a mean story,'" she said.

"Amen to that," said Lottie. "It's a shame that woman run off like that. But I guess Nina was old enough to fend for herself by then."

"I don't think I knew that," said Grace. "You'll have to forgive me. I'm out in Houston now. I feel so out of touch."

"Houston? I could never live in the big city," she said. "Waco's as much as I can handle."

"Where did Susie run off to?"

"Beats me," said Lottie. "It's like she up and disappeared one day."

"Did you like her? Get along?"

"As much as anyone does, I suppose," said Lottie. "She kinda kept to herself. 'Course my brother can be pretty domineering."

"I know the type," Grace said. "Didn't like her going out, having her own friends, that sorta thing?"

"Yes," said Lottie. "He does the same thing with the woman he's with now. Tiny Tina, I call her. Norman tends to like them small. You remember how petite Susie was."

"I do," said Grace. She had two images of Norman Jeffers, one from Nina's Photoshopped obit and the other from the high school yearbook. He looked large and imposing in both of them. The idea of him lording over much smaller women gave Grace a chill down her back.

"Lottie, I have some bad news," Grace said. "It's about Nina."

"I was just wondering why you'd called. We got to talking, and I forgot to ask."

"I'm so sorry, Lottie, but I have bad news. I'm afraid it's your niece. She's no longer with us."

Silence on the other end. "But how? She was young, healthy…"

"She was murdered."

Lottie made a noise as if she couldn't breathe. It came out as a strangled whistle. "No," she finally said. "It's just a coincidence..."

"What is?"

"I'm sorry, no. That's not what I meant to say. You'll have to excuse me… I-I didn't even catch your name."

Grace ignored the name request. "Lottie, if you have information about Nina's death, please tell me."

"What? No. I don't have anything. I have to go. I'm so sorry about Nina. It's such a shame."

With that, she hung up.

>>>

265

Grace thought it was odd that Robin hadn't mentioned Nina's mother, so she went over to talk to Robin about it. The PI didn't expect Robin to refuse to answer the door for her, but that seemed to be the case.

Grace thought she heard someone step toward the door, as if they were looking through the peephole. But whoever it was didn't open it. Robin's car was in the driveway behind Nina's, which had been there since the murder, appearing unmoved. Grace noted its tires looked a bit deflated.

"Robin?" she called out. "Are you in there? Listen, dear, I really need to talk to you. Cat and I are looking for Nina's murderer, and we're onto something. But we need your help."

Nothing.

"Robin, please. Don't you want to know who really did this? Don't you owe it to Nina?"

After a couple of minutes went by, the door finally creaked open. "You have five minutes to convince me." She held up her wristwatch to emphasize the point.

"What can you tell me about Nina's mother?"

"Really? You're still digging around in her past? How's that going to catch whoever killed her in the present?"

"Was she looking for her? Did she find her? Were they in contact?"

"No," said Robin. "That bitch abandoned Nina right before she went off to college. She hasn't seen her since."

"So, except for this trip to Waco that Nina

neglected to tell you about, your wife was estranged from both her parents, with no contact whatsoever with either of them or anyone else in the family for the past twenty years."

"Nina would have told me about Waco when she was ready, if Sam hadn't … changed her. She cut herself off from everyone and started a new life for herself with me. Just me. That's how she wanted it."

"Robin," Grace said, as calmly as she could. "I know you're grieving. But I'm not sure that's what really happened. You seem to be in denial about how Nina was, before her death."

Robin slammed the door in her face.

Chapter Twenty-One

Cat walked into a bar and immediately realized she was dreaming, or rather, that she'd slipped into Jacob's dream.

She looked down at her feet and spotted his familiar dress shoes, black slip-ons with tiny silver tabs over each big toe. These were the shiny dress shoes he wore to work at his uncle's art gallery. Looking out of Jacob's eyes, Cat spotted his dream version of herself standing at the bar, with a giant Space Needle floating above her head. The fact that Jacob dreamed about her felt flattering, though the Space Needle nearly made her giggle. She had on some slinky dress she didn't actually own. Cat made a mental note to look for something like that the next time she went shopping.

Jacob walked toward Dream Cat, and she could feel his sizzling anticipation. But then his gaze shifted from Cat to some other woman standing on the other side of the bar. The Empire State Building floated above her head. He went to her instead of Cat.

Cat recognized the woman immediately from another dream of Jacob's that she had slipped into back in Miami. Cat had gotten the impression then that the woman was important to him, but that his feelings about her were complicated.

Now Jacob was clearly flustered by the woman, who stood there sipping a martini. She took the toothpick out of her glass and wrapped her tongue around the olive, sort of pulling the olive off the pick with her lips. Cat could feel Jacob's reac-

tion to this. He glanced over at Cat, the one who was basically a character in his dream, and then back at the other woman. Jacob's dream version of Cat called his name. But he ignored her, his gaze pulled to the woman with the martini.

"What do you think of Cat?" Jacob asked the woman at the bar.

"Oh, I think she's been a good distraction for you," she said, her glossy red lips curving into a wicked smile.

The scene changed, and now Jacob stood before dream Cat, who was lying on a bed covered in Space Needle-themed bed sheets. Jacob was flushed with lust, and the real Cat was glad to see things were focused back on just the two of them.

But he hesitated, turning around.

Behind him stood the blonde woman, eating an enormous red apple.

"You don't belong here," she said, her teeth piercing the fruit's skin.

The dream must have ended then, as everything went black.

>>>

That morning, Cat and Jacob made love like they always did, with Cat riding atop him, her favorite position. But something was off about their sex, and she attributed it to the dream. She didn't know if it was her own mind suggesting it or something she sensed in Jacob, but she wondered for a fleeting moment if their relationship would make it after all.

She shook off the thought. There she was in San Francisco, which was quickly becoming her new favorite city, and they had the day ahead of them. It was a welcome break from all the stress of the previous month—her grandmother's spill on the ice, her parents' impromptu visit, her bad dating experience, and most importantly, the case she couldn't seem to crack.

Jacob took her to a Mexican bakery for breakfast. Feeling playful, she blew powdered sugar all over his face, and he kissed her, getting the powder on her face as well. They walked through an arcade of old-time games at Fisherman's Wharf. Feeling like she'd fallen back into a good groove with Jacob, she reasoned that not every dream had to mean something. In her experience, a great many of them didn't mean a thing. Whatever Jacob's psyche worked on in the wee hours, he was perfectly attentive and affectionate to her when they were together.

This was her third trip there in six months, and Jacob had also been to see her three times. So theirs was a once-a-month liaison. She was aware that they couldn't keep up the long-distance thing forever. But Jacob couldn't leave San Francisco—his uncle was planning to leave his well-established art gallery in Jacob's hands when he retired. So Cat had to consider whether or not she could leave Seattle for him. She could be a private investigator anywhere, she reasoned. Her Uncle Mick and Granny Grace had each other now; they would be okay without her.

But she felt comfortable in Seattle. For now, it suited her. She didn't like the thought of leaving her family, or being entirely dependent on Jacob and *his* family in a city where she knew no one else. She loved her uncle and grandmother. Simon and Dave were her friends, too, and now she had a new friend in Bethany, as long as she didn't screw it up. And Greg, as long as she didn't screw that up, too.

As if on cue, Cat received a text message from Bethany, AKA Mistress Mary, inviting her to happy hour.

In San Fran, Cat texted back. She felt guilty that she hadn't been in touch with her friend since the night they ran into each other at The Warehouse. But it was kind of awkward, finding out your new friend engages in puppy play, even if she wasn't the one in the puppy costume. Relationship-wise, Cat didn't think they were at the sharing-our-fetishes stage, if there even was such a thing. And since Cat didn't really have any fetishes, outside of slipping into her partners' dreams, if that counted, she felt the situation was really one-sided. Not to mention that Bethany thought she was a schoolteacher and had no idea Cat had been undercover that night at the club.

Bethany replied. *San Fran? Vacay?*

Cat realized she'd never mentioned her long-distance romance with Jacob to her new bestie. She really didn't want to get into it now, especially over text. *Long story*, she wrote. *Tell you when I get back? Over turmeric beers. I'm sure that's a thing.*

She and Jacob went to Ghirardelli Square, where they bought chocolate bars and fed them to each other, pausing to watch a band of musicians from the Andes play, one with a bamboo flute. She stretched out on a spit of grass near a water fountain, resting her head on Jacob's chest. She could stay there forever, she thought. The taste of chocolate lingered on her lips, and it seemed to be the taste of possibility, of promise.

"Why are you looking at me like that?" Jacob asked, his tone teasing.

"Like what?"

Jacob stroked her hair. "Like you want to say something."

"Oh, don't flatter yourself," she said, lightly punching him in the arm.

"You're really great, Cat," he said.

His words let her down somewhat. They paled in comparison with what she'd nearly said, and that made her feel foolish. But in her experience, it was hard for a man to express his feelings, so she didn't dwell on it too much. There would be another moment.

At lunch, Jacob ordered a bottle of wine. This seemed a bit much for so early in the day, but Jacob said he wanted to linger over the meal, which was divine, the best steamed mussels she'd ever tasted. There was saffron, not turmeric, in the broth. They talked about Jacob's trip to visit her in Seattle next month. He planned it to coincide with Art Walk. But he seemed preoccupied with his thoughts, and he kept her wine glass full.

Cat realized as they talked that there was something he wanted to say to her. She grew excited but anxious at the same time, anticipating that Jacob might want more than she could give.

By the time the wine was only a strip of dark liquid at the bottom of the green bottle, Jacob had moved his chair closer to hers and was stroking the inside of her elbow, sending shivers across her arm and into her fingertips.

"Cat, there's something I need to tell you." He cleared his throat.

He seemed nervous, and that endeared him to her all the more.

"Of course," she said, leaning in toward him.

"Actually," he said, "I've been struggling with this for a while."

Was he going to formally ask her to move to San Francisco? He continued to stroke the inside of her elbow.

"If you keep doing that, you can ask me anything." She closed her eyes, savoring his touch.

"It's just…" he hesitated.

She opened her eyes. "Jacob, you can tell me anything."

He sighed. "I'm thinking of going back to New York."

She hadn't seen that coming, but as soon as he said it, she flashed on the floating Space Needle and Empire State Building in his dream. The sheets, too. And the apple.

"But what about your uncle?"

He looked away, out the window at the wharf beyond. "Yeah, that's the thing. There's a reason you don't do business with family."

Cat recalled Jacob's complaints when he first got to San Francisco, but she thought they'd worked out their differences.

"Who will take over his business?"

Jacob met her eyes. "Not me, as it turns out."

She could see the pain in them. And … something else. Longing … for something. The woman in the dream? She flashed angry, thinking about what she'd said about Cat.

"What have I been to you, then?" Cat demanded. "Just a *distraction*?"

He looked as if he'd been caught in the act. "What?"

"You heard me."

"God," he said, running his hand through his hair. "I can't believe you just said that. What are the odds…"

"Is this really about your uncle? Or is it about someone else?"

"Cat…"

She kept going. "Because if it's about someone else, I wish you'd just tell me."

"There's no one else," he said. "What gave you that idea?"

She stopped, realizing what she'd done. There was no good way to answer that question. So she sat there, fuming. Hurting.

After a few breaths, she said, "I don't hear you asking me to move there with you."

He was quiet, studying his fingers, which were splayed wide on the white tablecloth. Then he glanced up at her and said, "I don't hear you offering to move there with me."

"I think someone's already there, waiting for you," Cat said, her voice low, nearly a whisper.

He sighed. "I-I don't know. It's complicated."

"I'm not it for you, am I?"

"Am I for you?"

Cat did not respond at first. She thought of her attraction to Greg and realized the answer was no. Slowly, she shook her head.

Jacob reached up, put his hand to her cheek. "It's been so lovely. In Miami. And here."

She grabbed his hand and couldn't help her tears spilling down. "Yes."

>>>

On the flight home the next day, Cat at first didn't notice the man next to her on the plane until he struck up a flirty conversation with her. He seemed manly and rough, with "clavicle bush" peeking profusely out of the top of his Western shirt. His hands were calloused from hard work. When he got up to use the restroom, she noticed the tight jeans and boots.

"What, are you like a cowboy or something?" she asked when he returned.

He laughed. "Or something. I'm a farm-equipment distributor, headed to Seattle for a conference. But you can pretend I'm a cowboy if it helps."

It was not a long flight from San Francisco to Seattle, but the man moved fast, with Cat giving him the green light. She didn't know why, exactly, except that she wanted to know if she could do this, simply follow her physical attraction without her heart getting in the way.

By the time they landed at Sea-Tac, they'd made out, and she had an invitation to head back to his hotel room, which she did.

Their sex was frantic, the two of them smashing up against and into each other as if the force of their enthusiasm could make up for the fact that they were strangers.

"You can stay if you like," he said when they were done. He traced a finger across her lips. "What you do with that mouth should be illegal."

"I think in some states it still is," she said, smiling. She liked him, but he was only in town overnight, and she didn't want to stay and risk slipping into his dreams. She needed to go home.

>>>

There were three more family members for Grace to call from the Waco list. She opted next to try the youngest one, a cousin around Nina's age. This would be Lottie's daughter, who was forty-two.

Doreen Johnson proved hard to get hold of at first, but she left Grace a cell-phone number and mentioned she worked rotations as a nurse. Grace followed up, and the two connected while Doreen was on break.

"I'm supposed to be sleeping," she said. Grace could hear the squeak of metal bedsprings and imagined Doreen in one of those sleep station rooms they have for hospital staff.

"This won't take long. I just—"

"Are you the one who got my mother all riled up?"

"Well, I spoke with her. It certainly wasn't my intention to upset her."

"Look," Doreen said with a sigh. "I don't socialize with the family much. I don't socialize with anyone, really. I've got forty K in student loans I'm trying to pay off, so I work about eighty hours a week, no exaggeration. And I ain't no spring chicken. I went to school late, after burning my life away in retail."

"I really appreciate you taking the time for this call," Grace said. She sensed the woman had something else to say, and some motivation for making such a concerted effort to be available for Grace. Her instincts told her to come clean about who she was and what she was doing.

"I'm a private investigator," Grace said. "Looking into Nina's murder."

"I thought that line you gave my mom about high school was bullshit," Doreen said. "But listen. Here's what she wouldn't tell ya. My Uncle Norm's a fucking creep. Not that anyone ever asks me. You have to understand how things are in this family. Denial is not just a river in Egypt, if you know what I mean."

"I can imagine," Grace said. "But are you talking about the Tiny Tina stuff? He likes women he can physically control?"

Doreen laughed. "I wish that were all. Believe me. Look, Nina was right to come back here and tell everybody what a monster he was."

"Is that why she came back?" Grace asked. "Her father says it was a friendly visit."

"Friendly? That was Nina's first trip back since she left more than twenty years ago."

277

"Oh," Grace said. "I hadn't realized."

"Yeah, she went and told everyone in the family what he did, and she confronted the bastard himself. Said she had to in order to finally get past what he did to her. If it weren't for her, I would have gone right on thinking I was the only one he—" The woman broke off.

There was a long silence. Grace didn't want to intrude.

"Goddamnit," Doreen finally said, sniffing loudly. "I thought I had this under control."

"It's okay," Grace said. "Take your time."

"That's just it. I don't have time. My next shift starts in ten minutes."

"Doreen," Grace said, "I think you want to tell me that your uncle abused you when you were a girl. Is that right?"

"Yes," Doreen said, her voice catching in her throat. "He did. And you want to know what? I told my mama about it at the time, and she accused me of making up stories."

"Oh," Grace said. "I'm so sorry."

"Yeah. How about that. Family values, that's what Waco's known for."

"Why didn't you move away?"

"I did," Doreen said. "Went to Dallas. Lasted about twelve years before my mama got sick, and I had to come back. Since my daddy's a no-good deadbeat, I'm all she's got. I was struggling anyway. It's a lot cheaper here in Waco."

"Did you ever think of taking your Uncle Norm to court?"

278

"Nina and I talked about it. Argued about it, more like. But she came to see what a joke that would be. Uncle Norm's a good old country boy, in thick with the police and the judges. Hell, when Aunt Susie run off, they gave him a divorce without her present, on the grounds of abandonment, no questions asked."

"It would be a tough trial, too," Grace said. "Hard on you."

"'Raped again in court,' isn't that the saying? That is definitely not something I can afford, financially or otherwise. Waco's a small town, basically. I don't need that. I'm just trying to survive as it is."

"You're taking care of your mother, too?"

"Yeah, she's got MS. Some weeks she's fine, but then she gets these paralysis spells. But at least she's stuck by me. Not like Nina's mama, running off like. She left Nina to pick herself up after what basically must have been a nuclear bomb going off in her family."

"I'm so sorry you have to deal with all of this," Grace said. "It's unfair. You don't deserve it."

"Where are you calling from?" asked Doreen. "You sure don't talk like folks around here."

"Seattle," said Grace. And that gave her a thought. "Did Nina think of bringing suit against your uncle in Washington State?"

"Yeah, she did. But the statute of limitations ran out for both of us about eight years ago. We couldn't sue him even if we thought we could survive the trial, or win. It's just too late."

Grace felt heavy with the impossibility. It wasn't often that she couldn't see a way out, somewhere.

"Just one more question," Grace said, remembering the strange dream Cat had. "It's a bit of an odd question, too. Has anyone in your family ... believed they were abducted by aliens?"

"Excuse me?" She laughed bitterly. "That must have something to do with Uncle Norm's little you-fo hobby. Nina told me once that he read one book in his entire career and then set up his whole life around it. Damn, I can't remember the name of that book... Oh, yeah. *What If Spacemen Really Did Colonize the Earth?*"

"Doreen," she said. "Thank you so much for your time. I want to tell you something. You are an amazing person, strong and resilient. Your mother should be proud. Your god should be proud. The world should be proud."

Doreen laughed nervously, but her loud sniffs gave away that she was crying. "Jesus, you're something else, lady. I-I've got to get back to work. Um, thank you? I hope you catch Nina's killer. I hope it wasn't Uncle Norm, for my mama's sake. Honestly, I don't know that he's capable of murder, but I wouldn't rule him out."

>>>

It was late when Cat traipsed into the Victorian and dropped her carry-ons in the entryway. Famished, she made for the Terra- Cotta Cocina and was surprised to find her grandmother there, peering at her laptop.

"You're up late, Gran."

Granny Grace pulled off her reading glasses and jumped up to hug Cat.

"And you're back already! I thought you weren't coming home till the weekend."

"I decided to come home early." Cat marched over to the refrigerator, opened it, and grabbed a block of cheese.

"Oh, you don't want dairy this late," Granny Grace said, taking the cheese out of Cat's hands. "Let me make you some tea. In this week's organic box, we got one called Sleeping Moon. It'll be just the thing."

Cat stomped her foot. "Gran, I haven't eaten since lunch, and I managed to squeeze a one-night stand in between the time my plane landed and now. But I guess since I didn't stay the night, it's technically not a one-night stand. At any rate, I more than deserve a cheese sandwich right now because Jacob and I are no more."

At that, she collapsed into tears in her grandmother's arms. Cat felt Granny Grace squeeze her tight and then release. "Okay, let me make one for you. Grilled. On a thick slice of homemade bread."

"Only if it's got bacon on it, too," Cat sniffed, extracting herself from Granny Grace's arms.

Her grandmother took a pan down from the rack and turned on a stove burner. "How about some cocoa?"

"Oh, God no. I've had enough chocolate for today, Gran."

"Now tell me all about it."

Cat poured out her tale, and Granny Grace listened as she cooked, making soothing, sympathetic noises. She set the grilled cheese and bacon sandwich in front of Cat with a cup of Sleeping Moon tea. Cat consumed them both greedily.

Once Cat's story wound down, Granny Grace sighed heavily. The look she gave Cat seemed full of meaning.

"What?"

"I'm going to tell you something, Cat, but I don't want you to get upset."

"Go ahead, Gran." Cat braced herself. Her grandmother's wisdom was often enlightening, but it could also feel like ripping off a Band-Aid.

"You've been letting all of these men choose you. Lee Stone, Jacob, even today's cowboy. You're attractive and sweet, a bit flirty when you want to be. You draw them to you like bees to pollen, but what about what *you* want?"

Cat looked up at her. "I knew I didn't want to go to New York."

"That's a start, knowing what you don't want."

"I like Greg."

"Well, good, but take your time."

"I will," said Cat. "Believe me." She stopped short of telling her grandmother she'd been thinking about going back to The Warehouse, and not undercover.

But Granny Grace switched topics anyway. "I have some rather upsetting things to tell you about my phone canvassing."

Her grandmother shared what she'd learned in the conversation with Doreen.

They mulled that over for a few minutes.

"I have an idea," said Cat. "I'm sure Nina paid her membership at The Warehouse in cash, so as not to alert Robin's suspicions. I'll need Sasha and the other board members there to attest to Nina's membership. Do you think ze will agree to it?"

"I think ze will."

"Once I've got that, there's one more thing I can do. It will solve both our problems, hopefully giving us an income source and access to police files."

Chapter Twenty-Two

Detective David Spencer agreed to see Cat immediately. He appeared in the waiting area with his hands on his hips and nodded for her to follow him back to a meeting room.

"You said you had information?" he prompted.

"I'm no longer working for Robin Howell," Cat said. "So I'd like to offer my services to you, to consult on this case as an independent investigator."

Spencer laughed. "Wait. Let me get this straight. You want me to pay you for your information?"

"I want you to pay me for my help," said Cat. "Just like you do with any other contractor."

"Look, when we bring in experts, they're not..." He stopped.

"What?" she challenged him. "Women?"

"We've got women on the force, lesbians even, so don't give me that."

"What then? Young?"

"Inexperienced."

"Really? Look, I've been running circles around you in this case. You need me. Let me give you an example," Cat retrieved a piece of paper from her bag. "This is an affidavit from an establishment known as The Warehouse. It's signed by the current executive director, and it attests to the fact that both Sam Waters and Nina Howell were members of the club."

Spencer took the paper, his jaw dropping, but just

a bit. He quickly recovered. "So you're back on this Sam bandwagon."

"No," Cat said. "My partner and I have pretty much cleared him."

"Really," he said. "How so?"

Cat swallowed hard. A lot of what she knew she couldn't tell him, since it came from dreams, not to mention her gut. "Eyewitness accounts at the club."

"How did you figure this out?"

"The pet collar," Cat said. "It's hers. Nina's. Dandelion was her club name. The two of them were having a romantic affair."

Spencer closed his eyes, taking in the information. "You do realize this is the cross, don't you?" He stood up. "I've got to get my people on this immediately. It's enough to bring Sam in."

This wasn't going exactly as Cat had planned, but in light of what she gave Spencer, she wasn't surprised he wanted to act on it.

"Fine," she said. "But you need me for this. You're going to waste your time investigating Sam now, when it's looking like the murderer was one of the spouses." Cat hesitated. "Or maybe even her own father."

Spencer laughed. "You don't say?" He sat down again. "You think you've got this all figured out, eh? Well, did you know her partner Simon Fletcher had a good motive for wanting Nina out of the picture?"

Cat reeled back at that one. She didn't know what to say.

"We also found evidence that links him to the crime scene."

That one stunned her.

"Tell you what, Ms. McCormick," continued Spencer. "I'll bring you on as a consultant, but I want everything you know out on the table here. Don't keep anything from me, or your contract will be replaced by an obstruction-of-justice charge."

She nodded, wondering what she could possibly have missed about Simon. She elected not to tell Spencer that Simon was one of her grandmother's dearest friends.

>>>

"Simon Fletcher? What on earth are you talking about? *Our* Simon?" Granny Grace grasped her long strand of pearls as if it could steady her.

"I'm afraid so," said Cat. "Fletcher Green and Howell is up for a multimillion-dollar contract with the state to rebuild the Seattle Ferry Terminal. David Green is their senior partner, but he's near retirement and ready to sell off his remaining partnership shares. After her tremendous success with the Puget Place Hotel project, Nina superseded Simon as the heir apparent."

"Simon's the majority partner now, but if Green had sold to Nina, she would be," said Granny Grace.

"Exactly," said Cat.

They were quiet a moment, the sound of the grandfather clock in one corner of the Daring Damask Den ticking loudly. Then Cat, who still felt schooled by Detective Spencer on this point, said, "I'm sorry I didn't think to talk to Nina's coworkers. The police followed up on the firm more than I did, and they have several staff members who can attest to arguments and tension between Nina and Simon."

"Well, I certainly didn't suggest it, either," admitted her grandmother. "Maybe we both had a blind spot there because we know Simon."

"Maybe," said Cat. "We'll have to see about this evidence linking him to the crime scene. I mean, maybe he and Nina had a professional rivalry, but so what? That doesn't make him a murderer."

"Still," said Granny Grace. "Simon never mentioned it to you, did he?"

"He only spoke well of Nina, except to say that she was very private about her background, her family history."

"And now we know why," said her grandmother.

"Do you think Simon is capable of murder?" asked Cat.

Her grandmother gave her a look that made her sorry she asked.

>>>

Detective David Spencer brought Sam Waters in for further questioning. They had conducted a cursory interview with him at the beginning of the investigation, at which point he'd claimed not to have ever met Nina Howell.

"You want to tell me why you lied to my officers?" David demanded.

Sam looked at Cat, as if for assistance. But she knew her role here. She dropped her gaze.

"Look, Detective," said Sam. "I'm sure you can understand the bind I'm in. I had nothing whatsoever to do with this murder, and I didn't want to cause upset to my family—"

"The bind you're in? How about the bind you put your victim in?" He laughed wretchedly. "You *sicko*. I don't give a shit about your reasons for lying. You were just protecting yourself."

"I won't stand for this," said Sam. "You have no right to speak to me this way."

David laughed. "You think I care that you're some hotshot what ... radio celebrity? Dude, didn't anyone tell you that radio's dead?"

A month ago, Cat would have cringed at this. But her admiration for Sam had pretty much dissolved. David was right about one thing: Sam was a self-interested coward not to come clean about his affair with Nina. His silence had only put distance between the killer and justice.

"We're going to interview Mrs. Waters, too," said David. "Don't think we're keeping your dirty little Warehouse secret."

Sam smiled, and that surprised Cat. "There's no secret," he said. "Cassidy knows about my membership there. I have her permission."

David laughed again. "No shit? Wow. How'd you work a deal like that, man? If I proposed to my wife that I take up membership in some sex club, she'd divorce me so fast…"

"Wait a minute," David continued. "If she already knows about your nasty nights over at The Warehouse, then why did you lie to my officers? Because you didn't want us to know you killed Nina."

Sam looked caught, but not for the murder. For something else.

Cat butted in. "You violated your deal with Cassidy, didn't you?"

The green eyes that had once seemed so charming gazed at Cat in defeat.

"Yes," he said. "It was supposed to be just sex, since Cassidy doesn't like any of that kind of play, won't let me so much as wrap her wrists with a silk tie. Our sex life died even before we got married, but we have a family together. The kids..." He ran a hand through his hair, dark brown like the bannister in Granny Grace's house.

"You weren't supposed to choose a partner in there," said Cat. "You weren't supposed to fall in love."

Sam nodded.

>>>

Detective Spencer got a warrant to search the Waters residence, and forensics would try to find evidence placing Sam at the scene of the crime.

In the meantime, Cat had access to the full case files, and certain details surprised her. The first was that the autopsy revealed no signs of sexual assault. Nina's death had been a murder, clean and simple, and the method was suffocation. Second was that at the scene they'd found a pink Gerber daisy in a pot. *Not a dandelion*, she noted. A pink daisy?

For weeks, the daisy had been merely a case oddity. No florist tag or any other identifiers gave it a trail, and there were no fingerprints on it besides Nina's. But finally, during a follow-up interview with Simon to ask him about the fights his staff reported took place between him and Nina, a detective noticed a bit of dirt on the floor between Simon's desk and a filing cabinet. It was out of the way of the vacuum cleaner. She bagged and tagged the sample, and it was a match for the dirt in the potted daisy found at the crime scene, down to the mineral content of the soil and its biological signature, which was as good as DNA evidence. The lab also determined that the plant had likely been purchased at a high-end grocery store in Belltown, near both the hotel and Simon and Nina's office. The store carried the plants for only that one week as a special; they were not a regular item.

Staff members reported seeing the pink daisy on his desk, so he couldn't deny it had been in his possession.

"I must've purchased the same plant as the one you found at the crime scene," he'd told them when giving his statement to police. David asked him to produce this plant, but Simon said it died, and he'd tossed it.

That didn't look good. Still, thought Cat, looking up from the report, this didn't prove Simon killed Nina. It hadn't been enough to charge him, either.

The police had failed to find Simon in the hotel footage. They didn't have a clear shot of Nina's hotel door, so they had flagged a few figures on camera who'd been at least close to her room near the time of the incident, and none resembled him in height or build.

Cat looked at the eight images printed out and hanging in a workroom at the downtown precinct. Two people she recognized from her own review so far of the security tapes: a hipster guy in thick glasses and a knit cap and a woman in a business suit. None stood out as a known suspect; none of the figures caught on camera resembled anyone in Nina's family, including her father.

Next she reviewed the forensic evidence from the crime scene. They'd found clothing fiber and several strands of hair that were not Nina's, but everything else was clean. The hair didn't match any DNA on file in police databases. One strand was a match for Robin's hair, but since the married couple lived together, it didn't necessarily prove Robin's presence at the crime scene, as the hair could easily have been attached to Nina's clothing. But Cat felt good about having this evidence on file. They could use it to place their suspects at the scene, which is what David was trying to do with Sam. The hair wasn't a match, but he was looking for the clothing fiber now.

Cat had shared with him everything they had on the case, from Robin's continued insistence that Sam was the killer to the information that Doreen had divulged.

She and Granny Grace had two operating theories. The first was that either Cassidy or Robin had killed Nina, as they both had motive. Robin could have done it to punish Nina for cheating on her with Sam. Originally they'd thought Cassidy could also have been motivated to punish a cheating spouse, but in light of the

291

new information Sam provided, Cat had amended Cassidy's motive to killing Nina to eliminate a perceived real threat to the marriage, since Nina and Sam had been in love. The second theory was that Nina's father did it, perhaps to keep Nina from telling the truth about her past, though that didn't seem likely, as he would certainly know the statute of limitations had long since passed for his crimes, and Nina had already broadcast the truth to everyone in Waco who cared.

With the information Sam provided and with Sam in a holding cell where he wouldn't be able to confer with his wife, the homicide captain gave them permission to bring in Cassidy for questioning. The woman had quickly ponied up a lawyer, who accompanied her to the interrogation room.

David's demeanor with Cassidy was a far cry from what it had been with Sam. In a tone verging on sweet, he said, "Mrs. Waters, I'm so sorry for the trouble this has caused you."

Cassidy merely nodded. Her lawyer had a pen in one hand that he twirled as if it were a baton.

"It must be upsetting to learn that your husband has been cheating on you," said David. Cat found his approach interesting. He already knew she knew, but he was going to see how she would play it.

Cassidy's response was to say nothing.

"I mean, especially *that way*," said David. "In a kink club. What if someone recognized him?"

Cassidy glanced at her lawyer, who nodded. "Detective Spencer," she said, "my husband never took his mask off in that club. People there knew him only as

292

Mr. Master." She shrugged it off and laughed, as if to say it was all very amusing but hardly to be taken seriously.

"What if he killed her?"David met her shrug with a more dramatic version of his own, his hands held out to his sides. "Would that have been part of your … what was it, exactly? Some agreement the two of you had? Because if murder was part of it, then you're an accessory to the crime."

Cassidy opened her mouth to say something, but her lawyer put his hand on her arm. "Don't respond to that."

She pursed her lips.

"Look," said David. "I don't give a shit about whatever kinky arrangement the two of you had. I'll leave that for *The Stranger* to suss out."

His referral to the weekly tabloid known for its snark caused Cassidy's eyebrows to rise in alarm, so he must have hit a nerve.

David continued. "But if you and your sicko husband get off on killing people, I'm taking you down."

Cassidy touched her lawyer's arm. "You represent me in this case, not Sam," she said. "Don't forget that." Then to David, she said, "Other than giving in to my husband's demand that I let him express his kink within the confines of The Warehouse, I had nothing to do with his activity."

Cat couldn't stay silent any longer. She caught David's eye, and he nodded. "How'd you know about the mask?" Cat asked.

A bit flustered, Cassidy responded, "Well, we did discuss that. Neither of us wanted him outed. I know that cell phones aren't allowed in there, but you can never be too careful. When he went back recently, he saw one of our kids' teachers! Can you imagine? It's a good thing she didn't recognize him through the mask. I swear, is everyone in Seattle but me secretly into kinky sex?"

Cat treated her question as rhetorical, even though it was one she'd asked as well. "Did you think about getting a divorce?" she continued. "I mean, why stay married to a man who wants something you don't?"

"Sam and I have a great affection for each other," said Cassidy. "We signed on for life. Commitment means something."

David broke in. "You've got to be kidding me, lady. Your husband can't keep it in his pants, and you're trying to tell me commitment means something."

"We have young children," said Cassidy. "Neither of us wanted them to be raised in a broken home."

Cat remembered one of Sam's "Watershed Moments" monologues about the rise in divorce and how that had contributed to the dissolution of society. She had only half-listened at the time since she had no connection to the subject matter. Her parents were still together, and other than a vague feeling that she was lucky in that regard, the topic hadn't resonated with her. But she now remembered Sam questioning how quickly and easily people seemed to file for divorce. He had actually called on his listening audience to take their commitments more seriously and to go to great lengths to work out their differences before calling it quits.

David shook his head. "As a child of divorced parents, I find this 'broken home' thing patently offensive, by the way." He laughed. "Look what the two of you have accomplished. Oh, no, your home's not 'broken.' But your kids will be raised in a fucked-up household, in the full spotlight of the public eye. Congratulations."

The detective got up and left the room.

Cat followed him into the break room, where he poured himself a cup of coffee.

"Those two sure are a pair," he said. "Today's modern marriage. Give me a break."

"You don't think it can work, these 'open marriages'? It's kind of a thing here in Seattle."

"It's just your garden-variety cheating, dressed up as something else."

"But Cassidy gave her consent to it."

"Yeah, and look what it got her."

"You have a point."

She watched as he walked away with his coffee, still shaking his head.

Cat wondered what the forensics would reveal. They'd taken a hair sample from Cassidy, but she was a blonde. And the sample found at the crime scene was brunette, and not dyed.

Chapter Twenty-Three

Cat ran through a field toward the trees on the edge of a clearing. If she could get there, she'd be free of them.

But as she approached the clearing, more of them appeared. One after the other. Pennington James, Pennington James, Pennington James. An army of them, all alike. They came after her, stumbling, their eyes blank, their mouths twisted in gruesome poses.

Wait a minute, *she thought.* I must've slipped into Uncle Mick's dream.

Luckily, she knew what to do. At this point in her dreamslipping practice, she was an old pro at ejecting herself from someone else's dream when she didn't want to be there. She concentrated on the image of her uncle in his studio bedroom in the Adorable Amber Attic, and when he ran to charge at a James zombie with a two-by-four, she stood still with all her might, ripping herself away from him.

Agh, she muttered, sitting up in bed. Then, still feeling groggy, she jogged up the two flights of stairs to the top of the old Victorian and through the door to Mick's studio. There he was, still fighting zombies, thrashing under the covers, his legs and arms kicking.

"Uncle Mick," she cried out, touching his shoulder. "Wake up! You're having a nightmare."

"Wha—?" he opened his eyes. "Cat? What are you doing here?"

"I slipped into your zombie nightmare. I didn't

mean to, believe me."

"Oh," he said, sitting up. "Sorry. Not that I can help my dreams."

"I'm sorry I slipped into it. I guess my forcefield didn't work." With Mick, she'd taken to setting up a glowing forcefield in her mind between herself and him before falling asleep every night. But this dream must have busted through it.

"I'm pretty tired of these nightmares." He sighed.

She noticed he had dark circles under his eyes.

"Maybe you should get some counseling."

"Right," he said.

She sat down next to him. "I get it, though. I mean, James did a number on you. He's lucky you didn't kill him."

"I still might," said Mick.

"I think you are," Cat said. "In your nightmares. Over and over and over again."

"Maybe I *need* to have these dreams, then," he said. "To, you know, work it all out."

"As long as you don't beat up poor Cecily."

"I know," he said.

>>>

After falling back to sleep and finally getting a bit of rest, Mick awakened, and the first thought on his mind was that maybe his grand-niece was right. He'd availed himself of counseling services before, back when he and Candy broke up for the last time and he'd taken too hard to drinking. He wasn't opposed to the idea. The

297

dreamslipping thing meant he could never be totally open with any therapist, but he wanted to talk about his own dreams, not someone else's. So maybe it would work.

He had no idea how to find a therapist in Seattle, so he waltzed into the den where Cat was mulling over her case board and asked her to help him.

"I'm kinda busy with this case," she said, trying to beg off.

"Aw, come on," he said. "It'll take you two minutes. Me, a lifetime."

"Fine," she said, rolling her eyes. "You elderly people just can't do anything related to computers for yourselves anymore."

"That's not fair," said Mick. "Pris is pretty good."

"Then why didn't you ask *her*?"

He shrugged.

Mick watched as his grand-niece pulled up a registry of "wellness practitioners" and began to check out the Web sites of each one.

Which immediately sent her into hysterics. "Oh, God," she said. "This one says she will 'help you find your spirit animal in order to live the life of purpose and divine animal ecstasy your soul craves.'" Cat grabbed his arm. "Please see her, Uncle Mick. Please. I could use the comic relief."

"You're not helping," he said, taking the laptop from her. He scrolled down, and one entry caught his eye.

DREAM THERAPIST, it said. I ACCESS YOUR DREAMS IN ORDER TO HELP YOU INTERPRET THEIR MESSAGES AND

OVERCOME YOUR FEARS. He turned the screen back toward Cat.

"Is this perfect for me, or what?" he asked.

"Perfectly ridiculous," Cat said. "Who seriously calls herself a 'dream therapist'?" She clicked the link and searched around till she found the therapist's credentials.

"She does have a PhD in psychology, so she's at least legit. Or she was before she came to Seattle and lost her mind. It looks like she moved here from Chicago."

"Cool," said Mick. "I'll give her a try."

"Have fun with that," Cat said as she got up and left the room.

>>>

The police had already taken a hair sample from Simon Fletcher to compare to that found at the scene of the crime.

Grace wanted to speak to him herself, less as a PI and more as a friend. Cat had given her a copy of the interrogation transcript, and what she'd read there troubled her.

As she pulled up to their lovely home in Siddhartha, she noted a few straggly weeds growing out of the top of Simon and Dave's green roof. She rang the antique school bell that functioned as their doorbell, and Simon greeted her, his manner subdued. He led her into the grand foyer and through to a crescent-shaped couch by a fireplace that had gone cold. They were alone; the house was still. Grace wondered where Dave was.

"Grace ... my God," Simon said, taking off his

glasses and rubbing his eyes. He put the glasses back on and peered at her through them. "You know I didn't kill Nina."

"Of course," she said gently. "But what accounts for that pink daisy?"

Simon stood up, sticking his hands into the pockets of his pleated chinos.

"I want to hire you to find the real killer," he said. "Whatever Robin's paying you, I'll double it."

"Well, as it so happens, I'm not at the moment working with Robin. She fired us because we couldn't pin this on Sam."

"Then let's make it official," he said, offering his hand. "I'm trusting you, Grace. With this handshake, our contract begins, but you can send over the paperwork later."

Grace rose to take his hand. She held it. "You're not going to tell me anything until client privilege is in effect, are you?"

"I just want you on my side first." He smiled. "You're a force to be reckoned with. You and Cat both."

She let go of his hand. "I'm afraid this contract between us won't include Cat. Conflict of interest. She's consulting with the police now."

"Damn," he said, though it was uncharacteristic of him to swear. "This is risky, if she's working for them, but you're my best option."

"It'll be okay," Grace said.

He sighed, sitting down. "One day this man walked into our office. It was late, and really nasty outside, the rain coming down harder than usual and the fog thick enough to cover the neon market sign."

"He was well-dressed and … how can I describe him? Disarming. He carried a potted plant. A pink Gerber daisy."

"He introduced himself as Norm, and I thought of that character on *Cheers*, the one whose name everyone shouted when he came in."

Grace felt chills run down her spine. "Norm" had to be Nina's father, Norman Jeffers.

"He was such a sad sack, Grace," Simon said, as if he were pleading with her to see Norm the way he saw him that night. "Standing there in his wet trench coat, the flower seeming silly and out of place against the super-serious backdrop of my firm's offices."

"He wanted to leave the flower in Nina's office, but then he said she'd just throw it away…"

Simon choked up, placing his fist against his lips as if he didn't want to have to tell her what happened next. "I felt so bad for him."

"He must have been a good actor," said Grace.

Simon looked at her, surprised. "Who? Norm?"

"Her father," she said.

"So you know who he is."

"Yes, and I'm beginning to get an idea of *what* he is, too."

Simon broke down. He slipped off his glasses and buried his face in his hands. "I had no idea—I was just trying to help her—"

"What did you do, Simon?"

"I invited Norm—Nina's father—back to my office. I had a little brandy there, a gift from a client. We opened it, and we talked. He was charming, Grace. I don't know how murderers are supposed to present themselves, but this guy didn't at all seem like a psycho. I … liked him, right off."

"Did he ask about Nina?"

"Yes, but only in the way you'd expect an estranged father to inquire about his daughter. He said he'd been a gambler, left her mother in debt. He said he wanted to make it up to her."

"You didn't…"

"I agreed to help him find a way back to Nina."

Grace couldn't help herself. "But that was Nina's choice to make, not yours."

He stood up again, began to pace in front of the fireplace. "I'd just gone through that self-actualization workshop, you know, the one sponsored by The Greenpoint Channel? They help you face all your demons, and if you're estranged from friends or family, that means getting square with them. So I wanted to help Nina, truly."

Grace did know the organization and had been through a couple of their programs herself. "Is that what the two of you were really fighting about, as witnessed by your staff?"

"Oh, not really. Nina hid it well, but I could tell she was struggling with something personal. She'd blown it with a mutual client of ours, and since our senior partner thought Nina walked on water, I knew this would come back to bite me instead of her. So that's what she and I had a fight about in front of the staff."

"But why the hotel?" she asked.

"Nina was my friend; you know that. I was concerned about her. When I saw she was struggling, I took her aside and asked if she needed anything. She looked me square in the face and said, 'Just one day to myself, when I can be Nina without all the demands.' So I encouraged her to check into the hotel. It's a lovely place, and she could stay there any time she wanted, the owners were so pleased with her work."

"Simon?" Grace asked. "You weren't angry at her for eclipsing you at the firm? Tell me the truth."

"Oh, angry doesn't describe it," Simon replied. "I'd been jealous of Nina, beside-myself-green-with-envy, for a long time. But the Channel helped me see that wasn't serving me at all. I mean, what's the point of being jealous of someone else's talent? So I let that go and worked harder at my own practice. Greenpoint really helps, Grace. I'm so glad you recommended it."

She'd forgotten she had. That must have been ages ago, though Simon was often slow to accept new ideas. Of course now she wished she hadn't. "So how did you get the plant there without being seen or caught on camera?"

"What?" he responded. "Oh, right, the security cameras. Even as an architect, I forget there are cameras everywhere, watching us. I use the gym at the hotel— they gave all of us access cards as a thank-you for our work on the project, but I'm the only one who's taken them up on the offer. Nina was partial to Rain even though it's not as close. So, anyway, I'm used to entering the hotel through the gym. I guess there aren't any cameras there. Or maybe that footage wasn't included

303

because that route is on the other side of the hotel from Nina's room? I don't know. I always enter through the gym-side door."

"But there were no fingerprints on the pot..." Grace said, just as she realized why, spying Simon's leather gloves sitting neatly in a tray on a table in the foyer. "Nina's father is from Waco, where it's already warm this time of year. He didn't think you'd be wearing gloves. He thought your fingerprints would be all over that plant."

"That's right, Grace. Through some divine intervention, I never touched that plant until I picked it up the day of Nina's death. And that was on the way to the hotel. I'd already put my gloves on."

"How did the dirt get onto the floor?"

"I don't know," he said. "All I could figure is that the cleaning staff knocked into it."

"How did Nina's father get into the hotel? Why isn't he on the footage?"

"I don't know," said Simon.

"I think Norm Jeffers meant to set you up all along," said Grace.

Simon narrowed his eyes. "I think so, too. I can't believe I fell for his act."

"I have a feeling people have been falling for that man's act all his life."

>>>

Forensics found a match to Simon from one of the hair samples, and that combined with the soil and the staff testimony was enough to charge him. Granny Grace was beside herself with upset, convinced that Simon was innocent. Cat reacted when her grandmother told her about Simon's Greenpoint Channel experience and how it led him to try to help Nina.

"I read about that stupid cult in college," she said. "We studied them as part of my criminal-justice curriculum. Their policies are totally irresponsible. They think it's a good idea for a rape victim to sit down to dinner with her rapist. Not only is that dangerous, but they effectively shift the responsibility for the crime back to the victim again, which is exactly where the perps try to put it in the first place."

"Now, Cat. They help so many people. You have no idea."

"Don't tell me you've drunk their Kool-Aid, too," said Cat.

Her grandmother bit her bottom lip and looked away.

"What, Gran?"

"Apparently I'm the one who recommended The Greenpoint Channel to Simon, originally. Though I don't really remember that conversation. It must have been years ago…"

"Seriously?"

"Yes." Her grandmother stuck her chin out. "The Channel helped Simon get over his jealousy."

"And what did it help you do?"

"Get out of my own way a bit … stop blaming others for my unhappiness."

"Really, Gran? Because you've never done those

305

things. They probably just reinforced what you already knew."

Her grandmother was quiet after that. Cat could see she'd given Granny Grace something to consider. Grace opened her mouth as if to say something and then stopped.

"I can't believe Simon needed the Channel to get past his jealousy," said Cat. "Why didn't he turn to the Church?" She remembered attending Mass with him at the beautiful old cathedral on Capitol Hill.

"You mean like you did when Lee died?"

Now it was Cat's turn to remain quiet. She'd let her spiritual life lapse, at least its formal aspects. She'd turned away—not toward—the Catholic Church when Lee died.

"Well," Cat said eventually, changing the subject, "Simon needs to come clean to the police about all this. It won't look good that he withheld information until they charged him, but there's nothing we can do about that."

"What if he ends up taking the fall for it?" Granny Grace said, her voice quavering. "He's been set up, but there's no evidence that points to Nina's father for the murder. All we've got is the fact that Nina was trying to talk to family members."

"Yeah, even if Doreen is willing to go on the record about what Norm did to her, that's a leap to murder."

"For some jurors, it would be a short leap," her grandmother said hopefully. "But that might not even be admissible in a murder trial. Oh, Cat. I'm so afraid for Simon."

Chapter Twenty-Four

Grace convinced Simon to tell the police everything, but that wasn't easy. He'd quickly lawyered up, and the attorney told his distraught, panicked client it was a bad idea. It took leveraging Simon's Catholic guilt to get him to agree to tell the police what had happened with Norman Jeffers.

"If you'd been truthful about this from the start, you might not be charged, Simon," Grace pointed out. "And we might've caught Nina's killer by now. You owe her that."

Detective David Spencer and Cat were bent over a table strewn with video stills when they brought Simon in for another conversation. Before they whisked the stills into a folder, Grace caught that they were from the hotel footage. Probably trying to spot one of the current suspects in them, she surmised.

"So you're Cat's grandmother," David said as he shook Grace's hand. "I see the apple doesn't fall far from the tree."

Cat had obviously come clean about the relationships between everyone, to spare them that bit of awkwardness, not to mention David's reaction should he be blindsided by them. "I'll take that as a compliment," Grace said.

"Now, listen, I'm not happy about how messy this is with everybody being friends with—or related to—everyone else here," David said. "I'm only overlooking it this time because Cat came up with the cross between Nina and Sam, and my team missed it." David cast an accusatory gaze over a couple of detectives who sat at the other end of the table with laptops.

"Mr. Fletcher," he continued, turning toward Simon. "We're all eager to hear about this new insight you have that will prove your innocence. Please, sit down."

Simon told them how he set Nina up to meet her father.

But after Simon's reluctance to go to the police all these weeks, and despite being shielded by a lawyer, by the end, he broke down in tears and contrition. "It's all my fault," he kept saying. "Nina's dead because of me."

His lawyer jumped in, telling him to stop talking.

"I hope you understand that was not a confession," the man said to David. "My client is experiencing heavy emotional strain."

Grace pressed her fingernails into the palms of her hands to keep herself from crying. Thinking of her granddaughter's anger over The Greenpoint Channel, Grace felt she'd had a hand in Nina's death as well. Her heart hurt with regret.

<<<

Cat, David, and the others pored over the images from the hotel footage, including that from a third camera, but it was trained on the workout rooms and not the entrance to the gym, so Simon's story couldn't be verified.

However, they got a break when the detective

who'd found the soil in Simon's office, a young redhead with a perpetual steely look, pointed out to everyone, using a 3-D map she'd created of the hotel, that a person could have come in from any of three entrances, traced a path through the hotel, and made it to Nina's suite, all the while dodging the hotel's cameras, if that individual followed a narrow path through the center and up a stairwell, avoiding the elevators.

David cleared his throat. "Good work, Detective Galen. This will help prosecutors nail Fletcher for the crime, since it doesn't matter that we don't have video proof he was there. Plus, he's an architect who worked on the design, so he could have known about the blind spots."

Cat remembered the fake obituary Nina had created for her father. It listed his occupation before retirement as chemical plant manager.

She raised her hand.

"Yes?" Galen waited.

"Due to the value and potential danger of the chemicals, chemical plants always boast robust security," said Cat. "The victim's father, top of the list of current suspects, worked his entire life as a chemical plant manager, so he'd be very familiar with the way security cameras function—and their limits. He might have known how to slip into the hotel undetected. Then all it would take was a knock on Nina's door, and he'd be in."

David continued. "As Ms. McCormick reminds us, the last shoe to drop here is following up on Fletcher's story about Howell's father. We're assuming Fletcher's grasping at straws, trying to finger someone else, but I don't want any surprises, from Ms. McCormick or anyone else. Let's get this case cleaned up."

David reached out to authorities in Waco, who said they'd assist in the investigation on their end, first checking with the state park authorities on Jeffers's alibi. Cat had already run a check on the passenger logs at Sea-Tac around that time and come up empty. Nina's father had either driven to Seattle or traveled under another identity, which would be difficult to do by air due to the heightened security. But ten days away from home gave him enough time to drive it round-trip, assuming three ten-hour days of driving each, there and back.

Cat had a feeling that leaving the case in the hands of the Waco authorities would get them nowhere. She remembered her grandmother's report from Doreen that Jeffers was in thick with the force there, and she told this to David. "Can't we go to Waco ourselves?"

He snorted. "You think that's how it works? We jet around the country following every lead?"

"This is more than a lead," she said. "Simon's innocent. Jeffers is a serious suspect, along with Cassidy. And Robin."

"It's not looking good for your nana's buddy, and you're biased," David growled.

Cat had grown used to his gruff manner, but she worried he was in too much of a rush to close the case. "Right," she said. "Meanwhile, Jeffers sits there at his ranch or whatever, plotting his next child victim."

"Knock it off," he said to Cat. "I don't need this."

"He killed Nina."

"Prove it," said David.

"Send me to Waco."

"You and your grandmother had ample opportunity to travel to Waco on your own before you dragged your whiny ass into my precinct."

Cat flinched. Was he even allowed to talk to her that way? She looked around at the other detectives, who busied themselves with their paperwork and laptops.

"You're just a contractor," he continued. "If you want to go to Waco, go. But it'll have to be on your own dime."

Cat grabbed her jacket and walked out.

>>>

"You've cost us not one, but two paychecks on this case so far," her grandmother said in answer to Cat's question.

"I asked you if we could go to Waco."

"And I'm telling you to see what we can do from here first."

"But we have to catch Jeffers."

"Yes," said her grandmother, who sat cross-legged in the Yoga Yolk, a small but cheery room painted yellow on the second floor of the old Victorian. Cat noted she had not made it back to full lotus since the fall and wondered if she ever would.

"Well, why can't Simon send us? You're working for him now. He wants you to vindicate him."

"Simon and Dave financed you in the beginning," Granny Grace said calmly. "Remember? Your startup costs. Your first case, one that required travel to St. Louis. Now he's a friend in need. We should be offering him our

311

services for free."

Cat felt humbled by her grandmother's words. "You're right, Gran. So let's use our savings. Or charge it. We can't catch Jeffers from here."

"Yes, we can." Her grandmother made the sound *ohm* and drew the forefingers and thumbs on both her hands together to touch, in *chin mudra*.

"But how?"

"You are a dreamslipper," she finally said, moving into a pose whose Sanskrit name Cat couldn't remember, but it sounded like Johnny-something. "You've been remote-dreaming, not to mention dreaming the dreams of the dead, through this whole case. If anyone can catch Jeffers from here, it's you, Cat."

"But, Gran…"

"Ohm," intoned her grandmother, followed by a chant in a singsongy voice. "Namah shivaya shanti…"

Feeling simultaneously challenged and defeated, Cat lay on the empty mat next to Granny Grace. *Dead body pose*, they called it. She closed her eyes, let go of her tense breath, and searched for Nina in the darkness behind her eyelids.

"Will you join me in sun salutation?"

Nina stood before her, clothed in gray from head to foot. A fog blew around them. Cat could see Nina instead of looking out of her eyes as if she were in Nina's head. So this was Cat's own dream, not one of Nina's.

The woman's arms floated up above her head, and she bent backward. Then she swooped down, bringing her head to touch her knees.

Cat followed her movements, syncing her sun salutation poses and breath with Nina's. "Ohm namah shivaya shanti," Nina chanted. Cat picked up the chant, their voices rising and falling in unison.

She remembered Granny Grace telling her what the chant meant: "Taken literally, it's 'I bow to Shiva,' but they don't mean it like bowing down before the Lord. Shiva is your inner self, your deep consciousness."

Cat felt a burning sensation in her chest and looked down. Between her breasts her skin glowed crimson, and it seemed as if her heart vibrated at a high frequency. She stopped chanting.

"Nina," she said. "What's happening?"

The red glow left her chest, filling the room as if it were a small sun, and then it disappeared.

Cat was alone. But she heard Nina's voice, this time chanting something else. "Through Him, with Him, in Him. In the unity of the Holy Spirit, all glory and honor is yours, almighty father, forever and ever…" Cat knew this chant from her Catholic masses, the high point of the Eucharist, when the offering becomes the body and blood of Christ.

"Help me, God," Cat said. "Show me the way."

Nina reappeared, right in front of her. She stuck her finger into Cat's chest. "You still don't get it, do you? He's not out there, like a parent who's supposed to protect you. He's in here, inside you."

Cat gazed down at the place where Nina's finger touched her chest, which glowed again.

Nina walked away from her, into a thick fog. She turned around once. "Parents don't always protect you, anyway," she said. "Sometimes they might as well be dead."

313

Cat woke up to find her grandmother sitting quietly next to her, watching.

"You fell asleep as soon as your head hit the mat," Granny Grace said. "You must be exhausted."

Cat rolled to her side and pushed herself to a sitting position. "I just had the strangest dream."

"You did?" her grandmother brightened. "Was it one of Nina's?"

"No. It was my own, but Nina was there."

"Anything insightful?"

"Yes," said Cat, who, realizing something shocking, got to her feet. "Gran, did you ever find anything else out about Nina's mother?"

"No, just that she disappeared sometime in the early nineties, and no one's seen her since. I don't know if she's living under an assumed name or what, but I haven't been able to find her anywhere."

"What if she's not missing?" Cat said. "What if she's dead, and Jeffers killed her all those years ago?"

>>>

Cat didn't feel she could go to Detective Spencer with her new theory about Nina's mother. But she felt like making a federal case out of this anyway, and she knew exactly who could help her.

Special Agent Roger Strickland answered on the first ring.

"Hello," she said. "This is Cat McCormick—"

"Cat! It's so nice to hear from you. How are things

in Seattle?"

"They're good. Granny Grace sends her regards. It was awesome working with you in Miami. I miss it."

"Likewise. I'm just sorry we couldn't lure you into the FBI. But you must have called for some other reason, though a guy can dream. Do I detect an ulterior motive?"

"I've got a situation here that involves a possible two-time murderer, his daughter and ex-wife the victims. But the wife would be a cold case, missing-persons, from twenty years ago. The daughter was killed here in Seattle recently. The father lives in Waco."

"Hmm…"

"There's something else. The father might be a serial pedophile."

"Was his daughter one of his victims as a child?"

"Yes."

Cat heard nothing on the line for longer than a minute, other than Strickland's breathing.

Finally, he cleared his throat. "I'll look into this and talk to my superior. Send me the details. I'll give you my email address."

After taking down the information, Cat said, "We have to move quickly. He knows we're looking at him for the murder, and he might also know we're aware of the abuse."

"I understand the situation," he said.

"Thank you," said Cat.

"On the contrary," he replied. "Thank *you*."

Something about his manner made her giggle, which she quickly stifled since it seemed inappropriate.

"By the way, Cat?" he began but paused.

"Yes?"

"Had any good dreams lately?"

This surprised her, and she wasn't sure how to respond. "Yes, as a matter of fact, I have."

"Me, too," he said. "I didn't understand what they meant until you called, so thank you."

At that, he hung up.

What he said gave her goosebumps.

>>>

The "dream therapist" held office hours in a converted Craftsman bungalow. Mick walked up to the door and, noting the sign that said PLEASE REMOVE YOUR SHOES INSIDE, was glad he wore slip-ons. Another sign instructed him to come in if the door was unlocked, and it was, so he did, toeing off his shoes and placing them in a tray left by the door for this purpose. Another sign inside the foyer read, NEWLY ARRIVING PATIENTS, PRESS DOORBELL. He looked around and finally found a doorbell on the far wall, nearly obscured by a trail of hanging vines that seemed to wrap around the room. He traced the plant's origin to a pot next to where he stood.

There was nowhere to sit, so he rang the doorbell and tried to stand to one side and look relaxed.

After a few minutes, the door opened, and a woman stepped out, with another woman behind her, holding the door. He recognized the latter as the therapist, Dr. Arfa Faruqi, from her business-profile shot.

"Thank you so much, once again," said the

patient. She placed her hands in prayer position and bowed her head, with her hands toward the middle of her face. "Namaste."

The therapist returned the gesture. "Namaste, Alice."

As the patient stooped to put her shoes on, Faruqi turned to Mick. "Thanks for waiting. I'm sorry I don't have a seating area, but sitting is the new smoking, so most of my patients now prefer to stand anyway."

Mick pondered this. *Sitting is the new smoking.* "No problem," he said, because there was nothing else to say.

"Let me clear the room, and we'll begin."

The other patient left, shutting the front door, just as Faruqi closed her office door again. Mick wasn't sure what needed to be cleared out of the room—until he smelled burning sage and thought of Pris's habit of "clearing" a room using a bundle of the herb lit enough to produce a thin stream of white smoke.

Soon she let him into her office, where a slight, sage-scented haze permeated the air. She sat in a tall leather armchair, and he took the couch opposite.

"Now then," she said. "You told me on the phone you'd like help with some symptoms of post-traumatic stress disorder. You mentioned nightmares. Are there any other signs?"

Mick wondered why she didn't have a pen and notebook. The only other therapist he'd seen in his life had taken notes as Mick talked. It unnerved him to have her full attention. She had deep brown eyes, like a coyote's.

317

"I don't think so," Mick said. But then he thought of how angry he felt all the time, even though Pennington James had been sent to jail. "Except being pissed off. But that's not PTSD. That's your average American."

She smiled. "Before we begin, do you have any questions for me?"

Mick cracked his knuckles nervously and thought about it. "I guess, just one. How exactly do you work with dreams?"

She smiled again. "That depends on how you'd most feel comfortable working with them. We can talk about your nightmares. That's a start."

"Okay," he said. It seemed pretty standard to him.

"When did the nightmares begin?"

"In Miami," he said. "After I stabbed an artist in the ear."

Faruqi didn't even bat an eye. "Tell me the story," she said, and he did.

>>>

Cat realized in the rush of events on the case that she'd been rude to her friend Bethany. So while she and Granny Grace waited, their hands tied, for either the authorities in Waco to make an arrest or the FBI to step in, she made a happy-hour date with Bethany.

Now that Sam had been pretty much cleared of the murder, Cat wondered if it was time to come clean about her true vocation. So far she'd avoided any specific questions about teaching by steering the conversation

318

away from "shop talk." But she couldn't keep that up forever.

Over rum-and-Cokes at the Rusty Pelican, Bethany conquered the first awkward topic of conversation, and that was their chance encounter at The Warehouse.

"So I guess I'm outed as a puppy player," she whispered, looking down. "I wasn't sure if you wanted to hang out again after that."

Cat smiled, her heart going out to her friend, especially because truthfully she was more worried about Bethany feeling betrayed by her teaching lie than she was about the fact that her friend liked to feed her dates treats. "It figures you'd be the one holding the leash."

Bethany laughed, relief softening her features. "You should see me with a rolled-up newspaper."

"Hey," Cat said, shrugging her shoulders. "Whatever works, right?"

"Right," said Bethany.

They were quiet a while. Then Cat asked, "But how'd you, you know, figure that out? It's not like … spanking, I guess. Like people know about that kink."

"I'm pretty out there, huh?" Bethany sipped her drink. "I guess I sort of identified with the classic dominatrix, but only to a point. I want to be the one in control, but I don't want to inflict pain, exactly. I want to cuddle with my pets. I like the affection. It's fun to pretend."

Cat noticed Bethany blushing.

"Sorry to pry," Cat said. "You don't have to explain yourself to me."

Bethany pushed Cat's shoulder. "What about you, mystery girl? What were you looking for at The Warehouse? And what's up with taking your *grandmother* with you?"

Cat weighed her options. If she told Bethany the truth that she'd only gone to The Warehouse to investigate Sam, she'd be drawing a line between herself and her friend. On the other hand, she liked Bethany, so honesty was probably the best policy. Maybe she could strike a middle ground.

She cleared her throat. "I have something to tell you. I'm not who you think I am."

Bethany's eyes grew as wide as the lime halves floating in Cat's glass.

"I'm not really a teacher," she continued. "I'm a private investigator."

Bethany put her glass down with a clatter. "Shut up."

"It's true," Cat said. She pulled out her wallet and showed Bethany her PI license.

"No way," Bethany said. "That. Is. So. Cool."

Cat smiled. "Thanks."

"Wait," Bethany said. "You weren't, like, investigating me or my date, were you? Following us? To *The Warehouse*?"

Cat laughed. "No, no. That was just a coincidence. Well, except you gave me the idea to go undercover there. So thanks for that."

"Awesome," said Bethany, and then the truth registered. "Oh, I get it. So you were just at The Warehouse on business." Her face went pink again.

"That's true," said Cat. "But you know? I didn't want to leave. I might go back sometime."

"Cool," said Bethany. "Anyway, enough with all that. It's like our friendship went from zero to sixty there pretty quick. Let's talk about something else. So why were you in San Fran?"

Cat blanched; she still felt sorrow at the loss. "I went down to visit my long-distance boyfriend, thinking I'd finally hear an expression of love. But instead, he's moving back to New York, where he's from."

"Oh, *no*."

"Yeah, and he said it was because things weren't working out for his career in San Fran, but I think he's in love with someone back home."

"So … things are over between you two? How'd you leave it?"

Cat sipped her drink. "It was okay. It turns out I didn't want to follow him to New York anyway."

"I'm sorry," said Bethany. "But you must've been into him to keep going down to San Fran to see him. So that's got to hurt. Tell you what: The next round's on me."

"Thanks." Cat smiled. Sometimes that's all you wanted from a friend: Not an attempt to fix your problems but just a little sympathy. The free drink helped, too.

Chapter Twenty-Five

She ran through a stand of mesquite trees, the sound of her own breathing loud in her ears. She inhaled the scent of the mesquite, like the cigarettes Susie used to chain-smoke all those years ago.

At the thought of "Susie," Cat wondered whose dream she'd slipped into this time. She looked at her hands. They belonged to a man. She remembered that Susie was Nina's mother's name. Could she have picked up Norm Jeffers's dream? She decided to remain in the dream.

He had to get to the burn circle, on the other side of the trees. The place where they land. He wanted to go with them, let them take him away. He was different from all the rest; they would see that. They would make him one of them.

She could hear the dogs barking behind her now. But ahead of her, the line of trees ended. A white light bathed the spot. She let her eyes travel up the beam to the dark underbelly of their ship, a row of green lights glowing. She launched herself into the light, and it carried her upward. To freedom.

Cat woke, so the dream must have ended. She puzzled over it for a moment. She couldn't shake the feeling of escape driving Jeffers as he dreamed, the sweet ecstasy of getting away.

He's going to try to escape, she thought. *Norm Jeffers is going to try to leave.*

She grabbed her cell phone off the bedside table. It was only three a.m., but she tried Special Agent

Strickland's work line anyway.

He didn't pick up, of course. She left a message: "Special Agent Strickland, this is Cat. I-I have reason to believe Norman Jeffers will soon try to leave the country, maybe cross the border into Mexico." She included her cell number and asked him to call her back.

She leapt out of bed. There was no way she could let that man get away, not after all this. She dressed in a hurry and then ran upstairs.

Gently, she awakened her grandmother, who seemed to expect her.

"I was in the dream, too," said Granny Grace, rubbing her eyes. "I saw it. I think I slipped into it because you were already there."

"I need to go to Waco," Cat said.

"I know, Cat. But that man seems dangerous. What are you going to do? Make a citizen's arrest?"

Her grandmother was right, she knew. She couldn't just go charging down to Texas without a plan, without evidence, without a reason to get him arrested.

She especially couldn't go down there to snoop around unarmed. She wished she'd followed up on her desire to possess a gun. Now it would take days, if not weeks, for her to get a permit after fingerprinting and a background check.

"What are you mulling over?"

"The need to get a gun."

"Cat, you know how I feel about them. I've made it all these years as a PI without one."

"Tell that to Lee."

Her grandmother, who'd remained in bed, threw

her covers off and stood up. "That's not fair."

Cat had been pacing around her grandmother's room. She stopped. "I'm sorry. I know. It's just—what if the cops down there don't get him in time? Or at all?"

They were both quiet.

"Greg," said Cat suddenly, thinking of how the man had just started his own security firm. "Greg Swenson."

"I-I'm not sure that's a good idea—" said Granny Grace, but Cat was already on her way out the door.

>>>

She couldn't find Greg's home address, but since privacy was his business, that didn't surprise her. At least she had his card, which listed his work address.

It was only 4:30 a.m. by the time she got to the Swenson Security office, so of course it was empty. Cat set up camp under a blue awning. She'd stopped for coffee at a drive-thru on the way over and thanked her lucky stars she lived in a city where you could get a great cup of joe before the sun came up. She kept checking her phone to see if there was a text from Special Agent Strickland. She'd left him her cell number, and since he was on East Coast time, he would get her message soon, if he hadn't already.

By the time Greg showed, she still hadn't heard from Strickland. It was 6 a.m., and the gray sky had lit from behind without any actual sunshine showing through the thick blanket of clouds.

"Well, whaddya know? It's Cathedral

McCormick." Greg flipped his jacket hood down, acting as if that would help him see her better.

"Hi," she said, letting his use of her full name pass. "I have kind of an emergency situation on my hands, and I wonder if you could help."

He frowned. "So that's all I am to you, then. Someone to come to for help."

Cat stood up. "Hey, I never asked you for help with the Seattle PD. You offered."

His face softened. "That is true." He dug into a pocket for his key and began to unlock the door. "Come on in," he said. "Tell me what's happening."

Just then she felt her phone buzz. It was a text from Strickland. *Sorry, Cat. Politics and bureaucracy. Be careful. Keep the nightmares confined to sleep.*

She puzzled over the cryptic dream talk once again as she followed Greg past a water dispenser and into a sparse office filled with boxes and not a single decoration on the walls.

Following her gaze, he said, "We just moved in."

"So here's the situation," Cat said, getting right to it. "I need your help catching a perp."

"I'm not a PI," Greg said. "I provide firms with private security."

"He's in Waco, Texas," she continued. "And he's about to flee to Mexico. We have to get him before he escapes, or he gets away with murdering his ex-wife and his daughter, not to mention child abuse."

Greg stared at Cat as if she'd lost her mind. "Who *are* you?"

"I've already alerted the Feds, but they're not

moving fast enough."

"And you think I can do what the FBI can't? Maybe you just missed me," he chuckled.

"The Waco police have been brought into the investigation, but they might be coopted by the perp."

"It's really cute the way you keep saying 'perp.' I bet you got that from hanging around my buddy Spencer."

That stopped Cat's train. "David told you I went to work with him?"

"Yeah," said Greg. "And that you walked off the job."

"I was 'just a contractor,'" said Cat, emphasizing David's own words with air quotes. "But he wasn't doing shit."

"Now, now," said Greg, amused. "Not everybody flies around by the seat of their pants like you do."

She glared at him. "Are you going to help me or not?"

He sighed. "Why don't you start from the beginning?"

>>>

After Cat left, Grace got up and went back to her list of addresses. A few things still bothered her about Nina's family in Texas. First was that she'd been unable to reach Tina Jeffers. The fact that Norman Jeffers seemed to be thinking of fleeing to Mexico without her, if his weird UFO metaphor was to be taken at face value, indicated she might be more receptive to Grace's approach. The second was that Dr. Berkman hadn't yet come around about sharing more information from Nina's sessions.

It was still only five a.m. in Waco, though, so she busied herself with more research. She double-checked her sources concerning Susie Charles, Nina's mother, who seemed to have dropped off the face of the earth in 1993. There was a record of her birth, but no death, and no trace of her after that year in the form of a license or rental or credit card. She wondered if Nina had tried to file a missing persons report on her. She might not have had any success getting help in Waco, or maybe she was angry for a long time if she thought her mother had abandoned her. Filing one all these years later would be difficult.

By six a.m., which would be eight a.m. Waco time, Grace decided it was late enough to make calls on a weekday.

First, she tried Doreen Jeffers. "Hello, Doreen. This is Grace again."

"Hi, Miss Grace. You just caught me between shifts. Hey, I guess you got the cops all riled up down here," she said. "My cousin says they brought Uncle Norm in for questioning. But they let 'im go already." Doreen's voice conveyed this was business as usual. Grace noted that they hadn't held him very long, certainly nowhere near the allotted seventy-two hours.

"I wonder if you could help me," said Grace. "Do you or your mother have a cell number for your Aunt Tina?"

Doreen scoffed. "*I* don't. But let me see if Mama does."

327

It sounded as if she'd set the phone down, so Grace waited through muffled sounds of movement on the other line, and then she picked up again.

"Here it is." She read off the number.

Just as Grace thanked her and was about to hang up, Doreen said this: "He did it, didn't he? Killed Nina."

"That's for a jury to decide," said Grace. "But I hope justice is done where your uncle is concerned."

"Me, too," said Doreen. "But I'm not gonna hold my breath."

As soon as she ended the call, Grace dialed Tina's number.

"Hello?" The woman breathed heavily. It sounded as if she were outside, with the wind whipping past her phone mic.

"Hi, Tina."

"Who is this?"

"Someone who just wants to help."

"Are you kidding me? I don't think anyone can help me right now. You have no idea. *Who is this*?"

"This is Grace. I tried to call you before, but you hung up on me."

"The private investigator?"

"Yes."

"You should be the one out here instead of me."

"Where are you, Tina?"

"Out in the pasture." More wind sounds. "Looking for bones. Human bones, that is."

Grace saw red, her pulse quickening. "Tina, I think you're in danger. You need to get somewhere safe. *Now*."

"One of the dogs brought this bone up onto the porch one day. I swear it looked like a femur."

"Tina, please. Go to a family member's house. You need—"

"—I asked Norm about it, and he said it was from one of his father's old medical skeletons. His daddy was a doctor, so who am I to act suspicious? But now the cops come here asking him about a murder. It got me thinking. I need to know—"

"Tina!" Grace heard a man's voice cry. "What the hell are you doing out there?"

Grace put her cell phone on speaker, and taking it with her, she ran to her landline, thanking the Buddha, Shiva, Yahweh, Jesus, and John Lennon's soul, may he rest in peace, that she still had one. She put her cell on mute and dialed 911.

"Looking for one of the dog's toys!" Tina yelled back.

Still breathing heavily, the woman kept talking to Grace. "I mean, it's one thing to get handsy with the girls —in my experience, that just comes with the territory of being female. But I don't want to live with some murderer."

It was a tough situation to explain, but Grace got through to the dispatcher, who contacted the Texas Department of Public Safety.

She took her cell off mute while the 911 operator stayed on the line with her. "Can you repeat that, Tina?" said Grace. "My phone cut out."

"The bone!" said Tina. "The dog had a bone that didn't look like it came from an animal. Looked like a leg

329

bone. My husband said it was from his daddy's medical skeleton. But why was it dirty, like it had been buried? I think there's more out here."

"Tina!" came the man's voice again, only louder, as if he were closer.

"What do you want, honey? I'm just looking for the dog's toy."

"I swear, that man won't let a person out of his sight for one second…"

The call ended.

"Hello?" said Grace. "Oh, no. I've lost her."

"I've got what she said recorded," said the dispatcher, whose voice was kind. "I'll relay that information to the state police. Are you okay? Do you have someone you can talk to? You're probably shaken up."

"Oh, I'm okay," said Grace. "This comes with the territory when you're in my line of work."

"I know what you mean," the woman said, and Grace realized her dispatcher must handle crisis after crisis. That would take a special kind of person.

"Is there anything else I can do for you, Ms. Grace? I'm sorry, but I need to clear the line now."

Grace said no, but in the silence after she hung up, she wanted to rush off to Waco as well. She felt impotent just sitting there, waiting for police in a distant state to do their jobs.

>>>

"What makes you so sure he's about to make for the

border?"

Greg asked a very good question, one she would ask if she were in his shoes. But Cat couldn't answer him without explaining her dream.

She thought about it for a split second. What a relief it would be if she could just say, *Because I'm totally psychic, and I can see people's dreams, and I was in Norm Jeffers's dream last night when he dreamed of taking off in a UFO, which for him probably means making a break for it.*

Yeah, that would go over well.

"Why *wouldn't* he?" Cat said instead. "He knows the Seattle PD is onto him. Even if he's still thick with the Waco force, they can't keep this thing clamped down forever."

Greg sighed. "There are a million reasons why I shouldn't help you. I just started this business. I can't afford to pick up and leave. I'm not qualified to do anything down there that would help you. You don't know what you're getting into, and you're not even armed. This guy could be seriously dangerous. I mean, hell, Cat. It's Texas. I'm sure *he's* got guns."

Cat stared at him. She could tell he wanted to help her.

"But you keep looking at me with those eyes."

Cat continued to gaze at him.

"I'm also trying to date you, not be your personal bodyguard."

"I know, but isn't that kind of hot?" Cat shot back.

Greg looked at her as if she'd scratched a needle across a record. "This guy sounds like a real asshole," he said. "If there's one thing I find fulfilling, it's making assholes pay."

"Great," said Cat. "When's the next flight to Waco?"

>>>

When Grace called Cat to tell her what had happened with Tina Jeffers, she got her granddaughter's voicemail. She did her best to relay the events in her message, and she also texted Cat for good measure. But where was that girl?

Remembering how she'd muttered "Greg Swenson" when she left, Grace searched him online but came up empty. Didn't Cat say he'd just opened a new security business? Maybe it was too soon to show up in registries.

By this point, it was getting close to seven a.m., and Grace was exhausted. She lay down, and before she knew it, she'd slipped into another dream.

She held fast to the bit of mane at the base of the neck as the headless horse galloped through the woods. Where its neck stopped was a soft, mounded-over spot covered in hair instead of a head. She touched the spot, delicately. The horse galloped faster. She squeezed her legs tighter around its body to keep from falling off. Even more quickly, it ran, and then it launched itself up into the sky. She steered the horse with her hands, pressing to either side of where its head should be to turn left or right.

The dream shifted, and she stood on a yoga mat in front of a mirror. Annie Lin looked back at her through dark eyes, her

*white hair swept into a tight bun. Grace admired the woman's
bird-like qualities in the reflection, her wiriness so different
from her own plump strength. She grabbed her foot and kicked
it out behind her while continuing to hold onto it until she saw
her foot rise up behind her head like a crown. A beautiful
standing bow. "Grace," she said into the mirror.*

*Grace felt so startled by hearing her name spoken, that
it woke her up, knocking her out of the dream.*

Shaking the sleep off, she got up, went back to her study,
and turned on her computer. While she waited for it to
boot up, she checked to see if Cat had texted back. It was
nine a.m. now, but still no word from her.

She logged onto Facebook and scrolled back
through her last chat session with Annie Lin. It had
already been a couple of weeks since they'd professed "I
wish" and "Me, too" to each other, with nothing from
either of them since then. She wanted to blame it on the
case, but the truth was she'd been both rattled by the
intimacy and intent on savoring it, and she wondered if
Annie felt the same way.

Hi, wrote Grace. *Sorry I haven't been here to chat. It
would be lovely to talk to you on the phone.* She left her
number and then switched over to Annie's page, where
she saw only one recent entry, a photograph of a painting
on an easel in Annie's studio. It was the headless horse
from the dream.

Chapter Twenty-Six

On the four-hour flight to Dallas, Cat filled Greg in on the rest of the details of the case, leaving out the dreamslipping aspects. She traced the path of the various suspects, from Sam to Robin and Cassidy to Simon and now Nina's own father.

"It's amazing how everyone who knew a person can suddenly look like a suspect when that person dies," he said. "It makes me wonder how'd they'd investigate if I were murdered."

"Yeah," Cat said, elbowing him softly. "Maybe they'd think *I* killed you."

"You're killing me right now with your humor."

"Sorry," she said. "Seriously, though, you're right. Most women are murdered by men they know."

"Thanks for the depressing statistic."

Cat gazed out the window at the patchwork quilt of farmland far below. "How are Sherrie and Ruthie?"

"They're doing well now. Sherrie works at a day care, and she loves it. Ruthie goes to school and then comes to the day care afterward. It's a nice setup."

"That's great," said Cat. "I guess Canada never panned out?"

"I was only trying to help her cross the border to get further away from Jim," said Greg. "But he'll be in jail for awhile."

"You don't still think of him as a threat, do you?"

Greg stared out the window past Cat, to the

clouds beyond. "Not really, no. Ruthie writes to him behind bars. But he's not her real father. He was only her stepfather for a short time. It's time to move on."

"It's sad, though," Cat said.

"You might be interested in this," he said, obviously changing the subject. "Sherrie's dating my friend Boyd. Remember? I hid her and the kid at his house in Tacoma."

"Aw, that's great. He seemed like a sweetheart."

"Yeah, but you know, she's my sister. I'm still getting used to the idea."

"Sherrie's lucky to have you as a brother," said Cat.

Greg looked at her in that moment, and a warm current passed between them. He smiled. "So far, I'm glad I came. I mean, if you're going to sit there and compliment me like that."

"Where are they living?" asked Cat, sidestepping the moment.

"Seattle's gotten so spendy," said Greg. "They can't afford a decent place on their own, not anywhere even close to the city center. So they're living with me."

"I know what you mean," said Cat. "If Gran hadn't bought her Victorian in the early nineties, there's no way we could live in Seattle."

"She was good to get in early," Greg replied. "Probably paid—what? Thirty grand or so for that place? She could sell it for a million now, maybe more."

The thought jangled Cat. She knew her grandmother's investments had suffered considerably in the crash, and she'd only somewhat recovered over the

335

last few years. The woman's retirement was tied up in that house. Not that Cat expected her grandmother ever to stop working. She'd already long since passed retirement age.

"We should map out a strategy," Cat said, getting back to business. "I think we should pay a visit to Nina's therapist. He's the linchpin in this whole affair. We get him to unlock the details of Nina's treatment, and maybe we have cause to arrest her father."

They discussed the case for the rest of the flight, and when they landed in Dallas, Cat turned on her phone to find a text from Special Agent Strickland. *In Waco. Working with SP.*

There were also several messages from her grandmother.

"Oh, my God," Cat said aloud. She updated Greg as the two of them ran to catch their connecting flight to Waco. She had just a minute to text her grandmother before the puddle jumper rolled onto the runway.

Headed to Waco with Greg, she wrote. *FBI there. Promise I'll stay safe.*

>>>

During the short flight to Waco, Greg quizzed Cat on firearm safety, going over how much experience she'd logged at the shooting range. Cat didn't ask, and he didn't offer specifics, until they'd picked up a rental car and loaded their bags into the trunk, at which point Greg opened a small case that held his own pistol, plus one extra.

He handed her the extra. "This is for self-defense," he said. "It's actually designed to protect against home invasion. Hence the name: The Protector."

She took the gun, its stubbiness a good fit for her small hands. The rubber grip would cushion against recoil.

"Is this a .357 Magnum, or a .38 Special?" she asked.

"So the lady knows her weapons," he said, offering her a holster that would fit under her jacket. "It's a .357. And you're not permitted. So take this baby out only as a last resort." He shut the trunk and looked up at the sky. "God, I so hope I don't regret this."

She jumped behind the driver's seat and threw him her phone. "Navigate me to the Jeffers home," she said. "The address is right there."

The house was out of town a ways, set on a hill surrounded by acres of pastureland, with a few copses of mesquite trees dotting the landscape. As they got closer to the house, they saw a variety of law-enforcement vehicles clogging the circle drive, from a couple of state cars to a lone Waco PD car and an unmarked car that looked like FBI.

They parked and got out. "Should we just go in?" asked Greg as Cat charged toward the door. "I mean, maybe you should knock."

Cat compromised by knocking as she opened the door. "Hello," she called out. "This is Private Investigator Cat McCormick and..." She looked at Greg, who shrugged. "...Her partner, Greg Swenson. We're entering the house."

"Great timing!" called out a voice she recognized as Special Agent Roger Strickland's. "We're all back here in the den," he said. "Or is this a family room? Mr. Jeffers, what do you usually call this area of the house?"

"Our contractor called it a 'great room,'" came the reply just as Cat rounded the corner at the end of the entryway, which opened into a space with a tall, cathedral ceiling, skylights, and an enormous rock fireplace at one end, a rifle on display above the mantel. Two sets of French doors revealed a view of the valley beyond.

"It's marvelous the way they design living areas now, isn't it?" continued Strickland. "We used to crowd each domestic function into small rooms, separated by walls. You cooked in the kitchen, carried the food over to the dining room, and ate it there. Then you retired to the living room to watch TV. Now, look at this. It's all one big space, with each activity flowing into another. But this isn't how the house looked originally, is it, Mr. Jeffers? You paid for a costly renovation somewhere down the line, and what a good choice! I bet the feng shui is much improved."

A state trooper cleared his throat as if to signal he'd like to get on with the business at hand. Undeterred, Strickland turned to Cat. "It's wonderful you could join us, Ms. McCormick, though I must say I'm surprised."

He stepped over toward Greg and extended his hand. "Pleasure to meet you, Mr. Swenson. You're quite a change from her previous partner, I must say."

Greg took his hand firmly but didn't respond. Cat kept an eye on Jeffers, who sat quietly, subdued. There were two state troopers in the room, and they seemed both wary and a bit confused. The Waco sheriff and his deputy, the only ones besides Jeffers who'd taken seats in the great room, were obviously annoyed. Strickland's partner, a woman taller than he was, hung back but appeared nonplussed by the proceedings.

Strickland gave a round of introductions, as if they were at one big social gathering. Then he slipped into interrogation mode, likely picking up where he'd left off when Cat and Greg had arrived.

"Mr. Jeffers," he said, "could you please, for the benefit of our newly arrived guests, tell us where your wife Tina is again?"

"She went to the store," he said. "To pick something up for dinner."

"So Mrs. Jeffers is at the store running a rather routine errand," Agent Strickland said, with a flourish of his hand. "And you'd rather we get a warrant before searching your house and property."

Jeffers leaned back in his chair, raising his arms up above his head and clasping his hands behind his neck. "I don't mean anything by it, of course, Special Agent Strickland. But a man can't be too careful when it comes to his property rights and the federal government. After all, this *is* Waco." He gave them all a wide grin. An attractive man with graying temples but otherwise still sporting a full head of mostly brown hair, he seemed to possess a self-confident charm.

Cat noticed the bottoms of his jeans were wet and dirty, as if he'd been digging, but tried to wash it off.

"It seems our local authorities have not seen cause

to provide a warrant," Strickland said.

"We'd rather wait till Tina returns," said Sheriff Everly, a burly man whose cowboy boots either got a daily polishing or were just for show. "We'd like to question her about this conversation she allegedly had with your PI in Seattle, especially since the 911 operator was patched into the call with neither Tina's permission nor knowledge."

"That's unfortunate," said Strickland, taking his phone out of his pocket to check it for messages. "While I understand the wariness of government overreach—there certainly have been abuses of power that would lead one to take that stance—your skepticism in the face of evidence of foul play has cost us valuable time. Hopefully, it hasn't cost anyone her life."

"What about the state patrol?" asked Cat.

Strickland glanced at a tall black man, his head shaved beneath the sharp line of his hat, who must have been the senior SP officer.

The officer cleared his throat. "We tend to defer to Waco PD in situations like this," he said.

"Seriously?" Cat said. "We're waiting for a warrant, when Tina might be out there dead and buried in this psycho's pasture, right along with his first wife's bones?"

"That's right," said Special Agent Strickland. His eyes met hers with a fire of understanding that Cat could feel in her gut.

"Well, you'll have to arrest me for trespassing then, because I'm going out there," said Cat. Greg grabbed her by the shoulders to stop her.

Jeffers jumped up. "You do that, missy, and I've cause to defend myself." He made for the rifle over the fireplace.

Sheriff Everly put his arm out. "Norm, wait…"

Cat drew her new pistol out of its holster and pointed it at Jeffers, who responded by reaching for his rifle. But Greg was faster. He put the old man in a chokehold, his arms flailing for the rifle still hanging over the mantel.

Strickland walked over, took the rifle down, opened the chamber, and emptied the cartridges onto the floor.

"Mr. Jeffers," he said. "You exhibit a blatant disregard for gun safety. One should never have a loaded weapon out in the open in one's home. In light of your recklessness, I'm going to have to ask to see a permit."

"It's out in the barn," said Jeffers, pointing across the field to a structure on the edge of the property. "But I'll go get it just to shut you up."

"That'd be terrific," Strickland said brightly.

"Tell this monkey to let me go," said Jeffers.

Cat didn't hear the rest of the conversation. She ran out the back door before anyone could stop her.

She started moving across the field, looking for signs of disturbance in the ground.

Soon Greg had caught up to her. "Gutsy move, Bonnie," he said.

"Who's Bonnie?" she asked as she held her hand over her eyes to cut the glare. She gazed out at the Jeffers's property, looking.

"You know, 'Bonnie and Clyde'?"

341

"Nope," said Cat. She spotted a clump of fresh earth on the ground and went to it.

"How are you a PI and have never seen 'Bonnie and Clyde'?"

She picked up the dirt. It was moist, as if it had recently been turned over from deep in the ground, well below the dry, dusty surface. "You go that way," she said, pointing Greg to the left. "I'll look over here."

Out of the corner of her eye, she saw Jeffers, flanked by two officers, making their way to the barn on the other side.

>>>

"Mr. Berkman, a woman's life may be in danger. I'm talking about Tina Jeffers, Nina's father's wife. I'm going to have to ask you to rethink your patient-doctor confidentiality agreement where Nina Howell is concerned."

Grace had the psychologist on the phone again, and this time, she needed answers.

He sighed. "It's really not up to me..." he said, but his voice sounded weak.

"Did Nina ever think her mother had been murdered?"

There was a long pause.

"Yes," he finally said.

"Did she suspect her father as the murderer?"

"Yes," he said. "But not until just before Nina was ... killed. That was something she only began to suspect when she came down here for a visit. She told me during a session we had here, in person."

"When was that?"

"Just before her death."

"What tipped her off?" Grace asked.

"You have to understand, it's not as if she got some 'tip.' Nina was a trauma victim. She put things together when she came back here after so long away. Talking to her cousins, seeing the physical place where she grew up. And by that time, she'd exhausted all her efforts to find her mother."

Grace wondered why Nina had never come to her about the search for her missing mother. Maybe that's how private she felt she had to be, not even telling Robin what she was doing. She didn't feel she could trust anyone with her truth. Yet she couldn't let it go, either.

"Did she see her father when she was here? He says they had a visit."

"I wouldn't call it a visit." Berkman sighed. "She didn't want to have anything to do with him until she suspected he might have killed her mother. Then she decided to confront him."

"What happened?"

"She described him as slick and manipulative. I've only ever seen the man in person a few times, at a distance, in public here in Waco. But according to Nina, he's very convincing. He of course denied everything, deflecting it all back on Nina, trying to make her mother out to be the crazy one."

"Did it work?"

"Nina was incredibly strong," he said. "She'd done all the work in therapy, demanding a successful life

343

for herself. She stood up to him. She had her moment, to tell him everything she'd held back for so long."

He paused for moment. "If she weren't now dead, I'd say the confrontation had been very good for her."

"Mr. Berkman, what was the nature of your work with Nina, originally? What was her trauma?"

Mr. Berkman cleared his throat. "How will this help you keep Tina Jeffers safe? By the way, Nina believed that woman knew about her father's crimes and chose to look the other way."

"I think we're talking about at least two different crimes here," Grace said. "We think Nina may have been right, that her father killed her mother all those years ago. And I'm afraid he may harm his current wife, too. She might have uncovered the remains. When I was on the phone with her, she mentioned one of their dogs finding what looked like a femur."

"Oh, God!" said Berkman. "That's horrifying. Nina's past literally won't stay buried."

"No," said Grace. "It won't. The more you can tell me, the better. It's been hard to piece together Nina's story because of how private she was."

"Nina first came to see me when she was a student at Baylor," Berkman began in a resigned but cautious tone. "She'd moved out of her parents' home even though it would have been better, financially speaking, to live with them while she earned her degree. But she said she couldn't stand it, that she had to get out. She begged her mother to leave her father, but nothing she did or said produced results. I can't comment on the state of Nina's mother since she wasn't a patient of mine, and I only know her through Nina's interpretation. But Nina often said she wished she could give her mother some of her own strength."

"But Nina was also her father's victim."

"Yes," said Berkman. "She had all the symptoms of post-traumatic stress disorder back then. She described having terrifying nightmares every night, ranging from the metaphorical to the literal. Her startle response was high after growing up in that house with Jeffers. It affected her health. She suffered from severe depression and suicidal ideation."

"What was that you said about metaphor and Nina's nightmares?"

"It's often the case with trauma victims that their dreamtime imagination reiterates the traumatic event to them in some other guise. For Nina, it was often the trope of alien abduction."

"But Nina did not herself believe that she'd been abducted by aliens."

Berkman laughed bitterly. "Not at all. She was too smart for that. She'd done the research even before she got to college, read Carl Sagan and others who debunked alien conspiracy theories even if they were sympathetic to them. I suspect it might have been a kind of bizarre gaslighting on the part of her father. Maybe he fed that alien nonsense to her to refocus her complaints about what he himself was doing. Her father reads like a classic sociopathic narcissist. They're very good at deflecting the blame for their actions onto their victims."

"Nina was a smart cookie," said Grace.

"You knew her, personally?"

"Yes, and her wife, Robin. We shared a social circle here in Seattle."

"How has Robin taken Nina's death?"

"Not ... well."

"I feel some responsibility here... I think I might have made a mistake. A few weeks before her death, Nina called me for some check-in therapy, for help with a decision she had to make ... about whether or not to leave Robin. I cautioned her against it..."

"Did you know about her affair with Sam?"

"Yes."

"I see," said Grace. "Well, I'm sure you just wanted to help. It sounds like you did, too. What would Nina have done without you? You said she was suicidal, and I know she's had some serious struggles even recently."

"It's just—the thinking on fetishes—it's a tough one for psychology. There's been a lot of debate.... We know choosing a BDSM lifestyle isn't a result of childhood abuse. But some theorists still aren't convinced, especially in feminist psychology, that a person's need to play in those dynamics isn't a result of internalizing a misogynistic cultural framework. Nina talked to me about her desires even in the beginning, twenty years ago. I don't think I helped her. I thought they were part of her programming, from her father's abuse. I was wrong."

>>>

Cat kept a razor-sharp lookout for more clumps of dirt.

She'd gone down several paths in the shin-length prairie grass only to have to backtrack. She cast a look toward Greg, whose head was turned down, intent. He hadn't found anything, either. Norm Jeffers and the others were just now making it to the barn.

She didn't think Jeffers was a very smart man. Devious, yes. But not the intellectual his daughter had been. Cat tried to put herself in his muddy boots. What would he have done out here, so quickly before the cops showed up? She closed her eyes, felt the breeze on her face, the sun warm on her black jacket. She saw a shovel in his hands, Tina hit on the head. But where was her body? Where were the bones?

Then she heard it: the gurgling of a stream.

Cat jogged toward the copse of mesquite trees. They'd grown up because of a seasonal stream running through a section of the property. That's why his jeans were wet, not because he'd tried to wash off mud. She saw fresh tracks, drag marks. She waded into the water, and there, pressed down beneath several small boulders, was the body of a woman. The water was clear, like glass, and Cat could see her face. Her eyes were pale blue, vacant, her mouth open. She stared out at Cat as if to reproach her for being too late.

Cat felt bile creep up her throat. She turned to the side just in time to vomit into the rushing water.

Greg ran up behind Cat and touched her back. "You okay?"

She nodded, wiping her mouth.

"I'll go back up, get them to arrest Jeffers."

But gunshots rang out in the distance. Cat looked

347

at Greg, and at the same time, they both said, "Jeffers." They ran in the direction of the barn.

It was a long way off, and by the time they got there, Jeffers was already in handcuffs, a bloody tourniquet on one leg. Sheriff Everly held a shop rag on his own arm. It was also soaked with blood.

"It seems Norman here discovered the limitations of his friendship with local law enforcement," said Special Agent Strickland. "They're apparently unwilling to aid and abet a suspect's escape, especially after he's drawn a weapon on them."

Cat saw the car in the barn, a load of boxes and luggage pressing up against the windows. "He tried to flee," she said. "He was going to try to make it to the border."

"We found his passport in the glove box," Strickland said. "But I doubt he would have made it. Not today."

"There's a woman in the creek out there," said Cat. "Dead. Killed recently."

Strickland nodded. "This isn't how you wanted to go, is it?" he said to Jeffers. "Tina was your wild card, and you didn't even know it."

Then he turned to Sheriff Everly and his partner. "If that's Tina Jeffers in that creek, her blood is on your hands."

Then a glance over at the two state troopers. "And yours, too."

>>>

348

Cat showed them to the body. It seemed as if every law-enforcement officer in the state of Texas had descended upon the Jeffers ranch. They'd brought dogs, which were sniffing the pasture for another buried body.

She stood away from the crowd, fighting tears as they pulled Tina Jeffers from the creek. Special Agent Strickland walked over to Cat, offering her a handkerchief.

"Just like in my dream," he said, but it sounded as if he were talking to himself instead of her.

She took the handkerchief, noting the monogram *RS* in blue embroidery. She shivered as the breeze caught her damp clothes. "Your dream?"

"Déjà vu," he said. "I have it often, powerfully. Except that I'm able to remember my déjà vu dreams before they occur in real life, as it were. That's partly why we're all here. This case wouldn't necessary warrant FBI involvement on its own, not on the evidence you related to me. Luckily, my track record at the Bureau speaks for itself. People listen to me, and they don't know I'm listening to my dreams."

"That's remarkable," she said. "Yeah, and I wondered..."

"That's not how it is with you, though, is it?" he asked.

"How do you mean?"

"My sense is that you're a powerful dreamer." He peered into her face, his eyes squinting against the sun. She focused on the sharp line of his part, his hair neat despite the breeze. Next to him, Cat felt wild and amateur.

When she didn't reply, Strickland continued. "The dogs are going to find bones, at least if my dream was correct."

"I didn't screw anything up, did I?" Cat asked. "I mean, by trespassing."

"No," said Strickland. "You certainly did not. My superiors granted the warrant as soon as you walked out onto that pasture. At least that's how it will read in my report." He showed her the screen on his phone. "I have the warrant in hand right now."

She breathed a sigh of relief.

He smiled at her. "If it weren't for you, Cat, I think Jeffers would've got away. My dreams weren't enough. You filled in the missing pieces."

Chapter Twenty-Seven

Cat woke in the Grand Green Griffin feeling better rested than she had in a long time. Her sleep had been thankfully devoid of dreamslipping, and her own dreams contained satisfying images of Jeffers behind bars.

She stretched, got out of bed, and went over to her dresser. Opening the top drawer, she took out The Protector. Greg had given her the gun as a gift once they got back to Seattle. "This fits you better than it does me," he said. "You should keep it."

She still needed to get a permit. She weighed its heft in her hands. It was small and did fit her well. Of course, she hadn't fired it in the Jeffers case, so maybe her grandmother was right that she didn't need one. She put it back and closed the drawer.

The house was quiet. Her grandmother wasn't up yet, and Mick was likely at Cecily's; he hardly ever slept at home anymore. Cat stuffed her arms through her robe and wandered into the kitchen to make breakfast.

>>>

She sharpens her beak on the rock, making a sawing sound. Beak shavings fly. She closes her eyes.

Her wings, mighty, taking her up into the air. She lands on the roof of his station. Her worm, such a fat, juicy thing. Her beak pierces the top, splits it open like a tin can. There he is inside, the worm, squirming in his chair. It's not neat, though. It's bloody when she eats him. She hears the crunching of bones, feels the blood run down her feathers. Die, die, die, worm. This is for Nina.

Grace woke with a start. She launched herself out of bed and ran downstairs, barefoot. But Cat wasn't in bed. Grace smelled bacon and padded into the kitchen.

"Good morning!" her granddaughter called out. "I hope you're hungry, because I've gotten all domestic on you this morning."

"Cat," Grace said, panting. "I think Robin's going to try to kill Sam."

Grace described her dream. The intensity of the hatred she felt from Robin was still with her, the woman's murderous rage reverberating in her chest.

"I'll call over to Robin's," Cat said, grabbing her phone off the kitchen table. There was no one home.

"His live talk show starts in twenty minutes," Cat said, looking at the clock.

"We've got to get over to his station," Grace said. "I just know she's going after him."

They dressed in a hurry and jumped into Siddhartha for the drive across Lake Washington to the Eastside.

As soon as they pulled into the parking lot at the station, Grace recognized what had been Nina's car, a sleek black Mini Cooper. She turned to Cat, who put her hand on her grandmother's arm.

"Gran," Cat said. "Let me go in first, okay?"

"But—"

"No buts," Cat said, taking off her seatbelt. "I'm

352

armed." She dashed to the door before Grace could protest.

But Grace followed close behind as Cat burst through the station door and searched for Sam.

"Stay back," her granddaughter commanded. Grace could see she held a gun in her hands.

"Cat, please—" Grace said. She felt in her heart that this was not the way. But her granddaughter ignored her.

They came upon a bank of glass windows, with the "on air" room behind them. Sam sat behind a desk, padded headphones covering his ears. Robin stood before him, holding a knife up over her head. A staff member outside the room was already on the phone with a 911 operator.

"...I think she's lost it," the woman said. "She's got a knife..."

Grace watched as Cat made eye contact with the staff member, nodded, and then opened the door. Grace slipped into the room after her.

"I'm sorry, Robin," Sam said. "I didn't mean for you to get hurt. You and I, we're the same. I loved her, too."

"You killed her! You animal!"

"Robin," said Cat, drawing her gun. "Put down the knife."

Robin looked at Cat. "What are you doing here? You were supposed to catch him! You didn't do your job, so I have to do it for you."

"No, Robin," said Cat. "I did my job. Sam's innocent. Nina's father murdered her. He killed her mother, too. We caught him, down in Waco. It'll be all over the news today."

Robin faltered. "Her father...?"

"That's right," said Cat. "We found her mother's remains buried on his land."

"You're just trying to trick me," Robin said. "He's got you under his spell, too."

"No, she's not," said Grace, her voice calm. "We would never try to trick you, Robin. You and I are friends. That's why I'm going to tell you the truth. I saw your dream this morning, the one of you as a bird, eating wormy Sam here."

Robin dropped the knife, and Cat rushed in to grab it. The staff member went to Sam. "We're still on the air," she said.

"You saw my dream?" asked Robin.

"Yes," said Grace. "And Cat here saw Nina's dreams. It's time to stop denying the truth, Robin."

"Wh-what truth?" A tear slid down Robin's cheek.

"Nina wasn't happy with you," Grace said. "She cheated on you with Sam. She wanted to leave you."

"No," Robin said. "No. No. I gave Nina everything." But then her face crumpled in despair, and she began to wail. "Why? Why didn't she love me anymore?"

Grace went to Robin, who collapsed in her arms. "I'm sorry, Robin," Grace said. "It hurts so much when love dies."

The police arrived soon after, and they took Robin into custody.

Grace and Cat talked briefly to Sam, who was

shaken but otherwise fine.

"What's your plan for the future?" Grace asked him. "Are you and Cassidy going to forge a new agreement, as it were?"

Sam looked from Grace to Cat, and back again, and then sighed. "I don't know. We're … reevaluating where we stand."

When they got back into Siddhartha to head home, Cat said, "Whoa, Gran. That was some crazy stuff in there. You know half of Seattle—okay maybe a quarter, the conservative quarter—just heard you say we're both, like, psychic dreamers?"

"The few who believe it won't get it right anyway," Grace said with a laugh. "It was the only way to startle Robin out of her fog of denial."

"I thought I had the situation under control." Cat still had the gun in her hands. She looked at it as if trying to understand it.

"Would you have shot her? If she'd charged at Sam?"

Cat ejected the clip. Grace could see the gun hadn't been loaded. "I don't have any ammo. I still have to get a permit."

Grace breathed a sigh of relief. "Well, you might've told me that. Where did you get it?"

"From Greg. It's a gift." She stowed it in a holster under her arm.

Grace smiled, leaning her head back as Cat started the car. "You're finding your own way, aren't you? It's not my way, but it's yours. It'll work for you as mine has for me."

"Thanks, Gran. I-I don't know if I want to keep it or not. The gun."

"It's your decision."

"What about your anti-gun policy?"

Grace put her seatbelt on. "It's time we had a talk, Cat. About your future. And mine."

>>>

Mick faced them again, a line of Pennington James zombies so long he lost sight of them around the corner at the end of the street. He set his rifle on the ledge of the Adorable Amber Attic's round window, using the scope to pick them off one at a time as they stumbled up the steep steps to the house.

"That's it, Mick," said a voice in his head. "You're in control here. Your bullets are filled with a serum that destroys the zombies' central nervous system. They die instantly."

Mick stopped shooting. He recognized the voice. It sounded like his therapist's. Dr. Faruqi.

"Don't stop now," she said. "You've got the advantage."

He tried to speak, but his tongue felt thick in his mouth, and outside, one of the James zombies had made it to the door.

"Shoot them, Mick," she said again.

He adjusted his scope and aimed at the one banging the door down. The zombie had already made it onto the porch, but Mick found a sight line under the eaves. He shot, and it crumpled to the porch, where it shuddered and died.

He redirected his gun at the seemingly never-ending line of zombies. "I-I need to talk," said Mick.

"So, talk," said Faruqi. "I'm listening."

"Th-they're zombies, but I'm not," he said as he felled one zombie after another. "I'm not! I'm not Pennington James."

"That's right," she said. "Their numbers are dwindling, Mick. Keep talking. And shooting."

"I'm not," Mick kept chanting. "I'm not like you, Pennington. You're a monster."

Bang, bang, bang. The zombies dropped, twitching on the cement sidewalk and stairs till they stopped.

"And what are you, Mick?"

He kept shooting. There were only a few left, big ones that would take more than one bullet to kill.

"What are you?" demanded Faruqi.

Mick shot them, three bullets each. They went down. "I am human."

Cecily shook him. "Mick, wake up."

His eyes flew open. Cecily bent over his face. "You were having another nightmare," she said, her voice obviously weary of Mick's midnight-dream drama. "This was different, though. You said out loud, 'I am human.'"

"I did?"

"Yeah," Cecily said, rubbing her face but smiling. "If it weren't for the fact that you woke me up again, I'd think it's pretty cute." She laughed. "'I am human.' What a thing to say."

Mick laughed, too. "Well, I am."

"What were you dreaming about?"

Mick told her as she snuggled under his arm,

throwing her leg across his body.

"Sounds like this therapy stuff is working," she said.

"Yeah, maybe," Mick said. "I guess we'll find out if my nightmares stop."

"Or at least lessen. It could take some time."

They were quiet a moment, and then Cecily said, "You're not that creep, you know. It must've been a real mind-bender to pretend to be his friend that night."

"It wasn't pleasant."

"You got so close to him. You went into the monster's lair. And with all the stupid online craziness, everyone thought *you* were the monster."

"Why am I seeing a therapist, when I have you?" Mick asked, tickling her.

She laughed, squirming away from him. "Because you can't afford my services."

"Is that so?" Mick teased. "As I see it, you've been servicing me for free."

"Only because you have what I need," Cecily said, reaching down.

He took her hand and moved it to his chest, over his heart. "I love you, CeeCee."

She smiled. "I love you, too, Mick."

Chapter Twenty-Eight

The Queen Anne Neighborhood Association christened Mick's mural with a ribbon-cutting ceremony. A good crowd turned up for the event, wearing knit caps and Gore-Tex hoods against the steady drizzle. The Association passed out organic apple cider in compostable celluloid cups, of course.

Mick beamed with happiness, Cecily there by his side. He'd painted the mural on a twenty-foot span of concrete, a retaining wall built to keep the hill from sliding down due to erosion.

The final image did not include a graveyard or electric-orange bolts hitting tombstones. But the alien mothership was still there, hovering in a bank of glowing lavender clouds, surrounded by birds, as if whoever came offered only peace.

Cat hadn't put it together before, but the coincidence of the alien ship made her wonder if her uncle had been taking artistic inspiration from his dreamslipping again. Could he have picked up one of Nina's alien dreams, too? She asked him, once the crowd of newfound fans had moved away, and she could get to him again.

"Oh, I don't know," he said. "I don't remember where the idea came from."

Her grandmother linked her arm through Cat's. "Sometimes, the coincidence is magic enough," she said.

>>>

The same day the FOR SALE sign went up in the front yard of the old Queen Anne Victorian, the murder trial against Norman Jeffers began. He faced charges in both Texas and Washington State. Special Agent Strickland told Cat that he'd convened a task force including law enforcement officials from McClennan County in Texas and King County in Washington, with representatives from the Texas Department of Public Safety and Waco PD who were involved in Jeffers's arrest. Since the evidence was strongest in the Tina Jeffers case, officials agreed to begin prosecution in McClennan County. First Jeffers would stand trial in Texas for the murders of his wife Tina Jeffers as well as his ex-wife, Susie Charles, whose remains were indeed found buried on the Jeffers property. Then he could be extradited to Washington to stand trial there for the murder of Nina Howell.

He would not be prosecuted for any other charges.

The FBI also began an inquiry into the procedures and policies of both the Waco Police Department and the Texas Department of Public Safety.

>>>

Grace watched Cat string a banner across the Daring Damask Den, the words BON VOYAGE spelled out in glittery red. The room never looked better. Now that the house had sold, they could go back to living like normal people instead of being careful to stow all their clutter out of sight so buyers traipsing through could have the space to imagine their own lives in the house. Her granddaughter had filled the mantel vases with flowers from Grace's own garden: clouds of pale blue hydrangeas punctuated by pops of orange tiger lilies. The sight made Grace tear up. What a hold this old house had on her! For one who'd traveled as much as she had in life, it seemed odd to her to suddenly realize how tethered she'd been, for more than twenty years, to this house on the hill.

A hand slipped into Grace's, warm and newly familiar. She turned to find Annie smiling at her, a knowing look on her face.

"The lilies are audacious," the woman said. "Just like you."

Grace leaned in to kiss her, the two holding their lips pressed together for longer than a moment.

"Oh, will you two get a room already?" said Cat, though her voice merely teased.

The two women separated, laughing, but continued to hold hands.

"Do you need any help?" Annie offered to Cat, who stood on a ladder.

"Oh, I think I've got it," said Cat, just as she secured the end of the banner. She jumped down from the ladder.

Grace wanted to say something, but so did Cat, apparently, who beat her to it.

"Grandmother," she said. "I've never seen you so happy."

Grace smiled. She'd been getting that a lot lately,

dancers in her Nia class telling her she "glowed," and even Mick taking note of the lilt in her step.

"I don't know that I've ever been this happy before," said Grace.

Annie beamed. "Me, neither."

Cat sniffed. "You two are going to make me cry, and I just put on mascara for the party."

Annie hugged Cat. "It's been wonderful getting to know you this way, you know, instead of as a PI who thinks I'm an arsonist."

Cat laughed. "I don't know if she told you, but I accused my grandmother of flirting with you that day."

Annie looked at Grace, who shrugged. "What can I say? I thought I was just trying to bond with one of our suspects, get her to trust me."

The doorbell rang, and Cat ran to get it. Over her head, Grace saw Greg, whose presence gave her hope. She had a little bit of business to attend to still, just one last meddling sort of matter before she and Annie went off to a Nia white-belt training together, the first ranking in the discipline. Grace had successfully convinced Annie to try the dance practice, and they were both hooked. As white belts, they'd be able to teach ... or not. Grace felt as if the last decade or so of her life—whatever she had left —was wide open with possibility. After the Nia training, they'd travel, see the places they'd always wanted to visit but hadn't had the chance to, and then settle down somewhere together.

Cecily and Mick came up the walk close behind, followed by Dave and Simon.

After greeting her brother and her friend, Grace

took Simon by the hand and pulled him in close to whisper in his ear. "Now, don't persecute yourself too much over Nina," she said. "Life is too short for that."

He nodded, but she knew it would take time for the sorrow lines in his face to relax again.

An hour and a half later, with the party in full swing, Grace summoned Greg and Cat to her study, where she closed the door on the festivities and presented Cat with an envelope.

"What's this?" Cat asked. "And why didn't Greg get one if he's included here?"

"It's my investment in your new business venture," said Grace. "A joint venture, between the two of you."

"Excuse me?" asked Greg. "I just opened a new business. I'm not looking for a second."

"And Gran, you know I've been dying to be a solo act."

"Be that as it may," said Grace. "But there's more strength in a partnership. The economic reality is that it's a lot harder for solo acts to survive than it used to be."

"As much as I like Cat," Greg said, "I'm not sure we should work together."

Grace shot him a hard look. "Is that because you'd rather be free to date her?"

He looked down, his face shading to pink.

"Look," said Grace, "the two of you work well together already, and in time, you'll be a formidable duo. The universe agrees." Grace spread her arms out wide, making the bracelets on her wrists jangle. "That's why you keep winding up on cases together."

"I thought that had more to do with Cat's need for a heavy," Greg said. "At least on this case."

Cat had opened her envelope and seemed to be rendered mute by its contents.

Greg cleared his throat. "Honestly, adding an investigation component to my security firm would be smart," he offered. "Instead of referring people who wanted the service, I could charge them more than I am for just the security work."

"Don't I get a say in this?" Cat finally spoke up. "I mean, wow. I feel like I'm being bought off here. Gran, this is a lot of money—"

"Yes, it is, but it's not a handout, Cat. I expect a return on my investment."

Cat stared at Grace. "What if Greg and I can't deliver?"

"That's not even a consideration," said Grace.

Her granddaughter crossed her arms. "Are you trying to throw us together? Fix us up?"

Grace laughed. "On the contrary. The possibility of your romantic entanglement is my only caveat as an investor. Those things often go awry, you see."

Cat looked at Greg, who shrugged. "What've we got to lose?"

The two stared at each other for a few seconds.

"I guess here goes nothing," Cat finally said, offering Greg her hand. "Partner."

He grasped her hand with his own, and Grace noted their hold lingered longer than needed to seal the deal.

Want to read more from Lisa Brunette? Try her short story series, *Out of the Blue*.

What readers are saying about it…

"This is amazing!"
AditiDankar

"I'm dead. Literally dead. I love your writing so much. Please continue."
ebails32

"Fabulous story - so much left to be said and discovered in that small longing voice. Families are always a puzzle. You've given delicate fragile threads of beauty here."
tamoja

Overview of *Spy Boy*…

The year is 1984, and Meredith's family moves to an Air Force base.
It's enough that she has to adjust to the weirdness of duck-and-cover and air raid sirens. But now there's something else: Meredith thinks she's discovered a spy.

More praise…

"This story is beautifully written! I absolutely love it!"
alexthymix

"Very distinct and well-thought-out characters."

austinlugo

"What a lovely story. You've captured all the interesting dynamics between the characters and I loved the way you've told the story. Short and sweet!"
Jing_Jing

An award-winning storyteller…

WINNER of the Miami Fiction Prize

WINNER of the Associated Writing Programs Intro Journals Project Award

FINALIST for the Faulkner/Wisdom Award

A Wattpad FEATURED AUTHOR

Recipient of a MAJOR GRANT from the Tacoma Arts Commission

You might also like…

Lisa Brunette's powerful poetry collection, *Broom of Anger*.

"I want to binge on every word."
Lisa Hickey
CEO, The Good Men Project

Acknowledgements

Thanks as always to my beta readers for their encouragement and insight, but most of all, their insistence that I keep pushing myself to do better. They are: Anna Dobritt, Beth Poole, Dianna Taylor, Ernest White II, Heidi Peroni, Janice Clark, Jennifer Hudak, Kay Neill, Mary Alderete, Rebeqa Rivers, and Sue Hollowell. Thanks also to Embody Movement Studio and especially owner Christina Mae Wolf, for giving me the gift of Nia, which I gave to Amazing Grace.

I'm also grateful to my line editor, Jim Thomsen, who keeps me in hypens, and to Elisa Mader for her passionate proofreading. I learn new nitty-gritty editorial bits every time they both take a swipe at one of my scripts.

Thanks above all to my one and only alpha reader, Tino, who believes in me even when my belief in myself falters.

About the Author

Lisa was born in Santa Rosa, California, but that was only home for a year. A so-called "military brat," she lived in nine different houses and attended nine different schools by the time she was 14. Through all of the moves, her one constant was books. She read everything, from the entire Nancy Drew and Trixie Belden mystery series to her mother's books by Daphne du Maurier and Taylor Caldwell.

A widely published author, game writer, and journalist, Lisa has interviewed homeless women, the designer of the Batmobile, and a sex expert, to name just a few colorful characters. This experience, not to mention her own large, quirky family, led her to create some truly memorable characters in her Dreamslippers Series and other works, whether books or games.

Always a vivid dreamer, not to mention a wannabe psychic, Lisa feels perfectly at home slipping into suspects' dreams, at least in her imagination. Her husband isn't so sure she can't pick up his dreams in real life, though.

With a hefty list of awards and publications to her name, Lisa now lives in a small town in Washington State, but who knows how long that will last…

SIGN UP:

Lisa publishes a bimonthly newsletter. Sign up and receive a free book!
http://forms.feedblitz.com/192

Book Club Discussion Questions

1. Go around the room and share your own dating horror stories, like Cat's in chapter five.

2. Were you Team Ed or Team Annie? What do you love/hate about Granny Grace's dates?

3. When did you figure out whodunit? What clues tipped you off? List your suspects as the story developed.

4. What's the strangest dream experience you've ever had?

5. Are you Team Greg? Why is or isn't he right for Cat?

6. Read aloud the fight scene between Mercy and Grace in chapter fourteen. Now go around the room and share your mother/daughter stories.

7. Who's your favorite dreamslipper, and why?

8. If Nina had lived, do you think she and Sam would have ended up together? Why or why not?

9. What would have saved Nina?

10. If you were on the jury to convict Norman Jeffers, what sentence would you want him to receive?

www.ingramcontent.com/pod-product-compliance
Lightning Source LLC
Chambersburg PA
CBHW070754280626
47162CB00016B/270